Praise for *Th*

Cynthia Newberry Martin's new novel is a bold transcendent meditation on desire, memory, motherhood, and the power of art to remake a life. I loved this book. I could not put it down. There's a spare lyric grace to Martin's writing, and in this story, she captures the nuances of ordinary life – what we love and fear to risk, what we lose and ache to hold. *The Art of Her Life* is a rare, exquisite work of fiction
—Dawn Tripp, author of *Georgia*, a novel of Georgia O'Keeffe

Cynthia Newberry Martin is a deeply gifted writer. *The Art of Her Life* should be placed on the same shelf as A.S. Byatt's *The Matisse Stories*. When tragic things happen to the character of Emily, she becomes devoted to a kind of Gospel of Henri Matisse, and she gets lost in the artist's life in order to find her own life again. This is a family story; this is a love story. But the novel combines these in profound and original ways. The splendid prose is tinted with the inimitable melancholy of Matisse's blue.
—Howard Norman, author of *The Ghost Clause*

In *The Art of Her Life*, Cynthia Newberry Martin tenderly and delicately shows how the unexpected turns of a life can most often only be steadied and moored by what we hold deepest inside. It is told with no punches pulled. No self-interrogation spared. Just a keen and blunt honesty. A lovely and moving novel that celebrates the legacy of the creative spirit, the power and salvation of art, and the challenges in balancing an intellectual life with an emotional life.
—Adam Braver, author of *Rejoice the Head of Paul McCartney*

With grace and clarity, Cynthia Newberry Martin paints in this novel a lasting portrait of love and family, of love and perseverance, of love and beauty and care and heart. Even in the face of loss, every brushstroke of life becomes somehow sacred, a blessing, an abundance.

—William Lychack, author of *Cargill Falls*

The Art of Her Life is a rare book about an adult woman with the full complement of responsibilities—children, job, love, passions—grappling with how to manage and juggle them. Matisse's art, and the painting *Breakfast* in particular, is a character in this gorgeous book—his use of color and channeling of emotion form lifelines for our protagonist. Matisse accompanies Emily on her journey as she learns that, paradoxically, it is only through surrender that we can feel life's wholeness. I loved this book.

—Lindsey Mead, editor of *On Being Forty(ish)*

Praise for *Tidal Flats*

Gold Medal in Literary Fiction, 2020 Independent Publisher Book Awards
14th Annual National Indie Excellence® Award for Fiction

"With deep insight and unending sensitivity, Cynthia Newberry Martin shows us to ourselves: our penchant for choosing lives that will crack us open, our resilience when our deepest fears come true. In scenes both vivid and emotionally complex, *Tidal Flats* excavates the interior of a long-term marriage, how it demands the impossible, offers the unimaginable. This book is a stunning, heart-expanding debut."

—Pam Houston, author of *Deep Creek: Finding Hope in the High Country*

"Cynthia Newberry Martin's *Tidal Flats* is written out of the rough wisdom that knows that love is a peculiar, dynamic force, and all we can do against it is to be alert and open and awake. This is a story of making and unmaking and making again, with no neat resolutions or pat answers. It's a beautiful book."
—Paul Lisicky, author of later and *The Narrow Door*

"Cynthia Newberry Martin is a tremendous writer, with a Woolfian talent for taking the full measure of small moments. Her work is both subtle and revelatory, and I've been waiting a long time for this book."
—Rebecca Makkai, author of *The Great Believers*

"For once, a novel of big ideas that is also filled with bold and uncommon events. In *Tidal Flats,* Cynthia Newberry Martin, a storyteller at the top of her game, creates a universe of betrayal, compassion, and regret in which two people's love for each other is surpassed only by their loyalty to their convictions."
—Jacquelyn Mitchard, author of *The Deep End of the Ocean*

"I admire Martin's capacity to render her characters with the dignity of complexity. And I double-admire that she takes that same care with her settings, turning Place into a player that has its own 'human' heart. The novel swirls with light and love."
—Joshua Mohr, author of *Sirens* and *Damascus*

"Exquisite! A gorgeously observed account of one woman's life, lived in our era of global reach, of international obligations, of domestic worries and domestic triumphs too. Cynthia Newberry Martin has found the perfect story through which to share her rare wisdom. Brava!"
—Robin Black, author of *Life Drawing*

Praise for *Love Like This*

"*Love Like This* is an astonishment. The novel comes on like a quiet exploration of the empty nest syndrome, but quickly deepens into an exploration of female identity, desire, and the utter unpredictability of love. Cynthia Newberry Martin's prose is confident, precise, and, when required, as bold as a billboard. The story she's crafted shocked and delighted me."

—Steve Almond, author of *All the Secrets of the World*

Cynthia Newberry Martin has written a well-crafted and sensitive story about the perils of assuming how things are going to be rather than talking them through. Angelina and Will are relatable people whose lives are changing in their middle age, but my heart was stolen by Lucy and her son John Milton, characters whose lives are unusual and compelling. I will reread the billboard scene many times.

—Alice Elliott Dark, author of *Fellowship Point and In the Gloaming*

So isolated by wealth, beauty, and family, her husband's house rules and her mother's agoraphobia, Angelina arrives at middle age believing only the rich know about poetry. Intimate, brutal and compelling, this beautifully-paced novel is her Buddha's journey down from the hilltop and into the world of women, the poor and the unbeautiful, who will teach her compassion, courage, open-mindedness and maybe a little self-love.

—Pam Houston, author of *Deep Creek, Finding Hope In The High Country*

Also by Cynthia Newberry Martin

Tidal Flats
Love Like This

The Art of Her Life

a novel

Cynthia Newberry Martin

Fomite
Burlington, VT

ISBN-978-1-953236-97-5
Library of Congress Control Number: 2023931780

Fomite
58 Peru Street
Burlington, VT 05401
www.fomitepress.com
09/29/2023

To

Kathleen, Bobby, Jack, and Sam

"Underlying this succession of moments
which constitutes the superficial existence of beings and things,
and which is continually modifying and transforming them,
one can search for a truer, more essential character …
a more lasting interpretation."

Henri Matisse,
from "Notes of a Painter"

"Lines connect in thin ways that last and last
and lives become generations
made out of pictures and words just kept."

Lucille Clifton,
from *Generations*

Breakfast

The picture seems complete, and yet I'm not in it.

Framed by the white door molding, Mark sits on the floor in front of the TV in jeans and a dark green shirt. Caroline, a yellow bow in her long hair, reclines in his lap. Elizabeth, in red overalls, stands behind him, the same height as his head, running her hands through his red hair.

I'm the observer, the spectator, the viewer. All pictures, and paintings, need viewers—to appreciate and search for what lies beneath.

Two brown paper bags, turned down and stapled, wait by the front door. Reminded of our plans, I push forward.

When she sees me, Caroline jumps up and says, "Now can we open them?"

"If it's okay with your mother," Mark says, smiling.

Caroline looks at me and then skips to the bags. Elizabeth toddles behind her, the plastic barrette I put in her hair thirty minutes ago already down to her ear.

Mark turns off the TV. We've been friends for what feels like forever. And for the last two years, we've been "an item," as my mother would say. Back when I *wanted* to get married, why didn't I marry him instead of Frank? Because back then Frank was my boyfriend, and the three of us were friends together. I used to tease Mark about when *he* was going to get married. He would say he was ready, that he was just waiting for the right girl. These days, he tells me that girl is, and always has been, me.

"I can't get it open," Caroline says, trying not to tear the bag. Before I can help her, Mark says, "Just rip it." Caroline pauses for a second and then rips, looking at me as if she's doing something wrong.

Elizabeth drags her bag to Mark. He picks her up, carries her and the bag to the sofa, brushes his hair off his forehead, and looks inside the bag along with Elizabeth as if he has no idea what they might find.

I sit on the floor by Caroline. One at a time, she hands me a metal bucket, a small plastic tray, a shovel, some Ziploc bags, and tongs. She glances at Elizabeth as if to confirm that she's receiving the same inexplicable items. Then Caroline asks if we're going to the beach.

"We're going on a dig," Mark says, "at the park."

Elizabeth, barely two years old, hears the word *park* and grins, clapping her hands. At five, Caroline wants more. "A dig?"

"Like I do for my work—to see what we can find that might help us understand the people who lived here before we did."

Caroline puts her hands on her knees and looks at me.

"Like a treasure hunt," I say.

At that, Caroline smiles.

Mark wads up the bags and pulls me from the floor. He's a head taller, and when I look up at him, I feel taken care of, even though I can take care of myself. The girls leave their buckets by the door and head to the gated porch to play. In the seconds the door is open, wet, sticky heat moves inside, ghost-like. Mark leans against the wall between the front door and the kitchen, resting his hand on my shoulder and drawing me in front of him. His hands slide to my waist, and he kisses me. I reach my hands to his hair.

"It looked like fun when Elizabeth was doing it," I say.

"I like it even better when you do it."

He grins and looks at me for only a second before he kisses me again—a long, deep kiss that wants something. That makes me want him. I lean my head into his chest and take a breath. He smells like soil, like the earth.

I give him a quick hug and lean away, my hands lingering for a second on his arms.

"Are you ready?" he asks.

"Almost."

"We'll be on the swings."

When I turn to scoop the mail off the hat stand by the door, I catch a glimpse of my thick black hair, but my eyes and mouth are so small I almost can't see them.

"Emily?"

I look at his hand on the doorknob, then his face.

"You're not going to forget we're out here, are you?"

A twinge of pressure, as if I've already forgotten something, but I smile at Mark, then make my way to my study, noticing in the mail two reminder cards—one for a six-month dentist appointment and the other for my annual GYN check-up. In my tiny study, one window, a framed portion of the day. I step to my desk, which is overflowing. A basket of things to do, little rectangles of color awaiting the next reminder, a rain-scented candle, thick ceramic pens in a museum mug, my laptop, attempts at the essay for the contest, and Jack Flam's *Matisse on Art*. I toss the mail into the basket. It will all have to wait a few more weeks, until summer is over and the girls are back in school. I reach for my purse. Around me everywhere—on posters and postcards and pages of magazines and stacks of books—the paintings of Henri Matisse. I want to be with Mark and the girls, I do, and yet I feel a pull to remain here, with Henri.

Several hours later at the park, the four of us are drenched in sweat and coated in dirt. At least August in Charleston is consistent—always hot and humid. We're set up in a somewhat shaded, flat area at the top of a small incline, bordered by large boulders on two sides and three weeping willows on the other. Buckets of water. Trays filled with dirt. Three Ziploc bags, labeled with date and place and finder. Mark made sure that Caroline and Elizabeth each found at least one item. For Caroline, it was a piece of an arrowhead, and for Elizabeth, a broken piece of pottery. Mark found the remains of an old blue Bic lighter.

I sit against a rock. In front of me, this picture. Elizabeth digs with her shovel, the dirt flying behind her onto my legs. Mark holds the ruler, while Caroline, her long hair in a ponytail, marks off a twelve-inch square with the bottom of her shovel handle. Mark is captivated. He loves a dig, anywhere, anytime, for anything.

And something else. Mark is right where he wants to be in the world. His face is relaxed, his shoulders rounded. He's doing what he loves with Caroline, with us. His hands connect with each thing they touch, and he transmits this contentment to her. They move together as they put toothpicks at each corner and reach for shovels to dig out the square.

"About one-inch down," Mark says, and Caroline stops to look at him. Responding to her confusion, he adds, "A finger, a finger down." She sticks her finger in the ground and, without looking up, digs and deposits the dirt on her tray. When she fills the tray, she hands it to Mark.

"Do you see anything?" she asks.

"Use your hands to feel around."

She stares at her relatively clean hands. Mark looks over at me raising his eyebrows, drawing me in. Then, pursing her lips, she sticks her hands in, her fingers picking through the dirt, squishing the little mounds.

"I feel something," she says.

Their heads practically bang together.

"Hold onto it," Mark says, "and rinse it off in your bucket."

"It's tiny wheels," Caroline yells.

"Like from a matchbox car," Mark adds from right beside her. "So what does finding this tell us?"

"Tell us?" Caroline repeats, still rinsing the wheels and her hands.

"About what might have happened here *before* we came along."

"Oh, yeah, yeah, like the lighter, like somebody trying to start a campfire. Well…." She sits down in my lap, staring at the tiny wheels. Then she looks up at me and begins. "Once upon a time, maybe there was a kid, like a boy, who was here with his mother and father, and he brought a toy car to play with, and he lost it in the dirt, and then—and then—it got left outside, and it fell apart and—and then I found the wheels!" She holds them high in the air.

I wrap my arms around her and hold tight.

"Let's label the wheels," Mark says, his face shining through the thick afternoon light.

When Caroline starts digging with Elizabeth, Mark comes to sit next to me. He stretches his legs all the way out and leans back on his arms. "Has Caroline always hated dirt? I thought kids liked to make mud pies and—"

"It's her hands. She's never liked to have messy hands. She hates finger painting too, so she has nothing specifically against archaeology."

After we watch the girls play for a while, he says, "I love them too, you know."

Caroline drops her shovel and comes toward us. "Did you bring any wipes?" she asks, her dirty hands out in front of her as if she's unable to understand how they could be a part of her.

I sit up, hand her a wipe, and pull my damp shirt away from my chest. Still, the heat presses in, molding itself to my body. Out beyond us, there's a thickening haze.

"Our Favorite Paintings." An exhibit of paintings chosen by people in the community—this was always to be my first exhibit as curator. Instead, I'm the registrar. At the Charleston Museum of Art. Where I suggested my dream as we were brainstorming for an exhibit to celebrate the direction the museum would be taking with Sam as the new director. And that's fine. I want to see my painting again.

Ever since the exhibit was announced, I've been trying to write an essay for the contest. At first, all I could do was stare at the instructions: "Name your favorite painting and write a thousand words or less about why it's your favorite and why it should be included in the exhibit." It took me weeks to think of a way to start, and then that's all I could think of, covering the dining room table with first sentences. I had no idea how to write the story of a little girl who fell in love with a painting.

But today, I close my eyes to remember what it felt like to be that little girl, climbing those steps, my mother's loose hand, the enormous rooms. And the words tumble into being.

At nine years old, the spell of once-upon-a-time had already made its mark. I would fall in love, get married, have children, and live happily ever after. But with that first trip to a museum, as I stood in front of Breakfast *by Henri Matisse, I knew—with the certainty that only a child can have—that this painting would be as much a part of my life story as falling in love and getting married. Twenty-seven years later, it still is.*

Henri was my first crush. I was the middle child, living in a cluttered house, and he created quiet spots. I chose French because of him and learned not to pronounce the H. His world—the world of art— enchanted me.

After Breakfast, *I discovered other paintings of girls by themselves. The colors seeping out of skin—green noses, yellow cheeks, blue blotches around the mouth. I wanted to be a* Girl Reading. *I wanted to be Marguerite. I didn't play music; I looked at paintings. I didn't collect albums but instead art books and postcards of paintings. And the things in the paintings. On my bedside table, I arranged a tray, a teapot, a dish of lemons. I imagined my bedroom as his canvas, ready for Henri to swoop in and make order. With shape and color. Warm light. Just like he did in* Breakfast. *Yes, there were other paintings, but I always returned to* Breakfast.

I was a girl who kept everything inside, and Henri showed me how to see what was there. When I saw colors explode on one of his paintings, I thought, I didn't even know; how did he?

When the calendar says September, I have to search for evidence to prove it's no longer summer—leaves on the ground instead of on trees, a cool breeze in the evening, a crispness to the morning. In Charleston, although the seasons change, they take their sweet time about it, as if they just haven't gotten around to flipping to the next month.

This September, both girls are in school for the first time— Caroline in kindergarten and Elizabeth in preschool. Back in the car after dropping Elizabeth for her first day at the Little Red Schoolhouse, Caroline is quieter than usual, sitting on the edge of her seat, biting her lip, and staring out the window. She looks pale, as if she might throw up, but when I let her window down from my side, she leans in and says, "Mommy, my hair!" I reverse the window direction but feel the thick slice of heat that snuck inside the car.

My first day of kindergarten I sat on a picnic table under an awning, fascinated by what seemed like a million other kids, all talking to somebody. I don't remember brushing my hair, much less caring how it looked. The principal rang the bell and called the kindergartners to form a line. I was behind somebody and in front of somebody else. By ten thirty I had made my first best friend, and ever since, I've always had one.

As soon as I stop in front of the school, Caroline jumps out, her new yellow backpack falling off her shoulder. She struggles to keep it on her arm while she swings the car door shut. "Bye, Mommy," she says, and then she's gone.

I want to watch her walk away, to see what she does first after shutting the door. See where her serious eyes look, back at me or ahead to her next moment. Instead, remembering the school letter, I move on because this is a drop-off area only. Park if you need to smooth their hair or kiss them good-bye or look into their eyes one last time.

I swallow, look ahead and behind me, and concentrate on finding a space between cars in the stream of one after another. The girls have school, then after-school care. I won't see them until six. Wherever I am, a pull from somewhere else.

Back home, I open doors, let up shades, and fill the house with light. I usually leave for the museum around eight thirty, but to celebrate the girls being back in school, I'm not going in until two. Even my study is full of light—the one window working extra hard in this space not much bigger than a large, walk-in closet, a space that the real estate agent billed as a "luxury" laundry room. After I took out the ugly cabinets and moved the washer and dryer into a hall closet, I had enough room for a small chest of drawers, two narrow bookshelves, a filing cabinet, and a desk, on top of which, almost always, sits my favorite book on Henri Matisse—*Matisse on Art*, his interviews and essays, his words, compiled and translated by Jack Flam. I've read *Matisse on Art* so many times that his words are a part of me now. It's from this book that I've conjured the man who at twenty-seven wore a corduroy suit, had curly red hair, a mustache and beard, who smiled without smiling, something about his eyes.

On top of *Matisse on Art*, in a clear plastic folder, my essay. All around it, the disorder of daily life. Magazine clippings, notes for the start of school, a shirt that needs to be returned, my overflowing to-do basket. I feel lopsided and long for the balance of Matisse's *Interior with a Top Hat,* a desk covered with books, papers, an empty flower vase, the top hat.

Matisse would begin with an abundance of color and then cut away the unnecessary details. Drawing with scissors, he called it. He didn't get things right on the first go either. Hundreds of sittings. Moving blocks of color until he found the shape and the composition felt right. Now, at thirty-six, I no longer know whether to pick up the brush or the scissors. I need to stand again in front of Breakfast, *and see, as Henri said, with the eyes of a child, as though I were seeing the painting for the first time.*

Ignoring my essay, I work on the basket. Every time I touch something, a paper falls to the floor. I give in and *move* to the floor, taking only my coffee and the basket, which I immediately turn upside down. Making piles is my favorite part of getting organized. I recently read an article that said the piles we make represent the contents of our brain. As I stack several envelopes from the bank, I hope there's more to me than what's in these piles.

I come across the reminder postcards, and I pick up my cell to call for appointments. But it's only eight forty-five. Maybe I shouldn't call just yet, at least not for the annual appointment. If I wait four weeks, I could lose the five pounds I gained over the summer. I create a reminder to call for appointments four weeks from today, throw the postcards away, and return to piling.

One of the catalogues from the basket is addressed to the name that was temporarily mine, Strickland. It shocks me, making me feel out of place or in the wrong time. After I left Frank, I tore him out of my life, the way I often tear a page out of a journal. I even changed the girls' last name to mine. The divorce was two years ago, right before Elizabeth was born. I don't talk about him. The girls rarely ask. Still, the rough edges remain.

The last time I saw him was the day I left, right after I found out I was pregnant again. He was standing in the doorway of our house. His blond hair was dull and dirty; and his once muscular body, out of shape. During the last months I was pregnant, the guilt I had buried about not telling him I was pregnant kept resurfacing. I knew it wasn't right, and yet I felt as if I needed to protect myself. After Elizabeth was born and I lay there watching her stretch her little arms, I knew it wasn't about me, and I picked up the phone.

Frank was working in New Mexico as a warden in the prison system. He would come see her, he said, and Caroline, as soon as he could get some time off. But before Elizabeth was three months old, he was killed in a car accident, his car careening off a bridge around two in the morning.

The essay is due today, and as I walk in from the lot behind the museum to the back door, I hold it with two hands close to my chest—which feels overly serious and ridiculous. So I drop my hands, hold the essay with only one, and when I step from the black asphalt to the pebbled concrete of the walkway, I force my gaze from the ground to the open sky, unearthing the feeling of possibility. Warm winds jump from here to there, the weather struggling to change, to push forward into fall. But inside, when the giant metal door shuts behind me with a loud, hollow sound, I feel uneasy, and trapped in the narrow gray stairwell. My teeth grind a SweeTART into powder. There's no reason to be this nervous about a contest in which my background gives me such an advantage. I start up the steps—SweeTARTs in one hand and words in the other. Words on paper are so permanent. And visible, out there for anyone to see.

On the third floor, I enter a short, low-ceilinged hallway. Without seeing anyone, I open the door to my office and switch on the overhead lights, then the lamp on my desk. I should turn the essay in now, but it clings to me like a pleading child. So I put it on top of my purse in the bottom drawer. I need coffee.

Once I leave the alcove of administrative offices, I'm out in the world of paintings. I cross the open galleria, going around the staircase to the opposite corner of the museum, where there are more offices and a break room. Arriving at the museum by nine gives me an hour to gradually adjust to the day before the lights are turned up in preparation for opening. Usually, I don't run into anybody on my first trip for coffee, but this morning, standing in front of the coffee maker, actually pouring a cup for himself, is

Ferrell Johnston, our curator—the person primarily responsible for the care, well-being, and future of the collection. Ferrell is famous for his aversion to clichés and anything that might suggest the current century. He's around fifty but seems far older. I stare at his bald head, and when he turns around, I'm staring at his bowtie and his wire-rimmed glasses, which frame and accentuate his tiny lips. He jerks his head in my direction without speaking, something I like about him, and then he slides out of the room.

At my desk, I have trouble concentrating. Attendance at the museum has doubled since the contest was announced. The local paper has run several articles about it, proudly claiming that since Charleston opened the first museum in the United States in 1773, it continues to set the standard for museums across the country. "'Our Favorite Paintings' has reached the hearts of the people," according to an editor at the *Charleston Post and Courier*. "People," the editor continued, "want to feel things again, and they are looking to art to show them the way."

I stand and look out the window. A man sits with two little girls on the wooden bench near the birdbath at the edge of the woods. Waiting for the museum to open, I imagine.

The feeling Henri Matisse created in Breakfast *reached out to me that day in the museum. I later learned that he was a private man who so disliked writing about or discussing his feelings that he was often considered not to have any. But when he picked up a paintbrush, feelings appeared on the canvas. As if he would paint to see how he felt, and once it was there in front of him, "Ah," he might say, "so I was confused."*

Henri also had a favorite painting, Cezanne's Three Bathers. *He said, "In the thirty-seven years I have owned this canvas, I have come to know it quite well, though not entirely, I hope.... I have drawn from it my faith and my perseverance." Matisse's* Breakfast *has been my favorite painting for almost thirty years. Yet I've seen the original only once. What it told me then was that there was more to life than the everyday. There was feeling.*

I turn around and face my desk, narrowing my focus to the bottom drawer, which I open. I grab the essay and head to Sam's office. Without really stopping, I hold it out toward his assistant. I feel her take it, and I make myself keep going.

Four weeks disappear, as do my summer pounds. From my study window, conclusive proof that a new season has begun—a light-filled day with golds, oranges, and reds flaming against the bluer than usual sky. My computer interrupts me with a reminder to make my appointments. I pick up my cell and take the first available—for the dentist, the next week, and for the gynecologist, the last week of October.

On Saturday afternoon, I'm curled up on the sofa in the den, my grandmother's knit throw covering me. I'm not asleep, but I'm not quite present either. Writing the essay reminded me of how, as a little girl, I used to paint the day in my head. Today I cover every inch of canvas with the gray of exhaustion.

"Mommy?" Caroline whispers from somewhere nearby.

I open my eyes. Without moving, I take in the cluttered room. Toys and books scattered on the floor. Sippy cups beside plastic bowls. No shades drawn. No lights on. The smell of burned popcorn permeating the air. Elizabeth woke up twice during the night for no apparent reason, and Caroline was up this morning at her usual time of six. It's naptime, and I'm trying to recover.

"Mommy?"

My canvas is devoid of lines and energy, making any movement impossible.

"Mom-mee," she sings now, like a child who has forgotten why she was calling out in the first place.

I focus to see the numbers on the clock. Four thirty-seven. Three hours and fifty-three minutes until I'll have a minute to myself. I love the girls, but I often wonder why I don't go to work for an hour or two on Saturday. It would give me a break, a few minutes I could control.

"Mom-mee."

I sit up and turn on the lamp by the sofa, feeling my book at my back. When naptime started, I wanted to read. I knew I was tired. Still, I hoped for a few pages. But the minute my body hit the couch, my eyes closed. The book is not even open.

"MOMMY!" Caroline screams.

As she creeps into the room, the color yellow appears on the canvas, covering over some of the gray.

"I think I hear Elizabeth," she says, sitting on the floor, collecting Legos into a pile.

I raise myself off the sofa by visualizing M&Ms, SweeTARTs, and sour jelly beans. I aim for the kitchen, for my candy drawer, the many colors of the little candies like pointillist dots of energy on the canvas. I grab a handful of M&Ms and shove them into my mouth. If Elizabeth is awake now, she'll go to bed early tonight.

And she is—playing in her bed. Red joins yellow, creating an image of life, with less space available for gray in its pure form.

Damn. I hate it when I eat before I'm all the way awake because I just cram, chew, and swallow. The M&Ms were in my mouth and down my throat before I even knew they were in my hand. I don't remember tasting the chocolate.

Since Elizabeth is content, I head for the bathroom to eke out one more minute of solitude. Or maybe I should leave the door open and use the time for transition. As I pass through the bedroom, my cell rings. I pick it up and sit on the bed, my upper body falling straight back.

Mark is already finished with his basketball game and offering to pick up pizza for later. Another color appears on the canvas—green—and a painting begins to emerge.

"Emily?"

"You're too nice, Mark."

"I know," he says.

I hear his smile. And I hate that I'm about to erase it. "I just don't think I can do it."

"What would you have to *do*?"

Respond to another human being.

"I can help put the girls to bed," he says.

"I'm too tired."

"You can't be too tired to just *be* with me." He's quiet for a minute and then adds, "You're always too tired."

I sit up on the bed. "I wasn't too tired last weekend when you came over."

Now the smile is on my face, remembering our evening in bed after the girls went to sleep. We heated leftovers and snuggled under the covers to watch an old movie.

"That's what I meant to say," he says. "You won't be too tired once I get there."

"I—Can you hold on a minute?" Things are too quiet.

I spot Caroline from the dining room—under the kitchen table with an entire box of chocolate chip cookies poured onto the floor.

Ignoring the cookie situation, I check on Elizabeth. When I inch open the door to their room, I see she's gone back to sleep. Now I'm torn between wanting to finish my conversation in peace and wanting that early bedtime.

"Mark?" I say, opening the door all the way.

"Still here."

I apologize for being distracted, then decline his offer for tonight. A beautiful blue bursts onto the canvas, over the green and around the yellow and red.

Switching my cell to speaker, I take heavy Elizabeth out of her crib and put her on the changing table. These are the last days of diapers. She's down to only one when she sleeps. Her eyes open for a moment but close right back.

"Emily, I miss you."

"I feel sure I'd miss you too if I ever had enough time for what I have to do *and* for myself."

I shouldn't have said that. I take off her diaper, but I can't get the wipe out. There, I have it.

"What do you mean *for yourself*?"

I'm relieved he's not focusing on my admission of not actually missing him. But I'm being sincere. If every minute of my life were not filled, I'd surely have an open place where I could feel the absence of him, and then I would miss him.

"Sometimes it's overwhelming to have to respond all the time," I say. Powder and tape and then a million snaps. I hate the snaps.

"Call me if you change your mind," he says, with little hope in his voice.

That pull again.

"I love you," I say.

Three snaps to go. Elizabeth's not happy. A little wisp of dark red hair, one with a thread of blonde in it, is stuck to her forehead, the blonde from her father. I free the hair and pick her up.

I never did make it to the bathroom, but I smile, remembering Caroline under the table.

As I walk toward the kitchen, carrying Elizabeth—who is too big to be carried—on my hip, I hear a scrunching noise. I bend down. The sight of Caroline, with her long black hair, half up and half down, propped on her elbows and lying on her stomach in a sea of cookies, breaks through my layers of exhaustion and numbness to reach the warmth underneath. I manage to squeeze under the table, and I put Elizabeth beside me, giving her the juice cup I grabbed off the counter.

"What are you doing?" I ask.

"Nothing," Caroline says.

"You look like you're having fun."

"This is *my* place."

Which surprises me. "You want me to leave?"

"Don't you want to lie down?" Caroline asks, wiping cookie crumbs off her elbow.

"I like it here with you."

Elizabeth rubs her eyes.

After a moment, Caroline says, "Do you like chocolate chip cookies?"

"I do."

"I do too," she says.

"What else do you like?" I ask.

She opens her mouth to speak, then stops. I wait, glancing at Elizabeth, now playing with her toes.

"I like it when you're not tired," she says.

This also takes me by surprise. And I see myself through her eyes—possibly for the first time. "I like it when I'm not tired too," I say. "You know what else I like?"

"What?"

"I like you."

"I like you too, Mommy," she says, hesitating before continuing. Then her brown eyes look straight at me. "Do you want just one chocolate chip cookie?"

A vision of Renoir's *Gabrielle with Jean and a Little Girl* settles over me, the two heads leaning in close and the baby right there beside them, the warm mixture of colors contributing to a feeling of goodness. As the color of contentment washes over me, I think to myself, this is why I don't go to work on Saturday.

At the end of the day, I inhale the stillness, giving the confusing oranges, purples, and teals—the feelings of crazy, loud, and too much—the calmness they need to separate. I'm glad I didn't accept Mark's offer of pizza and a movie. I turn down the comforter first on the far side of the bed and then on my side, where my note card of *Breakfast* sits framed on the night table.

I pull the sheet and blanket back and sit down. Why do I think of it as *my side?* The whole bed is mine. I move the pillows to the middle. I pick up *Breakfast* in its bulky plastic frame.

A woman sits by herself reading, her meal finished. The dark gray of the wall in the upper left of the painting appears in the floor on the bottom right, and the red-and-white flowered wallpaper in the upper right reflects the red-and-white striped cloth on the bottom left, dividing the painting into four small squares. The bureau, column, door, nightgown, cup, saucer, and napkin offer white breathing spaces, and act as magnets, drawing my eyes to the interior of the painting. The white circular doily on the back of the upholstered chair suggests a center. A white heart. The rectangular shapes of the door, bureau, table, and book exist along with the circular mirror, tray, cup, and saucer. Life is balanced, ordered. And safe. But my eyes always go to the woman, where the movement begins. As she curves forward, I follow to the book resting in her lap, then counterclockwise to the door, the mirror and wall, the flowers, the breakfast tray, and back to the woman.

I look up and away, into the breath of this house. The girls are not only in their beds but also asleep. I'm not only in my room, but also by myself.

After washing my face and changing into one of my favorite slip

22

nightgowns, all cotton and white, with wide straps and a square neck, I pick up the new notebook I left on the chest at the foot of the bed. Matisse kept notebooks too. Until a couple of years ago, that's all I did—collect them, storing them unused in a drawer in my study. My notebook drawer. I was afraid if I wrote in one, I would mess it up—ruin it—either with what I wrote or how I wrote it.

The day came when I couldn't fit one more notebook in that drawer. Staring at my collection, I saw journals not written and roads not taken. It was time, I persuaded myself, to overcome my fear. I could have a separate journal for each part of me. That day, as I was about to leave for a haircut, I grabbed a notebook—a dark green, nine and a half inch by six-inch, spiral bound with yellow paper and a hard back, including one front pocket—to be my first journal, on the subject of waiting. After all those years, it was as easy as that to commit to paper, which made me wonder if the preceding years were a necessary part of the process, or wasted.

I crawl into bed and slide my feet under the sheet, pulling its coolness over my legs. I place the hand-sized journal with its marbleized cover in my lap and stare at the blended colors and swirled layers. I can't keep the colors straight either. As each new color enters my consciousness, there's an automatic mixing of that color with what's already there, which prevents me from thinking and responding, or feeling and reacting.

Laying my head back, I stretch all the way to my toes, a rough toenail scratching the sheet. I've always needed time to myself.

Remembering the exception, I raise my head.

I was so open with Frank until the end that when I left him, I had to leave that me behind too. Those days right after, I felt nothing but a hollowed-out emptiness—the black form from *Jazz*, falling in blue, the scared red heart. I couldn't stand the ache of alone. Never again would I feel like that. Always, I would hold back.

A flicker of something, a missed heartbeat. I sit up, putting my feet on the floor, my hands on my knees, then I float through the darkened house to the kitchen for a glass of wine.

Back in the bedroom, the lamplight illuminates the picture of Caroline and Elizabeth and Mark from the day at the park. I put it in a frame this morning on the other bedside table. Mark has his arms around the girls, who hold shovels and look as if they're about to burst with excitement as they look up at him, Elizabeth with her head turned almost upside down. Mark looks straight at the camera, at me.

I should get out of bed to brush my teeth—I can hear my mother's voice. "Thirty-two is all you get; take good care of them." But I take my last sip of wine and reach to turn out the light, all in one motion.

The waiting room of my gynecologist's office is small and soothing, just like my doctor, Jack Matthew. Instead of a sign that forbids eating and drinking, an oak table anchors one corner, set up with never-burned-smelling coffee, some kind of real flowers, and a basket of fruit. Today, it's apples, with a tart, ripe smell. To the left of the table in the other corner is a water cooler and stacked on top are paper cups with proper bottoms, not the pointed funnels you have to hold until you drink all the water. Only two other women wait for appointments. I locate my journal in my purse and write as I wait.

Once in the examining room, I wait only a few minutes for Jack who, instead of shaking my hand, touches my shoulder. He reminds me of Mark, except that he's shorter and has curly blond hair. As we always do, we talk for a minute about growing up on St. Simons and about being in sixth grade together before he moved away.

The conversation narrows to my annual check-up. I tell him that during the year I only had one instance of abnormal bleeding. A few years ago, I had heavy bleeding between periods that were lasting longer than they should. Jack did an endometrial biopsy, which showed that the lining of the uterus was abnormally thick. He called it endometrial hyperplasia and gave me some pills, which solved the bleeding problem. I've had one other biopsy since then, and it was clear. He doesn't think that one instance of bleeding requires another biopsy.

He does say I can take a blood test, a screen for ovarian cancer. I would do a blood test for anything. It's too easy not to.

"Sorry I'm late," Alyssa says, coming from her monthly hair appointment and sliding into the other side of the booth at the Nacho Royal. Alyssa and I met three years ago when I was teaching art at the College of Charleston, where she was teaching French. Sometimes the only way I know what I'm thinking is to explain it to her. And she knows what I mean, even when my words aren't right.

"Your hair looks just the same," I say, taking a bite of my salad.

"Thank you, since you know that's the point." She smiles. At forty-five, she keeps her hair in line—shoulder length and straight. I can't do anything with mine. "And thanks for getting my salad." She picks up the packet of dressing but puts it back down. Then she puts her hands on the table and takes a deep breath.

"Did you not want a salad today?"

"I do. It's just—I seem to be lacking my normal *joie de vivre*. At first, I thought it was Ro leaving for school again, but he's doing great, and I really don't miss him too much. Teaching is fine. My weight's on the low end. And yet there's something not right. And the thing most not right is Richard. Yes. It's got to be Richard." She picks up the dressing again and this time opens it. "I feel better already."

"Last week you said he wasn't acting like himself."

"And now he's started pacing."

"Pacing?"

"In front of the TV. And the TV's always on. He comes in the door and goes straight to it."

"You hate TV."

Alyssa stares at her salad.

"I guess you pointed out the pacing?"

"He said he didn't know what I was talking about."

"So maybe it's nothing."

"It's not nothing." She pauses and then adds, "And he's drinking, a lot, way beyond taking the edge off. It's like he's trying to annihilate his feelings."

We look at each other.

"Okay," she says, taking a deep breath, "enough about me. Any news on the contest?"

I shake my head.

"And Mark?"

"Practically perfect in every way."

"You've been watching too much Disney. But does he have a brother for me?"

"You're already married."

"Oh yeah, too bad."

"Actually, he did have a brother. An older brother who died in a car accident his senior year in college. Mark was supposed to be with him."

"Jeez."

"I know." I collect the stray threads of lettuce from the table, tossing them on an extra napkin.

"Anyway," Alyssa says, picking up her unsweet tea, "Mark can't be perfect. Complain about something."

"Of course, he's not perfect. He likes to talk everything to death. Back and forth. Back and forth. And everything has to be decided together."

"There you go."

"And he's always asking me to marry him."

"Well, there's a problem a girl doesn't want."

"I'm serious." I pull the tray from the end of the table to the middle and put my basket on it.

"I know you are," she says. "I just don't understand. You love him, and he loves you."

"Well, would *you* get married again?"

Alyssa adds her salad remains to the tray. "I think I would," she says. "If I loved somebody, and he loved me."

"I loved Frank. And he loved me."

"Do you really want Frank to be your love stick?"

"My love stick?"

"The love by which you measure all future loves."

Laughing, I put my purse on my shoulder and pick up the tray. "Love stick is pretty good."

Outside, her car is next to mine. As we open our doors, I say, "I need time for Caroline and Elizabeth. And a little for me. And there's only so much."

Just like that, it's November. The day before Mark's birthday, I make the pimento cheese he loves, my grandmother's recipe. After work the next day, I pack a basket with sandwiches, chips, apples, wine, and candles. The red-and-white striped cloth.

Wynn—one of Alyssa's students at the College of Charleston and the girls' favorite sitter because, as Caroline says, she sits on the floor—will pick the girls up from after-school care at six.

Heading to my car, I look up. A strong blue sky. And there's a chill in the air perfect for a picnic. When I pull into Mark's apartment complex five minutes early, he's standing outside waiting.

"I was going to come to the door," I say.

"I couldn't wait," he says, throwing his sweater in the back and getting in.

I lean to kiss him. "Happy Birthday."

He keeps his hand on my leg as I drive to Waterfront Park. On our first pass, we find a parking place on a side street. Mark carries the basket, and I scoop up blankets and pillows. We set up under a tree, where we can see the water, the pier, the fountains, the sun on its way down. I sit and pull him beside me. He bends me backwards, kissing me. I run my hands through his hair, down his sweater, and then underneath his shirt. I nuzzle my nose into his neck and inhale Ivory soap.

"Don't take this the wrong way," he says. "But I wish you'd gotten a hotel room instead of a piece of grass."

I laugh and push him away. "Let's open the wine."

He tilts his head back, stretching, closing his eyes for a second. "It doesn't get any better than this."

I hand Mark a glass of wine, and he turns to face the water and the setting sun. I inch around too and lean against his shoulder.

"It goes so fast," he says, and takes my hand.

After baths are finished, while I help Elizabeth into her starry night big girl underwear and then into footy PJs, Caroline puts on her pink and white striped nightgown. When we moved into this house a year ago, I was worried it might be a problem for them to share a room since Elizabeth was still a baby. But she's not a baby anymore.

I sit half on and half off Caroline's bed, ready to spring away, although I'm attempting to act as if I have all night because little children being put to bed are like horses. They can sense your desire to flee.

With all the covers pulled up to her neck just like I like them, Caroline asks for "The Painting Story." Ordinarily, telling a story requires more energy than reading a book, but not this story.

> Once upon a time, a long time ago, there was a
> little girl named Emily Jane. One day when she
> was nine years old, her mother started packing to
> go on an airplane. She was the luckiest little girl

in the world because her mother wanted Emily Jane to go too. They were going together to a big city called Philadelphia. After they did this one sad thing and if she acted very grown-up, her mother was going to take her to a special place. Emily Jane acted very grown-up. So her mother took her to look at paintings in a museum. Emily Jane loved the museum and everything about it. But most of all, she loved a painting she saw that day when she was nine years old. The name of the painting was Breakfast. A man named Henri Matisse painted it. She liked the painting so much that her mother bought her a note card of it. When she got home, Emily Jane taped the card to the wall by her bed and imagined being the woman in the painting and someone painting her life. She knew then that this painting and Henri Matisse would always be important to her. And they were. The End. Good night.

"Mommy, tell about 'the sad thing.'"

"'The sad thing' was that we had to go to the hospital to tell my mother's sister good-bye. She was sick and about to die, and my mother said we would probably never see her again."

"Did you cry when you were little?"

"Sometimes, but I didn't then. My mother did. Last question."

"Did you see the Liberty Bell?" Caroline asks in her best teacher voice. She bursts into giggles even before I give the answer she knows is coming.

"Why would anybody want to see a stupid, old, cracked bell," I say in my best, obnoxious, little girl voice, "when they could spend more time looking at paintings in a museum?" Precisely what I said to my teacher almost thirty years ago when she asked the same question.

I'm sitting in my office at work when my cell vibrates. Moments later, I put it down and turn to my right expecting Mark to be there to catch me. With both hands, I grip the edge of my desk. Then I close one after another of the museum's old hand-written record books. Automatically and slowly, I stack the books, put the papers back in the file, and the pens back in my drawer. I go through the process of saving documents. The simplicity and familiarity of these small actions calm me, but I wonder how I'll be able to sit here doing nothing until Jack calls back. My heart beats too fast. I reach for my phone but let go of it as if it's too hot to hold.

My hand feels heavy when I pick up my notes. I breathe in as much air as I can. I took the blood test to rule out ovarian cancer, but instead, the results show there might be a problem. My CA125, whatever that is, is high—72. Normal is under 30. A high number could also mean, *in addition to cancer that is*, endometriosis or infection. I'm not supposed to panic. Usually with cancer the number is in the 100s. The next step is a pelvic ultrasound. Jack will call right back with an appointment time. If it shows a problem, and I turn out to have cancer, this is the dividing line, the transitional space between before and after.

Having cancer was not one of the options. My brain sprints ahead with feelings running in slow motion trying to catch up, but my body is still. I'm out of sync.

Caroline and Elizabeth. It's as if I've fallen off a fence and had the breath knocked out of me. When my cell vibrates again, I jump.

Not a good sign that the ultrasound is scheduled for two and a half hours from now.

I call Mark but get his voicemail. He's out of town, as he often is, on a dig and probably has no service. I try Alyssa. She's in class. I decide to get in my car and drive. Driving will force me to concentrate on a mindless task. And it will give me the illusion that I'm doing something.

This could be nothing, Jack said.

Another bad sign. The technician in the ultrasound room thinks my doctor is here. "Isn't Dr. Matthew the one with the gorgeous blond hair?" she says, as she spreads warm jelly on an area that could be loosely described as my stomach. I nod. I'm trying not to panic, but, after all, this would be an appropriate time to panic.

The technician rolls the probe below my waist, watching the screen and, I imagine, capturing images. My doctor *is* here. "Hi," he says. I do a kind of wave. I assume the other doctor is the radiologist. He studies the screen that faces away from me and toward the technician. Jack comes to stand by my left shoulder. He touches my arm. When he does, a breath comes out, and I relax a little. That's what Mark would be doing if he were here, holding on to me.

"I can't find her second ovary," the technician says.

"The first one looks fine," the radiologist says.

"Honey, can you raise your bottom off the table a little?" the technician asks.

I'm starting to sweat, as is the technician, I'm sure. She has two doctors watching her not find an ovary.

"Honey, you can put it down now," she says. "We're going to have to do a transvaginal."

The doctors leave, I get undressed, and I'm ready and waiting when the technician and doctors reenter the darkened room. Everybody resumes his or her positions, and the search continues. With one exception. Instead of moving the wand around on my stomach, the technician is now moving it around inside of me, by means of a long handle and with the sheet draped over me.

They relocate the same ovary and continue to look for my right one. I hear the hands on the giant wall clock tick and then jump. As if time did not move at a steady pace but periodically lurched forward either to catch up or to make itself move at all.

I perform the raised bottom lift again, and they find the missing ovary. All four of us exhale. And then again, the ticking of the clock, now against the hum of some machine. The technician continues to move the wand. "This one appears fine too," the radiologist says, but he is still studying the screen. Jack gives me a squeeze and goes around the table to look at the screen too.

"I don't see any tumors or abnormalities," the radiologist says. "I don't see any fluid. It all looks normal." And then he leaves, as does the technician.

Jack sits on the edge of the table. "I think we've done what we need to for now. As I told you on the phone, the CA125 test is known for false positives. That's why we follow up with ultrasound. Yours didn't show anything unusual. But to be on the safe side, come back next Friday—that would be two weeks—for another blood test."

"What is CA125 again?"

"It's a protein in the blood, an important tumor marker for ovarian cancer, but it's not totally reliable. I'm going to call an oncologist, a friend of mine, to see what he thinks. I'll call you after I talk to him. Are you okay?"

"What about that weird backache I was having? Could that be a sign?"

"Do you still have it?"

I shake my head.

"Good," he says.

Still, I think.

"It was really scary," I tell Mark, late that night when he calls.

"I should have been there," he says.

"I'm probably making too big a deal out of it." I put my book on the floor and turn out the light, sliding down in the bed with my phone.

"But you never know when it's going to be bad."

"Well, Jack was there."

"He's not me."

"I know he's not you. All I'm saying is I wasn't alone. Anyway, how's the dig?"

"I guess what *I'm* saying is that I wish I'd been there, and I wish you wished that too."

I roll from my side to my back. "Mark, I wanted you there. But you were out of town. I've had a rough day."

I hear him moving around.

"Sorry," he says, after a minute. "Is there anything else you should do? I don't understand why that number was so high."

"Jack called earlier. The oncologist he talked to wanted to know if anyone in my family had breast, uterine, or colon cancer. I told him that my mother's sister had breast cancer and my father's father had colon cancer."

"You never told me that."

I breathe. "But he meant closer family than that—like a mother or a sister, or a daughter. It gives me the shivers."

"Me, too."

"The oncologist said I didn't need to do anything else, but Jack still wants me to go in next Friday for another blood test."

"Good."

"I wish you were here," I say, rolling to my side, my phone next to me in the dark room.

"Me, too," he says.

The judges for the "Our Favorite Paintings" contest have completed step one, narrowing the almost five hundred entries to a hundred, one of which is mine. Out of these hundred, thirty-five winners will be announced in four weeks at a party in mid-December. I look for my phone to call Mark. I want to celebrate.

In a press conference back in June, wearing a charcoal gray pinstripe suit—a white handkerchief in his breast pocket—Sam announced the contest and the exhibit. He pointed to a large map resting on an easel and said, "It is our sincere hope that any person who lives or works in this designated area surrounding the museum will make an entry of his or her favorite painting. We're encouraging everyone who works at the museum to make an entry. We're encouraging children to enter. We want to know why each of you loves art. This contest is an opportunity for all of you to see the art you love hanging in this museum right here where you live. Please, whether you have a connection to the museum or not, whether you have any prior knowledge of art or not, enter a painting that means something to you."

Bobby Thomas, a reporter, stopped drawing circles on his notepad, flashed a smile, and said he was going to enter the contest.

"With what painting?" I asked.

"I'm not going to tell you," he said, still smiling, his navy blazer worn in a couple of spots and wrinkled, threads hanging off the bottom.

I returned the smile and looked back to Sam, who was still talking. "The essays will hang next to the paintings and will also be included in the catalogue."

Something to keep forever, I remember thinking. Something permanent.

I find my phone under the newspaper in the kitchen and call Mark, wondering if Bobby entered and if he's one of the finalists. When I give Mark the good news, he exhales. I imagine we're both relieved to have something to distract us while I wait for the second blood test. But Mark says, "The most amazing thing is that I happen to be in town at the same time that you actually want to see me."

"Very funny," I say.

We decide on dinner at Jake's, the neighborhood fish place, if I can get a sitter. Along with champagne, Mark offers to pick up chicken fingers for the girls. I thank him, but instead of *you're welcome*, he says, "As you know, I would do anything for you."

After hanging up, I push all thoughts of the blood test out of my mind. Henri and I are on course for a reunion, and Mark and I are side by side, lovely parallel lines. I smile again and again, feeling effervescent, as if I'd already drunk the champagne and its fizzing bubbles were rising, one after another, onto my face.

Later that night—after dinner, after celebrating, after everything—I bring us each a glass of champagne to bed. The room is cool with the windows open, but that makes being under the covers so much better. I lean back against Mark. He smooths my hair with one hand, while he turns on the TV and changes channels with the other. *The English Patient* is on—I loved the book—and we watch about ten minutes, the part around the fire, when Katharine reads from Herodotus and Almasy falls in love.

Mark sighs.

"What?" I ask.

"I wish I didn't have to get up and go back to my house."

"Well, stay then." The white gauze drapes billow into the room.

"I have stuff I need for work at my house."

"Can't you get it in the morning?"

But he's out of bed already, dressing, and is gone in less than a minute.

He doesn't say anything about how disjointed he feels not combining our lives, but I feel it in the shadows, and I leave it there, along with my fears about having cancer. I focus instead on the light and colors of the TV, as they flicker against the darkness.

I'm back at the doctor's office, the first patient to cross the threshold this morning. After signing in, I pour a cup of coffee and sit down to wait. I'm too nervous to write in my journal. I consider for a moment that writing might calm me. But I don't think I can hold a thought long enough to write it down. Maybe that's the calming part—making yourself hold the thought long enough. The process of writing forces your brain to slow down, and the slowness calms you.

With my purse on my lap, I unzip its inside pocket and take out one of those giant, individually wrapped Life Savers, which I will make last as long as possible. I dig for my journal and pen and begin to write. The nurse calls my name, and I bite the Life Saver in half.

Five women sit outside on Alyssa's patio on a November evening. After Victoria represented me during the divorce, I began to run into her downtown, and we'd have lunch together. Our conversations always included a friend whom the other didn't know. One day, around two years ago, she suggested that we all get together, her friends and my friends, and five of us had dinner at her house. Our dinners were a monthly event for a while, but more recently are only sporadic, due to increasingly complicated lives and temperaments. When five women get together, at least one will be in a rage.

"Nobody even thinks it's about men anymore," Victoria says, acting, as usual, as if she owns the universe. She's tall, with rich black hair, Black skin, and a purposeful walk.

"Growing up I don't remember one single discussion about *whether or not* to get married," Alyssa says, refilling glasses with white wine, offering another of her cream cocktail napkins with *Chez Alyssa* in black script. Until a few minutes ago she was in the kitchen, putting the finishing touches on her potato and leek soup.

"I certainly never looked at the pros and cons," Kari says, "like I do about everything else." Kari has that French red hair. Every time Alyssa sees her, she says she feels like she's back in Paris. Kari's an estate planning attorney in Victoria's law firm. Divorced with one son. I think she's a year younger than me, but she's in much better shape. She used to play soccer.

"Neither choice is the promised 'happily ever after,'" Victoria says.

"Is anybody doing anything fun this weekend?" I ask.

Growing up as the middle child of five, I was always the one trying to prevent pillows from flying. With a brother and a sister on each side, I would hold out my arms like a crossing guard and attempt to look like my father. I didn't like conflict.

And it's true what Frank said. I don't know how to *use* conflict. I don't know how to come out of it.

At dinner, Martha asks me when the winners for the contest will be announced, and I tell her next month. I would have to take a Xanax every four hours to be as calm as she is. Especially with four children. When she walks, she glides, never making any noise or any sudden movements. She's like this steady line we all bounce off of. She loves to read poetry. Maybe that's the secret.

"Like your painting is not going to be picked," Victoria says. "You work at the museum. You majored in art."

"That's not the point," I say, looking at my empty bowl. "The contest is about why people love art and what art they love. It's not about who knows the most or who works where."

"Yeah, yeah," Victoria says. "But Sam will make them pick yours."

"Sam doesn't get to pick. It's not up to him." I stand, asking, "Who else wants more soup?"

Monday morning, I'm in my study doing a little work I brought home to finish over the weekend. I'm also adding stuff to my calendar and going through my somehow full-again basket. But really, I'm just waiting for it to be 9:30 so I can call for the results of the blood test. When it's time, Jennifer, Dr. Matthew's nurse, is with a patient. I have to wait for her to call me back.

My cheeks are burning. I take a deep breath, but it doesn't help. According to Alyssa, the number will either be about the same or lower or higher. I think even I could have figured that out.

As I'm about to leave for work, my cell rings.

"The number's down," Jack says.

"Down?"

"Down."

"How down?"

"38."

"That's almost half of what it was before."

"I feel good about this," he says. "If it were cancer, it would have stayed high or gone higher. I don't think we need to do anything else, but I would feel better if you were to come back in two weeks for another test. Then if it's still down, I suggest we do the test every three months for a year. After that, we can check it every six months for a couple of years, and then annually."

"Why do you think it was so high the first time?"

"Probably an infection."

I thank him and make a note about the next test. Then I slump back, closing my eyes, feeling as if I've just finished a marathon. This makes more sense. I don't have cancer.

My younger sister, Susan, calls to tell me that her husband Peter doesn't know this yet, but they're about to have a big fight. Their daughter Beth, who just turned sixteen, wants to go to a party where, in an effort to prevent drunk driving, the car keys are confiscated, and the kids are locked up together all night. Negotiations have been ongoing for about six days as to whether or not Beth can go. What Susan is supposed to say to Beth when the subject comes up, as it does every day, is "I'm discussing it with your father." Susan said that was fine the first few days. This afternoon, however, when Susan gave the required response, Beth said, "Can't you make any decisions by yourself? Are you dependent on Dad?" Susan told me she just snapped. She told Beth, "Of course I can make a decision by myself. You can go."

I don't mention the blood test.

Susan and I are different. I keep my hair short and brush it once in the morning. Hers is always "fixed." I like to take a bath, but a quick one. She soaks for hours. I only wear mascara, a dot of cover-up, and a clear lipstick. Susan won't even walk to the mailbox without full make-up.

Of course, that's just the outside. On the inside, I don't know how she is. And it's weird to talk to her on the phone. I mean, we're supposed to be fighting over the bathroom and our clothes. Where does the time go?

It's a cold Saturday morning late in November, and I can't stop thinking about Frank. I get up to go to the bathroom, turn up the heat, then get back in bed, drawing the sheets and the blanket tight around my shoulders. The first time I saw him, September of our junior year, he was walking across campus with one of the cheerleaders, and he looked just like a young Robert Redford. I was lying in the grass, reading. Our eyes met. The next time I saw him, he was behind me in line at the cafeteria. We talked, but I have no idea what we said. No idea when I learned he was the quarterback and captain of the football team. The third time he was walking through the open door of my single room. Only one of those on every floor. Even then I needed time to myself.

Frank and Emily. That's who we were when we met Mark our senior year, when he transferred over. After that we were Frank and Emily and Mark. Always together. Even then, Mark knew he would be an archaeologist. Frank had no idea what he wanted to do. But Mark's always known what was important to him.

After Frank and I got married, I taught at a community college. I didn't notice anything for a while, but looking back on it, he was never the same after college, except when Mark would come visit. They always seemed as if they'd just spoken the day before, but they hadn't. I was the one who kept in touch with Mark, and he kept in touch with me. My being married to Frank changed nothing. Mark and I stayed friends, stayed connected.

We'd been married a couple of years when I began to notice the negative stuff. It was after Frank started selling insurance at a downtown company. Ugly stories about people from work. Then he lost his job and began selling cars. The stories continued. It seemed as if he were telling them to antagonize me, as if he wanted a fight—but I wouldn't do my part. I would keep the peace, keep things nice. I kept hoping Frank would find something to turn him back toward life. I thought a baby might break the spell. When I got pregnant with Caroline, things were hopeful for a while. We seemed to stabilize and hold.

But the Christmas before Caroline turned two, Frank won some money playing the lottery and quit his job. He was home all the time. When the money ran out, he started selling refrigerators, ovens, dishwashers, trash compactors. And he came home every day at four. If I wanted to eat early, he wanted to eat late. If I wanted to go out, he wanted to stay in. If I wanted Caroline to take a nap, he wanted to take her for a stroll. It was like Matisse's *Conversation*, with the highly saturated blues and greens expressing the heightened sense of tension under which we were living. We could still look each other in the eye as the man and woman do in the painting, but it was a standoff, each of us unwilling to move. And the open window in the painting was the space between us, taunting us with its abundance of fresh air, its possibility as a bridge of connection. If we could just meet in the middle, there would be trees and flowers—a natural harmony.

But we stayed on our sides, and it stayed cold.

This wasn't the way it was supposed to be.

Frank and I tried counseling, but it divided us even more, cementing our positions. I hated all the arguing. When I was around him, I felt so heavy and weighted that I could barely move or breathe. Even now, thinking about it, my hands go to my neck, as if somehow they could remove whatever invisible force was strangling me, taking my voice, holding me down.

I was worried for Caroline, and I smiled every time I looked at her, trying to smile enough for two parents. I was still teaching art but at the College of Charleston. One night she started crying, and I just lay in bed listening. Frank was downstairs watching TV. I listened and listened without doing anything. Then the crying changed to sobbing, and I jumped from the bed, understanding two things. Her life was in my hands, and my life was in my hands.

And always would be. I would never give myself over to anyone again. I'd been naïve. I was supposed to save a place for myself. I was supposed to be smart. With Frank, I didn't, and I wasn't. I had let my feelings lead the way.

Then, by accident, I was pregnant again. And the thought of the life inside me trying to grow in the midst of all this suffocation was too much.

I took a couple of days off and made a plan, packing stuff Frank wouldn't notice was missing. At the end of the third day, while Alyssa kept Caroline, I waited for him with the rest of my things packed in the car. As soon as he got home, I told him I was leaving. He seemed relieved, getting a beer out of the fridge and flopping on the sofa. Just as I was getting into my car, I turned back. He had come to the door after all and stood leaning against the house, curved in on himself, rotting.

In my new apartment that night, I missed him. Even as bad as it was, I couldn't believe it was over, that Frank wasn't going to be there—that night, or the next, or any other night ever again. What I felt then, and during the days that followed, was a shattering. Not only was the little castle smashed and the tiny slipper in shards, but the glass globe was cracked. As the water drained out, I could see that the snowflakes weren't real after all.

It was messy and for a while it took me down. I trusted no one but myself. I rediscovered small pleasures—losing myself in movies, books, wine, candy.

And Mark.

First he wrapped his words, then his body, and finally his whole life around me. He tried to talk to Frank too, but Frank never returned his calls or answered his letters. Mark said he didn't feel guilty about our relationship. Frank had had his chance, and now it was his turn. The second he finished graduate school, he drove from Boston to Charleston. And when Elizabeth was born on June 29th, my birthday, Mark was right beside me, holding my hand.

When Frank died, I was surprised I didn't feel anything. I had loved him; I'd been married to him; he was the father of my children. But nothing. I'd sealed that layer off and painted over it. When Mark asked me to marry him, I was surprised when I didn't want to. I wondered what had happened to that other person— that person who had wanted to be a part of the "they" in "they lived happily ever after."

Two weeks go by, and Jennifer calls to tell me that my second two-week check is down even more, to 35. She reminds me to come back in three months, around March 1st, for another check. I call Mark but get his voicemail. Then I return to this week's one-page interoffice memo, which helps everyone at the museum stay informed. For fun,

I always include an "art fact of the week," something interesting and short. This week it's that the original name of the Guggenheim was the Museum of Non-Objective Art. Recently, I began adding an art quote of the week, and I don't reveal the source until the following memo. Jere Allan, an artist and professor at The University of Mississippi, is known for working in a series—for exploring an idea with many paintings until he "exhausts every possibility." In answer to the question of how to know when a piece of art is finished, he said, "It just comes to you. Don't worry, you'll know."

The museum appears before us, sparkling white against the dark sky. Lights illuminate the walkway bordered by tea olives. On the front terrace, the water in the three fountains moves to the classical music performed by a string quartet and piped from the light-filled trees around us. I stop for a moment, despite the cool weather, mesmerized by the sensual power of it all.

Mark puts his hand on my back, and we move to the front doors to speak to Sam, who has on a striking tie and cummerbund of thin, horizontal, multi-colored pastel and black stripes.

"Artist designed, of course," he says, kissing my cheek and shaking Mark's hand.

I search his face for a sign but just get his normal smile. I'll have to wait like everyone else. Which makes me proud of our museum.

We enter on the second floor, and before we start down the staircase, we pause for a moment on the landing to look out at the three floors of the galleria ablaze with light and movement. Open rails, open staircases, open arches opening onto open spaces.

Clerestory windows border the top of the building, and looking down, there's the swirled brown marble floor in the middle of which is the sunken fountain, which sends intermittent jets of shimmering water up into the center of the atrium. All the walls of the galleria are white. The green plants and the many windows make this a transitional space between the outside and inside. Now, on the bottom floor, even the children's area is full of people.

No blatant Christmas decorations, just greenery and glittering lights. I rub my arms. I'm having trouble warming up.

"Bobby," I say, spotting the reporter I talked to the day the contest was announced. "This is Mark Hudson."

"We know each other," Mark says, shaking Bobby's hand, looking pleased to see him.

Bobby introduces his wife, Jenny. Then he looks at me and says, "I'm the older guy on Mark's soccer team."

"Oldest," Mark says.

"If you're lucky, you'll get to be as old as me," Bobby says.

"What painting?" I ask.

"*The Card Players*. Paul Cezanne. You?"

"*Breakfast*. Henri Matisse."

We raise our glasses in the air.

"What are you up to these days, Mark?" Bobby asks.

Mark tells him about a dig going on near Drayton Hall. Maybe Bobby might want to cover it for the newspaper? Mark says he found a small artifact, a pinch pot, two layers underground, which didn't make any sense until he dug down a few more layers and found other similar items. As he talks, he holds his hand out in front of him, cupped a little, as if he's holding the small object.

Until now, he says, historians had assumed that colonoware, hand-made pottery from the seventeenth and eighteenth centuries fired at low temperatures, like the pinch pot, was made elsewhere and brought to a plantation. Now it turns out it may have been made by slaves on the plantation itself. I look from his hand to his face. It's amazing, he says, how we just walk around on the surface without appreciating what went into its formation, without realizing what lies below.

A floodlight shines on Mark's hair, his green eyes sparkle and his cheeks glow. But the light seems to bounce off him. I look down at my body and then around to see where it might be. I turn back to Mark. His smile is so warm that when he turns to look at me, I feel as if he's wrapping me in a blanket. No longer cold, I relax. He puts his arm around me and squeezes. I love the way he's always touching me.

"What got you interested in being an archaeologist?" Bobby asks Mark.

This is one of my favorite stories.

"Well, I was always digging up the yard when I was little, finding pieces of stone. I would make these books, taping the stone on a page and calling it something. Then my brother would write a few sentences on the opposite page about the family we imagined it belonged to. And my father loved history. He was always reading to me and my brother about the past."

"And what does your brother do now?" Jenny asks.

"He wanted to be a writer, but he was killed in a car accident while we were in college."

"I'm sorry," Jenny says.

"It was a long time ago."

It's hard for me to listen to Mark talk about his brother. I always think of the night, our senior year in college, when he first told me about the accident. We were in his car, just the two of us.

"I'm really glad you invited me to go home with you," he said that night. It was Thanksgiving break, and Frank had to stay at school for football practice.

"Good," I said. But I thought I heard something else in his voice. Suspecting he was going to say he liked being alone with me, I asked, "Any special reason?" I wanted to hear him say it, even though we both knew I was Frank's girlfriend.

"This is probably going to creep you out," he said, glancing at me and then in the rearview mirror, passing the car ahead of us.

I looked at him, waiting.

"It was exactly this night, the Wednesday before Thanksgiving, two years ago, that my brother was killed in a car accident."

"I'm so sorry," I said. "I didn't know you had a brother."

"Harry. Two years older than me."

"Shouldn't you be going home—to be with your parents?"

"They didn't want me to come home."

"You don't get along with them?"

"I'm a senior, his age. He was on his way home for Thanksgiving."

Only later would he tell me how it happened. His brother apparently came around a curve on the interstate and had to slam on his brakes to avoid the traffic stopped in front of him. But the eighteen-wheeler behind him was unable to stop in time and swerved into the driver's side. Harry was alive when the paramedics got to him but died in the ambulance.

"I was supposed to be with him," Mark said, pulling slowly

back into the right lane. "But earlier in the day, I'd gotten a ride with a friend."

We rode in silence for a few minutes.

"Anyway, I'm glad not to be driving home tonight," he said, "and I'm glad not to be by myself." He turned and smiled at me.

Even then his smile could make me melt.

Years later, I would be able to say that Mark never crossed the line. But in those early days, I was kind of hoping he might and wondering what would happen if he did. Of course, in those days, I never thought about making a move myself.

In the dark car, all those years ago, I turned to face forward and slid down in the seat. "Tell me about Harry," I said, in that carefree college voice that was full of nights that went on and on, full of possibility.

"We did everything together," he said. "I even followed him to the same college. We didn't talk much. He was private, kept to himself. When I think about him, it doesn't seem like I knew him very well. I wish I had pushed him to talk more."

On the way to the auditorium for the announcement of the winners, I need a moment and pause by the bathroom, leaning against the wall. I'm afraid my name won't be called. And I'm also afraid it *will*—that my essay will hang for all to see.

When I enter the auditorium full of flashing cameras, Sam is already speaking. Mark's height and red hair make him easy to spot. Deep breaths. I'm chilled and wrap both my arms around Mark's arm as I join him.

The lights dim and the screen shows a stunning and huge "Our Favorite Paintings" logo in the museum colors of green and gold, with tiny, empty picture frames coming off the scripted letters. Sam picks up an envelope and breaks the seal. He announces the runners-up, in the order in which the museum will turn to them if the acquisition of one of the winners' paintings falls through. The lights are turned on. Sam motions for the runners-up to stand.

The lights dim again. "Ladies and gentlemen, our favorite paintings." The logo screen comes on again, this time with the little frames full of color and with a loud trumpet fanfare. The screen changes to show a woman in a white dress, reading. Sam says, "Taylor Adams, and her favorite painting, *Woman Reading in a Garden* by Mary Cassatt." Taylor walks to the stage with her hands on her mouth and shakes Sam's hand. The screen changes to a painting of mostly snow with a brown sky. The black outline of a roof is visible with gray smoke heading into the sky. Sam announces, "Chuck Battle, with his favorite painting, *Winter* by Ty Brooks." Then Claire Eprile, with her favorite painting, *Homecoming, 1995* by Bo Bartlett. Adams, Battle, Eprile—alphabetical order.

I don't hear anything else until I see her on the screen in her slip nightgown reading her book. Mark hugs me, and I see Sam looking straight at me. "Emily Hall, with her favorite painting, *Breakfast* by Henri Matisse." I head toward the stage. Before I'm conscious again, Sam is announcing Annie Levens, but I miss her painting. Next, "Suzannah McLin and her favorite painting *Trees in Winter* by Bruno Zupan. I try to find Mark's face in the crowd, but from where I'm sitting, I can't see him. Then Caleb Turner, and his favorite painting *The Storm* by Edvard Munch. I've recovered enough at this point to notice the dark painting projected onto the smaller screen set up for the people on stage. It's a painting I'm not familiar with, and there's no storm depicted.

I hear Bobby Thomas's name and look up to see Cezanne's *Card Players*. Two men in hats sit with their arms on a table, staring at their cards. My first impression is one of similarity, but, looking closer, I notice the individual characteristics of each—in the shapes of the hats, the degrees of leaning, the shades of darkness. Bobby nods to me as he takes his seat.

Applause and pictures, and then it's over. I can't get to Mark fast enough, fitting perfectly on his chest, with the top of my head coming to the top of his shoulder.

After a late dinner and celebration, when we're on the way to Mark's car, I shiver. Mark asks if I want his coat. I nod and he stops to take it off. He looks so handsome in his white tux shirt with the black tie, leaning over me to put the coat around my shoulders. When he gets into the driver's side, he just sits there.

"Mark?"

He starts the car and backs out. "First I'll take you home. Then I'll go home."

I reach for his arm, but look out the window.

He continues to drive.

And I continue to stare away.

"We should at least live together."

His words feel heavy, weighing me down. It's a feeling I remember, and it reminds me to be smart. I have to keep my life in my hands. And I have to protect the girls.

A couple of weeks after the announcement, I knock on the door to Mark's apartment, not waiting before I use my key. The whole room sparkles. Candles light every surface. Something smells spicy and hypnotic, as if a cartoon trail of smoke is about to lure me further into a lair. Captivated by the light, I push the door shut with my back.

Mark comes out of the kitchen, wiping his hands on a dishtowel.

"If it's sex you're after," I say, "wasn't this a lot of trouble?"

"Emily, you're so—" He shakes his head and laughs.

"Wonderful?" I say, still leaning against the door, hoping only after the fact that I haven't ruined the moment.

"Wary," he says, coming toward me, smiling. He puts his hands around my waist.

Relaxing, I reach up for his broad shoulders, noticing how solid he feels. I run my hands down his light brown corduroy shirt, which matches the freckles on his face.

"Anyway, sex is not what I'm *after*," he says. "Although I wouldn't refuse it." He gives me a kiss. Then we ease from the door into the room.

"So what's the occasion?" I ask.

"How about a glass of wine?"

I start to follow him to the kitchen, but he says he'll bring it to me. "I put that pinot grigio you like in the freezer a little while ago."

Sitting on the couch, I realize his chili is what smells spicy. I take off my shoes, lean back, and close my eyes. It's possible I fall asleep for a second. When I feel his legs nudging mine, I open my eyes to see him standing in front of me holding two glasses of wine. Mine is half-full, the way I like it. His is filled to the brim, as if it were a glass of milk.

The crisp taste of the wine revives me. "This is the life," I say, smiling. Then I pick up the small wooden boat on the coffee table.

Mark's grandfather, who was from Louisiana, taught him how to carve. I saw this boat in its various stages of becoming. "You can really tell it's a lobster boat now that it's finished," I say. The bottom is painted black; the little house part, white, with spaces for windows. One triangular sail at the back.

"I have another one I want to show you. I just found it."

Mark hands me a bigger boat, about a foot long, with a thick white bottom, a natural wood top, and a wooden canopy over where the driver would be.

"It smells good. Where'd you get this one?"

"It's one of my grandfather's, a copy of an old 1926 Richardson Cruiseabout. Made out of pine. This old Lyman motorboat is one of his, too." He hands me another boat, each white plank showing separately on the bottom. "I found them cleaning out a closet yesterday."

"Cleaning out a closet?"

He sits down too close for me to be comfortable. Then he leans forward, resting his elbows on his thighs. To the middle of the room, he says, "There *is* something I need to talk to you about—"

"I knew it," I say.

"Let me finish." He smiles, putting his hands on his knees for a minute. "I've wanted to do the candles for you for a while. I read about it in a magazine at the dentist's office. It *is* neat, isn't it?"

Leaning back, holding tight to my wine glass, I can almost feel the soft flames of light that surround us—no heat, just light. "I love it. It's kind of Christmassy, too, without being red and green." I give him a kiss and put my free hand on his knee, hoping he's not about to bring up marriage again. I swallow some wine quickly.

Still not looking at me, he says, "You know, I've been scouting around for my next job. Since I'm almost through with my work for the state. And for the museum." He pauses and takes a deep breath. "Well, some things have come up."

"What things?" I ask, realizing he was right. I am wary.

"Some opportunities."

I drain my glass.

"And I hadn't even had a chance to talk to you about options yet. I wasn't expecting to have to make a decision so soon." He looks at my glass. "Let me get you some more wine."

"I'll get it," I say, hopping up, realizing I need to move away from whatever this is that's getting too close too fast. I lift the cold bottle out of the freezer, fill my glass, take a sip, and then add another splash. It's a small glass.

"Hey, do you need some more?" I think to ask, holding the bottle and looking around his orderly little kitchen. Chili simmering on the stove. Half an onion chopped on the cutting board. A stack of bowls.

"No. I guess I've been doing all the talking, and you've been doing all the drinking."

"Funny," I say, putting the wine back in the freezer. When I sit back down, I say, "Okay, tell me."

"The chief archaeologist on the UCLA team studying the Black Sea in Turkey had a heart attack last week and died. They've offered me his spot." He turns to look at me only as he finishes his sentence.

"Mark, that's fantastic. I mean, not about the guy dying, of course, but for you." I put my hand on his back. "Congratulations. How long will you be gone?"

"Well, that's kind of the problem," he says, speaking to my eyes. "I have to commit for four years."

In that infinitesimally small moment before I register the words, I store the fact that when it came to the hard thing, he looked right in my eyes and told me.

"Four years?" I put my glass on the table and look at him. "Are you thinking about going?"

"I wouldn't choose to be gone for four years, but they need continuity. Robert Ballard, the famous underwater explorer, is in charge of the project and—"

"I can't believe it." I slump back into the sofa.

"Emily, I wanted to start this conversation talking about us, but I knew you wouldn't listen to that."

"I didn't know you wanted to go back over there."

He turns his body to face me. "I love you, and I don't want to leave you. I want us to get married. So we can be a family—you, me, Caroline and Elizabeth. Maybe have more children."

I tilt my head back for air, inhale, and then let out a long breath. I sit up. His dark green eyes seem to want to lock onto mine, but I look away before they can. I knew he wanted to get married. But I thought he understood how I felt about it. That I loved him, yes; that I wanted to blur the edges, mix his stuff with mine, have him around all the time, give myself over completely—no.

"I want to build a life with you," he says.

I look down at my clenched hands. I'm closing in on myself.

He calms his voice to say, "You know all this." Then he reaches over to take both my hands in his. He gently pulls them away from me, and my body follows, turning toward him.

"I know you love me, Emily. I also know you think you have your life organized just right." He grins. "Me here in my apartment and you in your house. Maybe you've never recovered from being married to Frank. Or maybe you're just different than everyone else. But I do know we love each other."

He pauses, takes his hands away, and pushes his hair back. "But here's the thing. This job is too good an opportunity to pass up just so I can *kind of* be with you. You don't have to decide tonight, but I've only got a week to let the team know my answer. I want to tell them my family is here. That I can't possibly leave. But if nothing's going to change, I'm going to take the job. And you know I should."

I hesitate before asking, "Did you go looking for this?"

He stands up and puts his hands in his pockets. He moves away from the sofa. Then he turns to look at me.

"I've followed the Black Sea Study since it started. But loving you and not having more of a life together has been rough on me lately. It's hard being so close to you, and yet not *with* you."

He comes over and kisses me gently on the lips, resting his hand on my head for a second. Then he goes into the kitchen. I'm stunned, no longer nervous. But I need to move. I head for the bathroom. Sitting on the toilet, I put my head in my hands.

When I come out, two big red bowls of chili face each other on the table. The yellow plastic squeeze bottle of French's mustard between them, surrounded by separate white bowls of oyster crackers, pickles, cubes of cheddar cheese, and chopped onions.

"Do you want to switch to beer for the chili?" he asks, rinsing the cutting board, as if the last thirty minutes hadn't happened.

"I'll stick with wine," I say, "but I need some water too. You want some?"

And my voice must sound as fragile to him as it does to me because he looks over and lets the cutting board fall into the sink. His wet hands reach for me as if I were an injured child. It's odd that I didn't notice feeling that way, but I heard it in my voice. I love this man. I can't bear for him to go.

He holds me for what feels like not nearly long enough. Although I want to hear about the job, I'm unable to ask questions. We agree not to talk about it anymore tonight. After supper, he follows me to my house so Wynn can go. We fall on the bed to watch TV. The next thing I know, it's dark and quiet. I look at the clock. 3:07. The TV's off. I'm covered up. Mark is gone.

The night after the candles, he comes for supper, and to talk, bearing a whole packet of information on the project that he received earlier in the day by FedEx. While I give the girls a bath and find them a Christmas show, he cleans up the kitchen. When I come back in, he has the information spread out on the table, and he's looking through a large notebook. I sit down, picking up one of the brochures, which shows a map of the world on one side and a large map of Turkey on the other. He shows me Cairo, where he did his graduate work. Then Sinop, in northern Turkey, bordering the Black Sea.

"What are y'all doing?" Caroline asks, wandering in. Her thick, black hair clashes with her thin body and serious eyes, but her nightgown, robe, and slippers all match. She wouldn't have it any other way.

"We're looking at maps of Turkey. Mark might go to work there."

"Can I see?"

He puts her on his lap and shows her where we are and where Turkey is, and then in comes Elizabeth.

"Ice cream?" she says, always getting right to the point.

I watch Elizabeth lean against Mark. Although both have red hair, Mark's is bright orange, but not as bright as it used to be. Elizabeth's is darker and brownish, with lots of blonde highlights. Actually, every time I notice it lately, it seems more blonde. I know she got the blonde from her father, but I like to think she got the red through osmosis, Mark being the one who was with me the last months of my pregnancy and the one who was there when she was born.

He reaches to pick her up too, one girl on each knee. He shows Elizabeth where Turkey is. "Gobble, gobble, gobble," she says and laughs. Then Caroline starts doing it. After they finish their ice cream, I put them to bed. When I come back to the kitchen, I pour each of us a glass of wine, also fixing myself a sparkling water with lime. I take a big sip of the water and sit down.

"This is incredibly exciting," he says, not looking up. "The goal of the project is to discover a possible trade route across the Black Sea. Then Ballard hopes to find shipwrecks that can tell us about civilizations from ancient Greece to Byzantium and the Ottoman Empire. But the Black Sea is huge." He turns a page in the notebook. "They've already discovered enough to suggest that there were Bronze Age, Greek, Hellenistic, Roman, Byzantine *and* Ottoman settlements around Sinop. Remains of a Hellenistic temple still exist, and those of a Roman bath complex." He pauses to take a sip of wine, finally looking at me.

"So you've decided to go?"

"My first choice is to stay here and marry you," he says grinning. "I'm really just a family man at heart."

I believe him. But I'm not smiling. This is not an easy subject for me. I watch him close the notebook. Looking into space, I listen to it slide as he pushes it away. My next breath is audible.

He reaches for my hand across the table, and I look into his face.

"I'm serious, Emily. I love you. I want to marry you. I don't want to leave you."

"But this project is something you shouldn't miss," I say, staring at the notebook.

"I'll turn it down in a second, happily." He puts his glass beside the map and takes my other hand, scooting his chair around the corner of the table.

Now there's nothing between us.

"Marry me, Emily."

Yes, I almost say, feeling as if he's drawing me toward him by a force over which I have no control.

I look down to see my hands. In his. But I can't feel them. Now I remember. I don't want to get married. I stand.

Mark's green eyes search mine for something to latch on to. Again, my heart wants to say *yes*.

You can't trust it.

"Mark, I love you," I say, backing toward the kitchen counter. "But I don't want to get married. You know that."

We look at each other, the sound of the TV from the den in the background—I forgot to turn it off.

"Don't you feel anything?" Mark asks.

"You don't know what it's like taking care of two small children.

I just do the next thing. I don't have time for a husband, for you being here all the time, for thinking about what you want." My voice trails off. "There wouldn't be any time for me."

"God, Emily." He spits the words out and scoots his chair back.

"You know I love you."

"After that speech?"

"I *do* love you. And I don't want you to leave."

"*Show me* you love me," Mark says, each word distinct.

I can't breathe. My heart feels tight, but I just stand there. When I feel tears escaping, I turn away so he doesn't see.

"Why Emily, why can't you show me you love me?"

He asks this, but as if he already knows the answer.

The TV seems louder, more insistent.

Mark whirls to the other side of the kitchen, yanks on a drawer, and then slams it shut.

I jump.

"You love me when you want to," he says, raising his voice. "It's like you keep me in a box that you open at your convenience. God forbid it should be open all the time and I should spill into your life and mess it up."

"Mark, please."

He turns to face me. "Please what? All this time you've said you love me. Hell, you even act like you love me most of the time. All these years—do I not mean anything to you?"

"Stay."

"Not this time. Not without more from you."

"Why are you making me feel that knowing what I want and being in control of what I want are bad things? There's no sense in getting carried away. I'm being realistic, and practical. I decide what I want and how I should feel. Then I make myself feel that way."

"Can you hear yourself?" Mark turns back to the counter and pops both fists on it.

"I don't want to be at the mercy of my feelings. I trust my head. What I know." Turning away from him, I pick up a spoon, squeeze it hard, and let it slip out of my hand. It barely makes a sound. Then I hear him coming toward me, and I turn quickly.

He stops where he is, then crumples into the chair as if the wind has just died.

"Why can't you let go?"

"I don't like to feel bad," I say, looking down at my bare feet.

I hear him shift in his chair. I feel him looking at me.

"I'll tell you right now that I'm afraid of losing you," he says. "I need you. I need someone I can turn to. We *know* each other. We take care of each other. We give each other a place in the world to belong."

I need air.

"Emily."

I don't look at him. I float above myself, leaving only my body in the kitchen. The sounds of his packing up the brochures and papers and replacing his chair under the table seem far away.

Then I feel him standing there, close, looking at me.

"Bye," he says.

And I'm back, but I stare into nothingness. I feel him pause again at the edge of the kitchen.

"I didn't think you'd let me go," he says.

The Yellow Curtain

Usually, I look at the new year as if I were looking at the first page of a notebook, excited and energized by the empty pages fresh and full of possibility. But this year the pages are already written on—I'll be checking my body every three months, and every day, I'll be without Mark.

That night in the kitchen, working with reason alone, I told myself to feel nothing, and I let him go. So now I'll make my own happiness. I'll be like the woman in my painting—having a nice breakfast in her hotel room and then reading. Having a perfectly fine time by herself.

Too fast, it seems, January is gone, the weather in Charleston unable to commit to winter. Each morning I turn on the TV to find out whether the high will be forty or seventy. And not a single drop of rain fell during the entire month. It surprises me that I would notice the absence of rain.

Still no letter from Mark. He's been gone about five weeks now. The girls are watching cartoons in the den. They probably didn't even notice I went outside. I sit down at the kitchen table, wishing I could take a nap. Instead, I cut a piece of lemon pie, conditioning myself to satisfy a basic need with an inappropriate response. I see this.

"Is there anything for me?" Caroline asks, coming into the kitchen, looking through the mail. "Did we get anything from Mark?"

"I don't know." Not the truth, of course.

She looks, and then asks, "Will you fix me some juice?"

I hand her a box drink from the fridge and she goes back to the TV, and I let her.

Later, when I'm watching with the girls, I remember that one of my New Year's resolutions was to do things I love with them. "How about we go to the museum tomorrow?" I say. Both have been before, but never on purpose, just for them.

"Yes," Elizabeth says, smiling and nodding. She talks so much more than Caroline did at her age. I guess that's partly her personality and partly having an older sister to talk to.

"Caroline, would you like to go?"

"What will we do while you work?" she says.

"I don't have to work. It's Saturday. We'll go for fun. Then go to lunch."

The next morning, sitting on my unmade bed next to a laundry basket full of clean, but unfolded clothes, I button the last button on the back of Caroline's longish blue and green plaid dress that I love. I turn her around. She just stands there, arms by her side, waiting for the next instruction. "You look nice," I say. "You just need your shoes."

"Elizabeth, come here," I say, starting to look through the basket for a pair of tights without a hole in them. Elizabeth, still in her PJs, gets up off the floor where she was trying to put tiny red shorts and a tiny red shirt on a Barbie doll because Caroline told her the doll should be dressed.

As I throw a pair of tights in the trash, I see that Caroline is picking out a different color shirt for Barbie.

"Caroline, shoes."

"Where are they?" she asks from the floor.

"In your room, maybe?"

"Hold still," I say to Elizabeth, wrestling her red dress over her head. "Now I need to do the buttons." She's constant motion, always running everywhere, with hardly any baby fat left. She's grinning when I turn her back around, and I hold her in place with my legs while I reach for the tights.

Caroline comes back without her shoes. "They're not in my room."

"Did you look in your closet?" I ask, as I roll up the tights.

"Where are we going?" Elizabeth asks.

"They're not in my closet," Caroline says.

"Where are we going?" Elizabeth asks again.

"You know, *your* shoes are *your* responsibility," I yell to Caroline as she mopes down the hall.

"Where are we going?" Elizabeth asks again in the same even tone of voice.

"Bend your knees," I say, trying to force two little legs into tights that are too small.

Caroline reappears with her hands on her hips, glaring.

"You're supposed to put your shoes in your closet," I say. "If you'd done what you were supposed to, you wouldn't be wasting everybody's time. Look under your bed."

A minute or two later, I hear her shout, "I found them!"

When I look up, I see her standing in the doorway holding her shoes and covered in dust. She looks from my face to her dress.

To distract myself from saying anything to Caroline, I pick up the brush to run it through Elizabeth's hair. I turn her around to face me.

"Why are we going to Bend-Your-Knees?" she asks.

In the first room of the museum, off to the right, nine paintings hang on gray walls. In about five minutes we've looked at each one.

Then we start to play. We count how many of the paintings have trees in them—six. Four have snow.

"Let's find red," Elizabeth says.

But none have red in them.

"That's just in this room," I say. "In some rooms, almost all have red in them. Sometimes it has to do with when the picture was painted, what the style was then."

"Let's count how many have people in them," Caroline says.

In a room full of landscapes, amazingly we find two with people.

Then we go back to the first painting. I point out one thing I like about it—the way the sunlight shines on one small area of the forest.

"Why don't you walk around one more time and pick your favorite painting," I say.

Elizabeth points to the first painting she looks at. I tell her to wait for Caroline to finish, which takes some time because Caroline looks at each painting again before she decides.

When they're both ready, Elizabeth goes first. I show them where to see the artist's name, the title, and when it was painted. Since Elizabeth can't read yet, I read, "*Nantucket* by Theodore Robinson."

"Red," she says, pointing to a dot of red for the man's tie.

"Is that why this is your favorite?" I ask.

"Yes," she says, "and the horse."

Caroline takes us to her favorite painting and reads slowly, syllable by syllable, "*The Road to Lambertville* by Edward Willis Redfield, 1908."

"Why do you like it?" I ask.

"The little buildings and the colors of the buildings. And the snow looks real. And there are no people in the painting. Everybody's inside because of the snow. And it's not fuzzy."

"What color is the snow?" I ask.

"White," Elizabeth says, and then seeing Caroline looking, she looks too.

"White and yellow and blue and gray," Caroline says. "That's cool."

As we head to the children's area, which is downstairs, she says, "We just did one room. How many are there?"

"Actually, I'm not sure," I say.

"Can we come here every Saturday?" she asks.

Cooler weather is supposed to follow the rain we woke up to this morning and that we're coming home in now. At six, it's already dark. As I reach to the mailbox, my arm gets soaked. I drop the disappointing mail on the empty seat next to me. Six weeks.

"Did Mark write us?" Caroline asks.

I shake my head and glance in the rearview mirror. She's sitting still, in her yellow slicker with her hood still on her head. Elizabeth, in shiny red, is pulling at her raincoat sleeves. Her hood was off as soon as I put her in the car seat.

The girls go straight into the tub and then into their nightgowns. Soup and grilled cheese sandwiches for supper. While I clean up the mess, Caroline and Elizabeth play with Legos in the den. As I'm about to empty a Barbie lunchbox, I notice what looks like the corner of a real letter stuck in a magazine in the stack of mail. I put down the lunchbox and pick up the soggy envelope. I turn it over. Mark's writing. Foreign stamps. My heart jumps. I sit and open the damp envelope that feels thick with paper.

Five sheets.

January 23
Dear Emily,

I'm finally able to finish a letter to you. You'll see I tried before. But I didn't feel as if I'd gotten to the bottom of the way I felt or that I had the starting point I wanted. Now, after four weeks of working outside every daylight hour— using my body and letting the precision of the staking and the digging occupy my mind—I woke up thinking about you this morning. So I pulled out the two pictures I brought—one of you and one of you and the girls. I looked at your face in each one. I'm not angry anymore.

Emily, I didn't realize until I left how draining our relationship has been on me. I know that was my fault, doing more than I should have. I realize now I can't do it enough for both of us.

I'm giving you my address, and the phone number for the office in Sinop. I don't have a phone. I'm asking you not to email or write, even to respond to these letters. I'll write again when I feel like I can.

I need to move forward.

Please give Caroline and Elizabeth a kiss from me.

Take care of yourself.
Love,
Mark

Tel. 0368 260 1 323
blackseastudy@gmail.com
Add. Meydankapı Mah. Range Range: 23 SİNOP

January 3
Dear Emily,

It's hard for me to think about the trip away from
you. I left Charleston less than twenty-four hours after
I left your house. By the time I was in my seat on the
plane, I was exhausted. Knowing how much I loved
you and that I was leaving you—I could hardly bear
it. My whole body ached.

At JFK, I remember the roughness of the paper towel
on my skin and then seeing my face in the mirror of the
airport bathroom. I don't know how long I stood there
staring, holding that brown paper towel. Then I boarded
a Turkish Airlines jet for a nine-hour flight that would
take me 5000 miles away from you.

January 6
Dear Emily,

Please tell Caroline and Elizabeth I said goodbye. I regret
not stopping to do that.
But I couldn't

January 10
Dear Emily,

Now real distance separates us.

January 18
Dear Emily,

From the first time we met, even all through your marriage to Frank, you've been a part of my life. I've always
been able to talk to you. Fifteen years. And then really
being together with you, knowing how we are together—
how could you let me leave?

And all this time, I thought he was too busy to write.

"Mommy."

I jump, my hands diving under the table. "Time for bed.
Tell Elizabeth too. I'll be right there." I hide the letters under the
magazine.

My legs feel heavy as I recheck the front door to make sure it's
locked. Out the windows, darkness. I pull down the shades. I want
to put the girls to bed in a hurry, but I can't find the energy. Caroline
hands me a book, my voice monotone as I read:

> One morning the Little Red Hen was pecking in the
> barnyard when she came across some grains of wheat...
> 'Who will help me plant this wheat?' 'Not I,' quacked
> the Duck. 'Not I,' meowed the Cat. 'Not I,' grunted the
> Pig. So the Little Red Hen planted the grains of wheat all
> by herself....

I turn out their light and call Alyssa, who comes right over. While
she's reading, I pour a glass of wine for each of us. Then I watch her
slide one sheet underneath another. Her eyes flicker over the words.

After she puts the letters down on the couch, she looks at me. "So, how are you?"

"I'm the one who let him go," I say.

"Emily."

I look down at my hands and remember my words that night in the kitchen, Mark slamming the drawer. I wonder who I am.

"Sad, mad, happy?" Alyssa asks.

"I feel like I fell off a fence and had the breath knocked out of me."

"Shocked and scared then."

I stand and move to the window, staring out at the darkness. "It sounds like our relationship is over."

"*You* ended it."

"But I didn't," I say, moving closer and sitting on the arm of the couch, the white rectangles lying there like something neither one of us wants to touch.

"You mean you didn't use the words 'it's over'?"

"I mean I didn't intend for our relationship to be over just because he was leaving."

Alyssa grabs up the letters and rereads. "I don't understand why no phone, no email."

"I'm not surprised about that. He's always disliked 'illusions of closeness.'"

"But email could help keep you close," Alyssa says, trailing off at the word *close* and raising her eyebrows at me.

We look at each other. I slide into the corner of the sofa, feeling like a child.

"Okay," she says, "Let's summarize. All he's really saying is that he needs some time."

"Not actually."

"Yes, but—"

"I had no idea. But then, I deliberately avoided thinking about it."

Alyssa sets her empty glass on the table.

"I'll get you some more," I say, without moving.

She shakes her head. "If I drink another glass, I'll have to spend the night."

"He's trying to make a life without me," I say, holding tight to my glass.

"But he says he'll write again." Alyssa looks at me. "Are you okay?"

I force a smile.

"I need to go," she says, yawning.

I hold on to the door and watch her get in the car. Leaving all the lights on, I pour another glass of wine. As I pass the sofa, I see Mark's handwriting and reach for the pages to reread his words. There's something familiar in the January 23rd letter. A tone I recognize. A determination.

Back at work after Mark's letters, I also try to move forward in the world. Today I'm processing a request from a client outside the museum for information on one of our paintings, including a photographic representation. After pulling up the painting on the computer, I document the request, filling in the title of the book in which the photograph will be included and the estimated print run.

"You know *you* should be doing all the work on this ridiculous contest."

I look up to see Ferrell standing in the doorway. "Surely, *you're* not actually doing it all," I say, not having had anything to do with the contest since offering the idea. "Don't you have an assistant or somebody who—"

"*You* are the one who should be working on it, with your organizational skills."

"Flattery will get you nowhere."

"Well, there's an original thought."

I put my pen down and stare at him.

"It's just like you to have entered this contest," he says.

"What do you mean? And why didn't you enter?"

"I don't have relationships with paintings."

"What does—"

He looks at the paper in his hand and reads, "The judges focused on the individual and his or her relationship to a favorite painting, as well as on the painting's intrinsic aesthetic value. The goal of the exhibit is to highlight the connection, to show which paintings mean something to people." Do you realize we've got to come up with some sort of coherent exhibit out of all this nonsense?"

I would love to be doing this. *I* should be the curator. And I will be one day. As soon as Caroline and Elizabeth get a little older. When they don't need me so much, I'm going to take this job away from him.

"Sam and I are spending all our time trying to find out if these paintings are available for the time of the exhibit, as well as the approximate cost of the loan. We're talking to Lloyd's about insurance. These are all things you should be doing."

I was worried that my painting might not be available, but it's not one of Matisse's more famous ones, which should also keep the cost down. "Are you putting all that information in a spreadsheet?"

He stares at me.

"That way, it will be easy to see the different ways to finish within budget."

Ferrell raises his eyebrows as he steps into my office. I'm not sure he's ever been in here before. He seems tall, maybe Mark's height, but then he bends to put the paper on my desk and make a note.

"I was just wondering…" I say, looking at his shiny head.

"What?"

"With these paintings, chronological order might not tell us anything. Maybe go in a different direction."

"For example?"

"Subject matter? Or color. Or the geographic location of the artists. Or the street address of the winners. Occupations. Reading the essays might give you more ideas."

When he looks up, he seems confused about where he is. "Yes, well," he says, fidgeting with his bowtie as he heads out. "Abhorrent little contest," he mutters near the door.

It was such a warm, spring-like January and February that the cold weather now makes it feel as if we're going backwards. On March first, an icy Saturday, my CA125 reminder shows up on my computer. I curl my feet underneath me as I make a note to go by the doctor's office on Monday.

On Tuesday afternoon, Jennifer calls to let me know the number is 47, close enough to 35 according to Dr. Matthew. She reminds me to come back in three months, at the beginning of June.

Later that night, watching a commercial—where a baseball player receives a letter from a little boy across the world, who then runs through cobblestone streets with a glove in his hand, arriving at a field just in time to catch the ball the player has hit across the ocean—tears spill out. Like when I was pregnant. I didn't worry about tears then. Hormones, everyone said. But maybe it wasn't hormones. Maybe I've buried as many feelings as I can hold, and now they will overflow.

After I tuck the girls in, I walk through the house, making the small adjustments that keep everything in order and signal the end of another day. With the time difference I guess Mark's about to start his day as I end mine. I take a deep breath to help me concentrate on my actions—book back on the coffee table, pillows on the couch, sneakers by the door. I turn on the outside light, check that the door is locked, and put on the chain. When I turn to look back at the den, only now do I see the few Legos that escaped the girls' attention. As the only adult in this house and the only person awake now, I can close things down. I turn off the lamp and carry cups to the kitchen, put them in the dishwasher, and turn it on. With water and a glass of wine, I head for my bed, cutting through the dark dining room.

In the bedroom, everything is in its place. No clothes draped over chairs, nothing that belongs to anyone else, nothing I can't control. Henri's words I know by heart. *"On the table, alone, a pencil sharpened with the greatest care. Everything, even the light, denotes a human presence that is careful about—no, in love with—order."* Just as I do every night, I drop my clothes in the hamper in the bathroom, and I reach for my nightshirt off the hook behind the door.

The next day, I toss the mail on the kitchen counter. Caroline meanders in from the den, trailing her finger on whatever she passes. "Can I have some Coke?" she asks, not as if she's thirsty, but as if she's bored. She walks over to where the mail is and asks, "Is there anything from Mark?"

I slam my unopened Perrier on the counter. "Will you please stop asking if there's anything from Mark?"

Too many seconds after my angry outburst, I take the few steps necessary to reach her and give her rigid body a hug. "I'm sorry," I say. "I'm upset about something that has nothing to do with you. Let's look at the mail and see if there's anything from Mark."

She helps me look, but, as I know will be the case, we find nothing.

I pour her some Coke, and we sit at the table. "You know, you could write Mark, and tell him you miss him." He didn't ask them not to write. He never would.

"I could?"

"Or you could draw him a picture and send it to him. Elizabeth could make him a picture too."

"Let's send pictures," she says, avoiding words, proving she's my daughter.

She goes to get Elizabeth and the paper and crayons. I get up for an envelope and a pen. All three of us sit at the table together, intent on our separate tasks. In the place for the return address, I write "Caroline and Elizabeth Hall," as if the letter has nothing to do with me.

And then, finally, another letter from Mark. I sit on a bench along the East Battery, holding it and staring at the seemingly endless ocean. As in Matisse's *Large Gray Seascape*, my eyes are drawn to the circular motion of the waves, to the desolate and haunting emptiness of the wide, open sea. I listen to the waves hitting the concrete and to the clock in the tower, now chiming five times. I'm cold, but I read his letter a second time, slower.

> February 17
> Dear Emily,
> I've been thinking about you.

I look up at the darkening sky, trying to feel his arms around me. I close my eyes and visualize his thick, dark red hair, strands out of place, with those lighter red highlights that almost look blond, and his perpetually flushed cheeks. I see his strong back and legs—not an ounce of fat on his body.

> It was disconcerting there for a while to deliberately avoid thinking about you, but I felt like that was the only way I could take care of myself.

And not saying *yes* felt like the only way I could take care of myself. But I can't think of a time that Mark was not thinking about me. Not even during the long, brief moment that I was married did he stop caring. The others all crossed me off. But not Mark. He would call to see how I liked being married or I'd get a postcard from some far-off place.

> The work here is better than I had even imagined. I think we've gotten over the awkwardness of my coming

in as chief to replace Billy. I have a great crew, three of us who are permanent, with others in and out. Tommy and Anna have been here since the project began. They're both young, 24, working on their dissertations. It'll be just the three of us for the next three months until May. Then for the summer, we'll have Robert Ballard, the marine explorer, the one I told you about, a new graduate from UCLA in Anthropology, and maybe a Turkish archaeologist.

I wonder why I think about Mark so wistfully now that he's gone, and yet when he was here, I acted as if he was allotted only so much of my time. I remember him saying, "Emily, we can go ahead and fool around now, so you can get back to your life."

Please tell the girls I said hi.
Love,
Mark

As I stand and face the street, the lights come on. I hear a horse's hooves and spot a carriage across the way on a cobblestone street. Mark doesn't even know the blood test came out okay—that I'm okay. Eventually I head back to my car, my eyes lingering on the steeples silhouetted against the evening sky.

Thinking of Matisse's *Large Gray Seascape* made reading Mark's letter easier. In my study, I pull out a copy of my essay. Then I look over at my notebook drawer. I choose a Moleskine, which claims to be the type of notebook Matisse used. This particular one has paper that's squared, like graph paper. When I showed it to Alyssa, she said that was very French. I put the notebook on top of my laptop, which is the only clear space on my desk. Then I pick up my heavy pen, the French one from Alyssa—creamy on the outside, black ink on the inside—and open the notebook.

I always leave the first page blank, perhaps as an additional buffer against the outside world, perhaps in case I think of something that should go first. With a journal, I have to be sure before I write because tearing out a page leaves a permanent mark and sometimes makes the whole thing fall apart. If I just cross out, the mistake remains.

The essay will be my starting point. I'll copy it into the journal. Safe, no thinking involved. The first sentence. *At nine years old, the spell of once-upon-a-time had already made its mark....* I copy all the way until the last. *There was feeling.*

Then I turn to a fresh page and veer into the unknown—the essay continued.

In paintings, colors can maintain their individuality and still create something more. Just look at Olive Trees, Collioure, *where "The different colors do not fuse into harmonious tonalities but maintain their own identities, clashing against one another and setting up 'movement' of their own as color..."*

March 16
Dear Emily,

How are you? Things here are amazing. I wake up in the morning and can't wait to get started, even after almost three months. These last few weeks we've been working on a site where we might be looking at artifacts from a previously undocumented period, which is very exciting. Layer by layer we continue to remove soil from sections. On Monday, we found a surprising artifact and had to go back and revise an earlier assumption. It's all so connected, with layers alternately buried and exposed.

Twice in the past week I've been so absorbed that I forgot to eat until Anna came to get me.

Lately we've been finding lots of fragments, which has been disappointing to Tommy, but I'm trying to show him how finding a fragment can be just as revealing as finding a complete artifact, sometimes more revealing. He knows that anyway. He's just easily discouraged.

If you feel like it, drop me a note about how y'all are doing. And how the blood test went—I remember you were supposed to have it again in March. I miss you and Caroline and Elizabeth.

Love,
Mark

Don't write me. Write me.

A note, not a letter. Something short and casual.

Perhaps all he's looking for is the perfunctory, "We're fine."

But I can't be angry. I understand. Seeing someone else do what I've been doing is like seeing myself from the outside. Like seeing myself on canvas.

Today was one of those rare days where every time I felt the warmth of the sun on my head, I wanted to stop and raise my face for more. Now as I sit on my favorite bench on the East Battery, I'm surrounded by little hints of spring. Clusters of daffodils and new leaves sprinkle yellow and green here and there. Occasionally I'll see a single daffodil, bending slightly in one direction or the other, and I'll think how fragile and unprotected it appears.

But it's the water I came here for. I look out and lose myself in its continuous sound, and it takes away the busyness of the world. It stills me.

In spite of the pleasantly warm day, a moist breeze keeps coming up, trying to chill me. I put on my jacket, then pull it tighter around me.

It's six fifteen here. One fifteen in the morning in Turkey. I guess Mark's asleep, unless he stays up later now. I don't know when he sleeps. Or where. Or if he sleeps alone. Stop.

I lure myself into movement by visualizing the couch in the den, where I can sit later with a glass of wine.

Where I'll be sitting next to cold empty space.

April 6
Dear Emily,

For the past three weeks Anna and I have been helping an archaeological crew on the Red Sea coast of Egypt, where I worked on my dissertation. It's so weird to be back. Tommy stayed in Sinop to take care of things there. This morning the two of us were digging in front of what we already knew was a twelfth century merchant's house. After a couple of hours, Anna found a reed mat in front of the entrance to the house. When she lifted the mat to get a closer look, I saw a wooden key. So well preserved that I could almost read the name on it. I had this overwhelming vision of a family who had lived in this house all those years ago, as if I could feel their presence still alive in this place. I thought of the four of us.

We go back to Sinop next week. I hope to hear from you soon. Tell the girls thanks for the pictures.

I miss talking to you.

Love always,
Mark

He's staying in the moment. Allowing the present to expand. Allowing the present to be everything.

But underneath the mat, the key.

April 27
Dear Mark,

After so long, I don't know what to say, where to start. Caroline, Elizabeth, and I are all fine. Elizabeth would rather be at the Little Red Schoolhouse than at home, and Caroline has enjoyed kindergarten. Life at the museum is the same. We're all preparing for the chaos of Spoleto. I'm sure you won't miss the crowds.

The girls and I enjoy hearing about your work, especially Caroline, who, after you first left, asked about you constantly. They're both making another picture to put in with this letter.

We all miss you, especially me. I miss you all the time. And my blood work came back normal. Thanks for asking.

love, Emily

This time last year, Mark and I took chairs and a picnic to the musical Finale at Middleton Place, the oldest landscaped gardens in the United States, just on the other side of the city limits. The evening temperature was perfect for being outside, and the Spoleto Festival Orchestra was better than usual, playing an all-American program, featuring Copeland and Gershwin. Mark and I were there for hours and hours, going through two bottles of wine and two candles. When the last of the fireworks colored the sky over the Ashley River, neither of us wanted to leave. We sat enjoying the night until almost everybody else was gone.

This May, in conjunction with Spoleto, I'm in charge of a special exhibit at the museum—a presentation of the posters of the *Festival dei Due Mondi*, which takes place in Spoleto, Italy, every year, and for which our arts festival is named. I've arranged the posters in chronological order from the first year, 1958, through this year, with a short biography of the artist underneath, and, to the right side, a short paragraph highlighting the events of that year's festival. I have two favorites. Willem De Kooning's 1974 poster is an abstract of thick colors of yellow, blue, brown, white, and red—almost as if he finger painted it. Joan Miro's, from 1981, is painted on a white background, outlined in a heavy black, and the subject is a color-blocked figure in some sort of musical or artistic endeavor.

Caroline and Elizabeth and I are on our way to an outdoor concert—we can already hear the music—sponsored by Piccolo Spoleto, which started in 1979 to celebrate the artists of South Carolina and of the South in general. As if in response to the festival, the magnolias are blooming. It's idyllic, really, like something you read about in a story book, hundreds of parents lying on multi-colored blankets on the grass, listening to the Charleston Symphony Orchestra and watching over children who wander around, holding on to dog leashes, red and yellow balloons or dripping ice cream.

Color and life.

May 4
Dear Emily,

I'm so happy to hear from you, to know that you're all fine, that your blood work was okay, that things are the same—to see your handwriting. Tell the girls I've put their pictures on the wall in my room.

The weather here is so much like Charleston, humidity included. It's weird to be so far away and have the same weather. You would love the green fields covered with wildflowers.

I've been working on mapping the Akliman Delta and on drawing in some of the artifacts we've discovered there. For some reason, that makes them more real to me and places them more accurately in their surroundings than does a photograph.

Today, this Turkish man was watching Anna as she worked, staring really. He was old with a light and dark gray beard, and despite the heat, he had on a black knit cap, a plaid flannel shirt and a blue work vest. He was carrying a stick with an orange and white woven basket on it and in his other hand, a suit coat. I was glad to be finished and move on. I wonder what these people think of us.

We moved to a different boarding house so that the three of us and the summer arrivals can all be together. The food here at the new place is great. Last night we had pide, Turkish pizza. Tell the girls. Almost every day for breakfast I have this yogurt drink called ayran. Anna and I found a tiny restaurant down by the wharf with just four tables and a view of the boats in the harbor. They serve only fish caught that day, along with grilled vegetables. I hardly miss American food anymore.

I hope you have a wonderful birthday.

Love,
Mark

On Saturday afternoon, as the girls and I settle on the couch to watch *Mary Poppins* for the millionth time, my mind drifts. It's 3:30 here. 10:30 at night there. Mark likes to eat late so he would have just finished dinner with Tommy and Anna, the people in his life now. But they would linger at the table. I imagine them sitting outside on a patio, each one's feet propped on the chair next to him, or her, sipping red wine from a new bottle they didn't really need, but which they opened toward the end of the meal at Mark's suggestion. The Turkish cook would have already gone home, having given up on waiting for them to leave the table. Darkness would be everywhere, except for the nubs of candles still burning around the patio and a few lights down in the village. It would be warm, but pleasant with a slight breeze. Mark would tilt his head back on his chair, not like I do, stiff and panicked for air, but slowly in a stretch, his eyes closed for a second.

I've seen him do it a thousand times. I would watch him do it in college when I was with Frank. It's as if he's allowing the moment to penetrate his entire body. And after he does this, it's impossible for him to contain his pleasure about being wherever he is. Right now, he might be saying something similar to "life couldn't be any better than this." And he would mean it. He might wish I were there, but such a feeling would be fleeting because he would reflexively bring himself back to the wine and the breeze and the sky and the friends, because that's what he has, that's what's real.

With the darkness nestled around them on the patio, the stars would be like a sparkling blanket above them. Mark might comment on that. I see Anna tilt her head back too as I leave the realm of the known and venture into the unknown. Tommy, sensing a change, looks up quickly and stands just as quickly, saying he can't stay awake a minute longer. And as he walks down the steps to his room, Mark and Anna look at each other. Mark thinks here is a woman who wants to be with me, and the pull between them is that fierce ache engendered by close contact, prolonged restraint, and unfamiliar sexual attraction.

Stop, I say. It was your decision. He loved *you*. He wanted to marry *you*. But you let him go. And now he's moved to the other side of the world and to another life.

Being in a doctor's office, even this ophthalmologist's office, reminds me of having my blood tested. It also makes me think of how much I weigh. Even though I hate to admit it, I'm often preoccupied with my weight, but I've never been more than fifteen pounds over what I would consider my ideal number. All fifteen pounds are candy.

Caroline, sitting beside me, holding a *Highlights* magazine, flicks her black hair behind her shoulders. I wonder where she got this gesture, probably from studying older girls. She watches people and knows which people wear what clothes, and then she knows what she wants to wear and more importantly what she will not wear.

"Teachers try to pay special attention to vision," Caroline's kindergarten teacher, Ruby James, said, calling to say that Caroline was squinting when she looked at the board. "Seeing is so important. What we see is our world."

She told me about this book she was reading, which says we can become more aware by *training* our eyes to see more—different shades of green and sharper edges. I wonder if that's true. I thought if I could see, if I had twenty-twenty vision, then I saw what was there. But if this book is right, there are things I'm not seeing. Things that I'm missing.

Ms. James told me about some of the exercises they've been doing as games at school. To increase your depth perception, you sit in one spot and intentionally look into the far distance. Next, you look right out in front of you. Then you concentrate on what's in the middle—the in-between space that we hardly ever pay attention to.

"It's amazing," she said, "how much more we see when we're actually looking for something to see."

When I called to make Caroline's appointment, I asked the nurse to find out when I had last had my eyes checked. Over ten years ago. So, combo visit. We've already been here twenty minutes and, in that time, only one person has been called back. There are three others ahead of us. In my purse, I find my "waiting" journal. When I don't have it, I write in my appointment book and then copy it into my journal. Sometimes I want to make changes during the copying process and wonder if that should be allowed.

Caroline waves to me as she moves over to the toy chest in the back corner of the waiting room. It strikes me how much she looks like me at that age—no fat anywhere on her body and thick black hair. The main difference is the shape of our faces, with hers being more rectangular and mine more of a circle. Noticing her hair, half up and half down in a black bow barrette, I realize that it looks just like it did after I fixed it this morning, even after recess and PE.

She touches several toys without picking anything up and then sits in a "child-size" chair. At six, she already seems to have outgrown the small chair. In front of her on the round table is a large, plastic, white and green dollhouse, complete with pool and outdoor furniture. She has her back to me as she picks up the members of the family—the mom, the dad, the girl, the boy. She positions the mom in the kitchen in front of the sink and puts the boy and girl at the kitchen table. She drops the dad on the ground by her feet.

"Here," I say, picking him up. "You dropped the dad."

"I don't need him," she says, holding on to the mom, turning her toward the children.

I feel this like a slap in the face. Instead of mission accomplished, I feel as if I've failed. "Maybe the children need the dad?" I say. It seems like the obvious next question in this make-believe world.

"Nope," she says.

I hold onto him until the nurse opens the door and calls Emily Hall and Caroline Hall, and together we head back to make sure that we can read the chart on the wall, so that we can at least have a chance at seeing and understanding our world.

The last day of May already, and once out of my car, I feel a disturbing warm breeze, as if time is running out and it will only be a matter of minutes before July is here to bake us to death. Without Mark,

I make my way up the pebbled concrete walkway to the museum's cocktail party announcing the paintings that have been acquired for the "Our Favorite Paintings" exhibit. Apparently, if a painting cannot be secured because of cost or availability, a plane ticket will be offered instead. My heart sinks at the possibility of not seeing *Breakfast* here.

In addition to those whose paintings were chosen back in December, patrons and top-level donors are also on the guest list. About a month ago, I bought a short black dress—with a low back and straps that angle in toward my neck. When I put it on an hour ago, the dress was a little tight around my stomach. It must be all the carbs, the comfort food. But I haven't gained any weight. In fact, I've lost some.

On the second floor of the galleria, Sam makes a speech thanking us for caring about art and community, and then he sends us off to the adjacent hall where, on large tables, a photograph of each of the paintings selected in December is set up on a brass easel, green and gold confetti sprinkled about, making it all more festive. Under each easel is an envelope.

The gasps and shouts recede into the background as I locate the copy of *Breakfast,* and in a fraction of a second take in how arresting it is to see it larger than my note card and in a context other than my bedroom. I reach underneath for the cream-colored envelope with my name on it and rip it open, making sure the envelope is empty of a plane ticket before I scan the words to discover that yes, Henri will be coming here to see me.

I close my eyes, and when I do, I see him in his hotel room in Nice during the winter of 1919, painting to the sound of the waves. He loved the winter light there. I open my eyes and look back at the photograph of his painting.

Six months ago, Mark and I were here together. In a little over a year, I'll be here with Matisse. And it was almost thirty years ago when my mother and I *first* stood in front of this painting.

When I looked up to see why my mother had stopped, I saw the woman. She had on a slip nightgown like the one my Aunt Evelyn wore when she came to our house for Christmas. And she was all by herself. I could tell she wasn't just sitting there having her picture made like all the other paintings of women we had seen that day. She was reading. And she had just eaten breakfast because the tray was still there. And she had eaten by herself because there was only one cup. I couldn't imagine getting to eat breakfast by myself.

By the time I took my eyes away, my mother was several paintings over. I looked back at the painting in front of me and noticed the tray. The woman must be in a hotel, like where we were staying, I thought. Or maybe she was rich, and her butler brought breakfast to her every morning in her bedroom.

I could hear my mother calling my name and turned toward her voice. She was coming back. Again, we stood in front of the painting, but this time she asked if I liked it, and I told her yes, that I wanted to be that woman. She laughed, but in a good way. She told me the name of the painting was *Breakfast*. That a man named Henri Matisse had painted it. I looked again at *Breakfast* and saw the flowers. Why would anybody have so many vases of flowers at one time in a bedroom or a hotel room? Then I remembered I had just seen lots of flowers in my aunt's hospital room. I liked the way it looked to have flowers in more than one vase.

My mother and I walked for hours in that museum, and I never noticed that my legs felt tired until we sat down for lunch in the ground floor cafeteria. All I could think about, or talk about, according to my mother, was that painting. She finally agreed to take me to see it one more time before we left.

On the way out of the museum, we passed the gift shop. My mother told me to sit down, that she needed to run into the shop for a minute. I put my head on the bench, and I can still feel the alternating ridges of the soft and rough fabric on my cheek.

When she came out, she said, "I bought you something to remember our trip with," and she handed me a flat, white paper bag, a sheared edge at the top, with "Philadelphia Museum of Art" printed in dark green on the outside, a bag I saved until I went to college. I reached in to find a shiny, smooth note card with *Breakfast* on it. I could take *my painting* home with me.

Still holding the ripped envelope, I feel a hand on my arm.

"Exciting, isn't it?" Sam says.

"Hard to believe."

"Well, it's true. I spoke to the people at the Philadelphia Museum of Art myself. Did you see we got almost all the top picks? Including *The Card Players* from the Musée d'Orsay."

"I was looking for Bobby while you were talking."

"He's out of town. This is going to be some exhibit. Eclectic, as Ferrell points out, but I think cohesive at the same time. And it's the essays that are holding it together."

I smile again, wishing it were my exhibit.

Sam leans over and whispers, "Now that the paintings are all locked up, how about jumping back in and helping Ferrell with the exhibit? He doesn't seem to get it."

Wanting a minute away from the craziness, I go upstairs to my office. Matisse is coming to see me. I pull out my phone wanting to call Mark. But outside my window, darkness. I open my journal.

My life is *full—but empty at the same time, like* The Yellow Curtain, *"one of the fullest and emptiest of Matisse's window pictures."*

My head says, I'm just lonely.

My heart, but I'm not.

Matisse said that empty space is meaningful, that it provides balance. But either Henri is wrong, or I've taken his words too far, my life now overflowing with empty space, my balance lost.

It's not other people I want to be with—it's only Mark. His smile, his arms, his red hair. His knowing Caroline doesn't like to have messy hands. His being here when *Breakfast* was chosen for the exhibit. It's as if I'm falling in love with Mark all over again.

I turn to the next page in my journal, looking from the blank rectangle of the new page to my curved hand, holding tight to the pen. And in a jolt, I begin to scratch out the emptiness on the page, marking through the whiteness, making a mistake I can't tear out. I want to see it, in front of me—what I did when I sent Mark away.

I grab a postcard from the top drawer. But then—nothing. Just like with the essay, I don't know where to start.

I made a mistake.

In my office the floor lamp I bought to soften the room stands by itself in a corner. Out of habit, I turned it on when I came in tonight, and it stands like a guard, unbending and sad.

I face what I've done—the angry, black marks in my journal.

Then I look at the blank space of the postcard. Not knowing whether to dig down into the past or reach forward into the future, I bury it all in my head.

> May 31
> Dear Mark,
>
> Breakfast is coming to Charleston! So are Bobby's <u>Card Players</u>. It's so exciting. I wish you were here.
>
> The postcard is of this year's Piccolo Spoleto poster by Henry Barnes from Atlanta. If you stare at the dark sky, you can just make out how the stars spell Piccolo Spoleto over the soft colors of the houses.
>
> It really feels like summer now with the girls out of school. And the weather here is stifling. Elizabeth says to tell you she likes pizza now.
>
> Your work sounds so interesting—you must love it.
>
> We miss you.
> love, Emily

I hold the postcard above my outbox. The dishonesty is there in front of me. In the exclamation point. Not what I feel, but what I think I should feel. I let the postcard fall.

I look at my watch—not quite seven thirty. Wynn is at the house babysitting. I pick up the phone.

"You're in luck," Alyssa says. "Richard's out of town as usual. Come on. Wait a minute. I almost forgot. What's the name of that Matisse painting that has something to do with Baudelaire?"

"*Luxe, Calme et Volupté.*"

"*Là, tout n'est qu'ordre et beauté/Luxe, calme et volupté.*"

"It sounds so much better when you say it."

"Will you bring a copy?" she asks. "I'm doing Baudelaire on Monday."

I check in with Wynn and relay the change in location. Then I flip through a book on Matisse to make sure the painting Alyssa wants is in there. As I do, I see one of Matisse's sculptures. He would sculpt to prepare himself to paint, "to put order into his sensations." I close the book and head to Alyssa's in the hopes of putting order into mine.

I leave my heels by the back door, and we settle in the upstairs sitting room. Joni Mitchell plays in the background. I have a *Chez Alyssa* with my wine.

"Here's to you and Matisse," Alyssa says, raising her glass. Then she leans back, putting her feet with their bright red toenails up on an ottoman. "I've heard you talk about this painting so much. And now I'm going to see it—live and in person."

"It's amazing," I say, "but—"

"But?" She sits up, putting her empty glass on the table between us.

"It should be the most exciting news, but when I heard it, I wanted to tell Mark. And then, when obviously I couldn't, I was disappointed instead of excited. I can't seem to move past him."

"What do you mean?"

"I keep thinking 'Okay, he's gone. Move on,' and then I'm thinking about him again. He's stuck in my head."

"That's the problem right there," Alyssa says, looking at me. "He never should have been in your head." She refills her glass.

"I made a mistake letting him go."

There. Finally, I admit it out loud. I made a mistake. A mistake

I can't cross out. A page I can't tear out. Words I can't unsay. I feel a tingling down my arms, at the tips of my fingers.

"How could it take you so long to figure this out?"

I shake my hands. "I tried to write to him before I came over here. I mean, I did write him a postcard to tell him about *Breakfast*. But all I could get on paper was the me who let him go, not this me, the one who wants him back."

Alyssa sighs and asks, "So now you want to get married?"

"Well, I don't know. I mean, even if I do, I can't. And he won't know anything has changed—not from that postcard."

Alyssa puts her glass down.

"I can't put my feelings in any order."

"Feelings aren't supposed to be in order," she says.

"I want more back and forth. I miss him all the time now."

"I thought you couldn't stand the back and forth." She picks up her glass.

"I know."

"Did you really banish someone who loved you and whom you loved because you wanted more time to yourself?"

The windows are filled with darkness.

"What are you going to do about it?" Alyssa says, like a dare, picking up her glass and draining it.

I stare at her.

"I've had too much wine," she says, standing up. Then she sits back down. "Richard doesn't care about me anymore."

"What happened?"

She stands up again. At the bar, she puts her hands in the pockets of her cropped pants, and, unusually, they pull tight across the back. She opens a sparkling water and takes a big, long drink. "That's better," she says, her red tank also a little tight.

"Your turn," I say. "Talk to me."

"I need to let it percolate. Next week, I promise. Now what made you switch from wanting time to yourself to wanting Mark back?"

"It's really your turn."

"It will be, soon. Now, c'mon."

"Well, when I had Mark and no time to myself, I wasn't happy. Now I have time to myself and no Mark, and I'm not happy." I stand up, gravitating to the window, distracting myself by trying to see stars. "I've really made a mess of things. I had no idea how much he meant to me."

"Even Victoria bet you'd get married rather than let him go."

"That's helpful," I say. I turn from the window to look into the room and then back at Alyssa. "You know what I said is not true. I *did* know how much he meant to me. But those moments during the day when I never felt like there was enough time seemed so constant and huge. I was always on the defensive. Not getting married was to protect me. There wasn't enough air for all of us."

"But wouldn't it be the same if he came back?" Alyssa asks.

"There's something I'm missing. Before, I was willing to give up the good parts in order to avoid the bad parts. Now I desperately want the good parts, and the bad parts seem unimportant."

"They're not; trust me."

"I didn't think I needed anybody," I say, taking a sip of wine. "I didn't think I was supposed to need anybody."

"You're right about that. *Be self-sufficient. And also, get married.* But nobody ever explained how the two go together."

I sit back down, rubbing the grain in the leather chair. "I miss telling Mark I'm worried about Caroline wanting to please everybody. I miss knowing whether he found what he was looking for. I miss telling him that my back is still bothering me. Eating with him. His green eyes. Knowing whether he's looking forward to a game. Threading my fingers through his red hair. Sitting with him on my couch watching TV in the dark with the girls asleep in their beds, and him checking on them while I pour us a glass of wine—I miss the belonging, what we created, the two of us." I pause for a minute. "And now there's this Anna person."

"Anna, Anna, Anna," Alyssa blows the name into the air.

I look up expecting, hoping, to see bubbles I can pop. "It's Anna this and Anna that, but as if he doesn't even know he's doing it. As if it's so natural."

"Did you talk about going out with other people before he left?"

"How could we? You know I thought we were still together. And the thought of going out with somebody besides Mark makes me ill. It would be like picking a random child to be mine, instead of Caroline and Elizabeth." I pause, waiting for the next song to start, but nothing does. "I guess he's going out with *her*. She's in every other sentence. And I don't even know what she looks like." As if that matters. Still, the visual. My way in, I realize.

"But wouldn't he tell you?"

"He always made sure our relationship was there. So I never felt the absence of it. Or the need for it. He was there so much that all I felt was a need to be by myself."

"Until he was gone," Alyssa says.

"Until he was gone." I'm quiet for a minute. "It seems like I've loved him forever but now it's more than that."

"What do you mean?"

"Well, I loved him, but I wanted to remain—intact."

Alyssa scoots up, sits on the edge of her chair.

"I didn't want to need him in order to be happy," I say, turning to the window but only seeing my reflection in the glass. "Mark was always ready to let go and see where the relationship would take us. He's loved me forever. And I loved him but—see, that's the way it's always been—I loved him *but*. Not too much. Not too close. Off to the side. Parallel lines. 'In a box I could open at my convenience' were his words."

"And now?"

"Now I think about him all the time. His pushing for and making connections. I want that back and I'm ready to do my part. To weave a relationship, to wrap a layer around myself and send it back to him, to wait for it to come back to me, to participate in the entwining." I pause for a breath and say, "That's what I mean."

Alyssa is staring at me. "You need to tell him this."

"I can't. It wouldn't be fair. Based on what I said, he made a commitment somewhere else."

Back home, I let Wynn go, check on the sleeping girls, turn out the lights. I stop in the small hallway, full of open doors, which makes me think of Henri.

Open doors and windows—opening from someplace dark onto a world of light. He said, "Windows have always interested me because they are a passageway between the exterior and the interior." In Open Door, Brittany, *the open door is the perfectly centered single subject of the painting. The door, the interior and the exterior are all painted the same colors. "[F]or me the space is one unity from the horizon right to the interior of my work room…and the wall with the window does not create two different worlds."*

He was a man as well as a painter, and he seems alive to me tonight, as if I might go through the door into the dark dining room and find him sitting at the table.

Instead, I go through the door into my bedroom and slip under the covers.

Matisse often kept a bad drawing "because I may be able to learn from it some day, just because I failed. One learns something every day; how could it be otherwise?"

Until now, I've never thought of Matisse as having made mistakes, as having failed.

I glance at the picture of Mark and the girls, and I flinch. On the other side of me, the note card of *Breakfast* now framed instead of taped to the wall. I pick it up and hold it with both hands.

"[T]he meanings of even the simplest of paintings may not be self-evident, but demand our patience…what it ultimately commands is our participation. We are invited to enter and explore…."

The woman is not by herself; she's alone. I lean my head back on the headboard and squeeze my eyes shut. When I raise my head again, I'm uncomfortable.

"A painter doesn't see everything that he has put in his painting. It is other people who find these treasures in it, one by one, and the richer a painting is in surprises of this sort, in treasures, the greater its author."

I look back at the painting. With those faraway eyes, she's not reading. She's not even looking at the book. She's staring off into the distance. To see this now is like looking in a mirror and not seeing myself. I close my eyes and my head falls back again.

When Henri was asked if the necessity to create the work of art begins when the individual realizes that something is missing, he answered, "It begins when the individual realizes…his solitude and has need of action to recover his equilibrium."

My heart knocks against my chest; my eyes shoot open. I lift my head. I am a woman who made a mistake. I am a woman alone.

I sit up and plant my feet on the solid wood of the floor. Beside the bed, the drawer that holds Mark's number is open a fraction of an inch. I open it wide. Keys, nail files, lip balm, scissors, and pens until finally, the scrap of paper I wrote his number on. As I reach for my phone, I knock my empty coaster off the table. Retrieving it, I discover an old bookmark of a light blue butterfly poking out from underneath the edge of the bed. I sit back up, ready to take a risk, telling myself, it's okay to be afraid and it's okay to ask for what you don't deserve. Then I punch in a number I've never used before. Because he asked me not to. Because until now I let my head control my heart. Because of reason.

As the number rings, I stare out my door into the dark hallway.

A man answers. I ask for Mark. He says to hold on. My heart beats with such force that I look at my chest to see the pulsing. The man comes back on the line to say that Mark is not there. If I'll leave a message, he'll give it to Mark when he returns.

"Returns?"

"Mark Hudson is out in the field. Couple of weeks gone."

I hesitate for a fraction of a second, letting it sink in that I can't talk to Mark now. Then I close my eyes and ask the man to please ask Mark to call Emily. I leave my number, start to hang up, and then ask the man if he'll add one more word to the message. "What word?" he says. "Yes," I say. "Please tell him I said *yes*."

The next morning, as I wake, I'm remembering the man's voice, and I roll to face my bedside table, the still empty coaster, the blue butterfly bookmark without a book, *couple of weeks gone*, the *yes* I spoke into silence.

When I sit up, my stomach hurts, and my head feels clogged and heavy. All three of us stay in our PJs all day, doing only the minimum, eating soup and saltines, leaving a trail of mess. Unable to find Kleenex anywhere, I go to the bathroom to unroll some toilet paper. As I bend down, I have a sharp, thin pain in my low back. Pausing for a slow breath, I discover the Kleenex on the back of the toilet, a redundancy I correct by moving the tissue to the table by the couch.

Too fast it's the last day of school and time for another blood test. Twenty minutes early, I sit in the car, periodically turning on the air conditioning and thumbing through the new *Arts & Antiques* magazine, where Emerging Artist of the month John Decker says he works on "several paintings simultaneously to give the pieces a chance to 'rest'...." The image of paintings gradually developing and unfolding captures my attention, but before I can see where it takes me, Jennifer motions me into the office, where her breakfast waits in a bag. I can smell the bacon. She takes my blood and says she should have the results the next afternoon. I bend my arm back and hold onto the cotton. Since I'm not bleeding, I decline the Band-Aid, which I don't want to have to explain. Then it's back to Caroline's school for the end of the year party. I won't be at work today until after lunch—after I've dropped Caroline at The Little Red Schoolhouse, Elizabeth's preschool that has a wonderful after-school, holiday, and summer program. Normally, their bus picks Caroline up every day after school. Today they're having a party and a movie to celebrate the beginning of summer.

The next afternoon Jennifer calls me at work to report that the CA125 is 54. "That's not good, is it?" I say. She says Dr. Matthew said for me not to worry but to come have the test again in two weeks instead of three months. I'm uneasy, realize I'm holding my breath. Mark will get my message in two weeks. I'll be okay in two weeks. I just have to make it two weeks.

Head down and back to work—photographing and cataloging the new painting that arrived this morning. A still life by George Forster, only slightly larger than a piece of notebook paper. Fruit and a tiny golden bird's nest full of translucent blue eggs. I let the light from my window fall at different angles onto the eggs.

May 18
Dear Emily,

> You won't believe how much is happening. Robert Ballard
> arrived, and we began the underwater work. We have
> four boats, two with side-scan sonar and two with ROVs,
> remotely operated vehicles, like the one they used in the
> movie Titanic. Tommy is working closely with Ballard, since
> his interests tend more toward underwater exploration.
> Anna and I are also involved in the underwater searches, as
> well as the continued mapping of the land sites.

But the most amazing thing happened last week. We were all on board when we discovered an ancient shoreline 500 feet below the current surface of the Black Sea, just above the anoxic dead zone. Unbelievable. And people are talking about Noah and the flood! I'm sending separate postcards to Caroline and Elizabeth telling them.

Now Ballard is gone for ten days and Tommy and Anna and I are going to take a break from work and the heat and head up into the mountain forests. It's even too hot on the beach. We're taking food and sleeping bags and we'll camp under the pine trees.

There are a bunch of journalists here. Look for something about all this in the paper.

Love,
Mark

I buy some vitamins and focus on Caroline and Elizabeth and fun summer things. On the weekends, we visit the library and swim at the neighborhood pool. After work each night, we sit on the front porch to watch the lightning bugs.

Time feels heavy.

May 28
Dear Emily,

I need to tell you that Anna and I have become more than friends. When her boyfriend was here in May, things didn't work out. Then she and I fell together naturally. I know I didn't have to tell you this, and I'm not

telling you to make a thing of it. I just—I don't know—
we've always told each other things like this.

How is "Our Favorite Paintings" coming along? Were
they able to borrow Breakfast for the exhibit?

Tell the girls hi.

Love,
Mark

Sitting on the bed, I push my bare feet into the floor. I've trained my
body well. No feelings, just thoughts. Mark and I had nothing bind-
ing us. He was perfectly free to begin another relationship.

I retract my feet and lie down, pulling the covers over my head.
How could I have let myself call? He and Anna will return together—
maybe even get the message together. I've made it all so much worse.

When I sit back up, my eyes go to *Matisse on Art*, his words. On
the cover of the paperback is a self-portrait. Against a background
of viridian, Henri is sitting in a straight-backed chair, painting. And
staring. Presumably at his subject. Red hair, dark eyes, beard. I rest
my palm on the cover, and I begin to settle down. I did the right
thing. Calling Mark was the right thing. I had to let him know *that
I know* I made a mistake.

Unaccountable creaking. The nighttime noises of the house
settling in.

But in the middle of the night, I wait for Mark on the front
porch, only he never arrives, and I wake in tears, trying to shake
off the dream I couldn't control as well as I control my emotions
during the day.

I love him, and he used to love me. I let him go, and now he's with someone else. Someone younger and not as stupid. I bunch up the sheets and hold them against me. No Mark. Just crumpled, empty white sheets.

Instead of hope, each day brings dread. A call from Mark, the blood test. But the days speed by, and the day of the test, as I'm looking at myself in the mirror brushing my teeth, I consider that "Two weeks gone" might mean he's *been gone* for two weeks rather than he's *going to be gone* for two weeks. Which means I have no idea when he'll get my message. I spit and rinse my mouth.

Too little Mark and too much body.

After the doctor's office, I go home instead of to work. My head cold is back and, as an added bonus today, my period. My stomach hurts. My clothes feel like they're full of weights. My body aches, and I can't breathe or think straight. Like Matisse's *French Window at Collioure*, where there's no light to lead me to the outside, just a wall of black, stopping me, closing me in on myself. Yesterday morning I turned on the TV in my bedroom, and it's still on. I guess I'm trying to situate myself in relation to the world, or to prove to myself that there is a world out there. Or maybe I leave it on for the voices.

Even when the exterminator says he thinks we have a mouse, I have trouble believing it. I'm paying bills as I listen to him tell me they don't use the cartoon cheese bait traps anymore. And when he shows me the adhesive paper they put out now, I think it's an effort to treat mice in a more humane fashion, a death with dignity kind of thing. I'm in a hurry to leave to pick up Caroline.

So it isn't until I'm in bed, trying to go to sleep that I realize I'm going to have to open the bathroom cabinet and maybe see a live mouse stuck to a piece of flypaper. And then what exactly?

Every time I close my eyes, I open them right back up. I'm afraid to look in the cabinet, and it's only after deciding to call the exterminator to do it that I'm able to sleep.

In the morning, after taking the girls to camp, as I'm about to put a bowl in the dishwasher, I remember the mouse. I sit down at the table, stunned by my ability to repress the mouse between waking and now.

I don't want to look in the cabinet, but somebody has to do it before the girls come home. I take small steps. I turn on the light. I bend over to put my hand on the cabinet door, keeping my face as far from the cabinet as possible. I open the door just a little, and when I do, something slides behind something else.

"Shit, shit, shit."

I leap from the bathroom and continue to time one exclamation with one small leap until I calm down.

The facts are that I have a little animal stuck to adhesive paper. Some part of her, an arm or a leg, must not be stuck. She doesn't understand what's happening. She's scared. She doesn't know what to do. She's in there right now wondering whether she will live or die, and she has nobody to ask for help. A quick death reaching for a piece of cheese has got to be better than this.

I imagine trying to help her—going back into the bathroom, opening the cabinet, reaching in and then picking her up. She'll be afraid and will try to get away from me. How will I get her to stop moving, and how will I pick her up, and if I get her outside to safety, how will I unstick her? Thinking about unsticking her the way you peel tape off of something is when I understand that unsticking was never a part of the plan.

Jack calls two days later to tell me that my CA125 is up to 64. He explains that he called with the results not because he's worried but to reassure me that I shouldn't be. He says to remember it's still down from 72. He's also checked again with an oncologist to be sure we're doing the right thing and we are. But he wants to do another blood test in two weeks.

The Washington Post
June 2

As the story is told in the Old Testament, the great flood lasted for 40 days and 40 nights, and submerged every living thing on Earth beneath 24 feet of water, sparing only Noah, his family, and the pairs of animals he protected on his ark.

Scientists have never found Noah or his ark, but they believe in his flood. It happened about 7,600 years ago, when the Mediterranean Sea, swollen by melted glaciers, breached a natural dam separating it from the freshwater lake known today as the Black Sea.

It was an apocalyptic event, in many respects much worse than anything described in Genesis. Every day for two years, 10 cubic miles of sea water cut through the narrow channel now known as the Bosporus and plunged into the lake—more than 200 times the flow over Niagara Falls. Every day the lake level rose six inches.

And every day the water marched another mile inland, forcing people and animals to flee or drown, killing freshwater fish and plants by the ton, inundating forests, villages and entire cities and spreading pestilence and death for miles.

But as the deluge filled the lake and transformed it into a sea, it also created an ecosystem unique in the world—an oxygenless abyss where shipwrecks could rest for thousands of years in chill, inert darkness uncorrupted by living creatures.

The possible presence of old ships in near-mint condition on the Black Sea floor has made Noah's flood the starting point for perhaps the most ambitious project ever undertaken in the emerging field of deep-water archaeology.

Marine explorer Robert Ballard along with UCLA chief land archaeologist, Mark Hudson, are combing the floor of the Black Sea in search of the remains of ancient dwellings. "If Hudson can find a trade route across the Black Sea," Ballard said, "then deep water archaeology can find the wrecks." Hudson said, "This was the most incredible thing I had ever heard. But the problem is that the Black Sea is huge."

This summer, the two of them, working together with a small team from project headquarters in the Turkish city of Synop, located an ancient coastline at a depth of 450 feet, just above the anoxic dead zone, confirming the flood theory. The pair hope to find evidence of human habitation beneath the cold waters of the Black Sea.

Caroline asks if she can take the article to school for Show and Tell. I print another copy for her and stick my copy in with Mark's letters. To her little pile by her bed, she adds the postcard that Mark sent her and a picture of the two of them together, that I took at the park on our dig.

When I go back into the kitchen for more coffee, I glance into the den. Both girls are now lying on the couch watching cartoons. As I reach for the coffee pot, my foot sticks to something on the floor. Then I see a trail of orange down the front of the cabinet drawers.

"Caroline," I yell. "Come in here."

She zigzags in, holding out the sides of her Spoleto t-shirt, which is so long on her that it's down to her knees. "Yeah?"

"I thought I told you to clean up your mess."

"I did."

"Then what is all this sticky stuff down the front of this cabinet, in these drawers and on the floor?"

She comes over to look where I'm pointing. "I guess I didn't see that."

"How could you not see it?"

"I guess I didn't look there."

"Why do you think you didn't look there?"

"I don't know."

"Is it maybe because you didn't want to see it?" As the words come out of my mouth, I sink into a chair, the same chair that Mark sank into six months ago, the last time he was in this house.

Alyssa and I are sitting in Martha's white kitchen, where this

111

summer day feels almost cheery. I've eaten every bite of my egg salad sandwich made with white bread that I didn't know anybody bought anymore.

"I'm going to plan a trip," I say. "I need something to perk me up, to look forward to. I mean, the egg salad worked great to get me through the morning, but I'm having a little trouble with summer."

Their landline rings, but Martha lets it go to voicemail. "It's probably Mack. We're having a little discussion about our new car— *my* new car. He was trying to find some information about the one I want and how it compares to the one *he* wants."

"If I don't rinse these chips down the disposal," Alyssa says, "I'm going to eat every one." And she gets up and carries her plate to the sink and turns on the disposal. "How about Paris?"

She always suggests Paris.

"I'm looking forward to Christmas," Martha says, as she wipes off the white countertop with a blue and white striped dishcloth that is just the tiniest bit faded.

"Already?" I ask.

"It's my favorite time of year. Because of everything that goes with it. You know, fires, family, hot chocolate, excitement, the magic…"

"But it's so much extra work," I say. "And the kids are home all day."

"Emily, have you lost weight?" she asks.

"Four pounds. And it's been so easy. I think my stomach is shrinking. Maybe we *should* go to Paris. We could do a different museum every day. Let's plan a trip for the fall."

"Paris," Alyssa says. "In the fall. Could you go too?" She looks at Martha.

"Maybe," she says. "I don't know. Let me talk to Mack about it."

I need to get back to work. We walk through the family room to the side door. Alyssa yells from her car that she'll call us with some dates for Paris.

The world on the verge of overflowing. The oppressive, humid heat of summer lodges in every breath I take, and I feel as if I might start pulling off my clothes to get it out of me. I haven't run in ages, but thinking a run might help, I pack a bag to take to work and leave my office early, changing into exercise clothes in the bathroom. I want to run downtown along the Battery, looking at the water.

I used to use running as a reset button, to get myself back on track. Today, as I feel my feet hit the pavement over and over again, I start to feel better. I've gotten out of the habit of exercise. From now on, a walk or something, thirty minutes every day.

After only a few minutes, I consider stopping. It's harder than I remember. But I said I was going to run. Surely, I can run at least one mile, at least ten minutes. Slowing down, I concentrate on the rhythm of the steps. As I push myself to go one step more, I feel as if I'm creating some discipline or endurance that I'll be able to reach back for if I ever need it.

A gift. Saturday arrives as one of those weird perfect-temperature days. After a visit to the museum, all three of us wearing dresses as requested by Caroline, we stroll down a cobblestone street in between tourists and students and cross the street to watch a basket weaver on the opposite sidewalk. With a towel folded over her skirt, she starts with two strands of sweetgrass, and before our mesmerized eyes, she connects them in this way and that, over and under, each strand continuing until the basket is complete, no gaps, strong enough for whatever anybody might put in it. Elizabeth is right up next to her, asking questions and even helping hold the bottom of the basket at one point. Caroline stands back with me, seeming older than six. It's not easy to know what she's thinking; I have to use clues other than words. Elizabeth runs over, grinning, wanting to know if we can buy some ice cream from the street vendor. I start to ask if she wouldn't rather have lunch first, but I know the answer to that. As I hand her five dollars, I smell jasmine and tea olive. Behind her, the opening buds of camellias push through a wrought iron gate bearing a Philip Simmons curlicue. The clock in the tower chimes twelve.

"How's 'Paris in the Fall' coming along?" I ask Alyssa, as the two of us relax on her patio with a glass of wine. The sun is setting on another cooler than normal summer day, one with a breeze running through it. Maybe the wine will relax my stomach. It feels bloated and like it does right before my period, but it's not time yet. Just a little indigestion, I guess. Or too much salt.

"We're set with the hotel for the first week in November. So far, it's you and me and Victoria for sure. Martha is out. She doesn't want to 'waste a trip to Paris without her husband,' which makes me ill."

"What about Kari?" Our friend's French red hair would make her an asset, helping us to blend in.

"A maybe."

"I wish we could go ahead and buy our tickets, so we would have another piece of evidence that we're going. I shouldn't say it out loud, but I'm always worried that something will happen before a trip. That I won't be able to go. Now that I think about it, it's only when I start packing that I stop worrying."

"I know, but I really think the fares are about to come way down. That's why I'm waiting. I'm also waiting to buy Ro's ticket home."

"Have you talked to him lately?"

"Yesterday. He sounds happy, not depressed like he did when he was here. I think being at boarding school agrees with him, and I don't blame him. I wish I could be away."

"I don't feel right either lately. But I can't even decide if it's my mind or my body that has the problem. Or both."

"Perhaps a *soupçon* more of wine will make you feel better?" Alyssa says, reaching for the bottle.

I slide my glass toward her as I burp quietly. Some of the ice from the ice bucket spills onto the table and mixes with a little of the pollen. It looks like a polluted river.

"How are the girls?" she asks.

"Last night we went to the grocery store, and each one got a 'Connect the Dots' coloring book. That's all we did after we got home. Dot to dot to dot."

"Speaking of connecting," Alyssa says.

"Where's Richard this time?"

"'This time' is right. I don't even know him anymore."

"Did something happen?"

"Nothing in particular. It's just everything in general. I don't know. His secretary called me at work earlier today to say he would be gone for a few days." She shakes her head.

"His secretary?"

"I couldn't bring myself to ask *her* where he was going." She pauses for a moment. "Here we are, living in the same house, seeing each other every day, and yet so far away from each other that I can't even touch him. Last night, lying in bed, I *wanted* to touch him, just touch him. I couldn't reach him without moving."

The vivid oranges and reds seep across the sky, then disappear.

"Maybe it's time to move on," she says.

"You're not really thinking of that, are you?"

"I *am* thinking about it. With Ro not here, I don't have to worry about him, but I also don't have the distraction of him. All I have is me, and it's not good." She pauses for a minute. "Maybe divorce should be the inevitable end of marriage, like death is to life. Maybe I should just accept it."

"Seriously?"

"Seriously," she says. "In my next life I want there to be somebody out in the world I can connect with, somebody who cares about me."

"I care about you," I say, grinning.

Alyssa looks at me. "We should do this more often."

"We should, but there's hardly ever time."

She puts her wine glass down in the middle of the polluted river. "Yeah, and we'd have even less time if we were married to wonderful men we connected with. Speaking of which, I assume there's still no word from Mark?"

I shake my head.

"I try not to ask."

I smile. "I try not to think about it. Maybe that call didn't really happen. Maybe I just dreamed it. The girls each got a postcard from him last week. I want to be happy for him. He deserves it."

"I cannot picture him with somebody besides you."

"I have a problem with that too," I say.

"It's so un-Mark-like that he didn't call."

"He's being kind. He wrote me about his relationship with Anna before he got my message. That saved him from having to call me back. We've been friends for a long time, since college. And when he first met me, I was with Frank. So I guess we can stay friends through this. It's weird to hear him talk about her, but it was weirder still when I didn't hear from him at all. And he feels a connection to Caroline and Elizabeth too, so I'm sure he wouldn't want to just disappear."

"Maybe he never got the message," Alyssa says.

"I never thought about that."

"I bet that's what happened," she says. "All these letters? It's obvious he's still in love with you. That's why he's staying in touch."

"Well, anyway," I say.

"I wonder what Anna thinks about his writing to you," Alyssa says.

"I imagine her as perfect, so she's probably completely understanding. You'd think I'd be over him by now, but it's the opposite. I miss him more and more."

Another cool breeze runs through, lifting the edges of my napkin.

"I didn't really see him before," I say.

"And now?"

"I see him."

June 15
Dear Emily,

It was the most exciting day I've ever had. I've never
seen anything like it. We were on the bridge of the ship
Northern Horizon, and Bob was directing the ROV—
with the ROVs it's like being underwater yourself. At
about 300 feet we saw a slightly raised, closed-in area.
When we went back more slowly, we could see that it
was rectangular in shape and we could also pick out
some large beams. It was a minute before I realized I was
looking at the closest thing I'd ever seen to a building
under water. We're the first to see this since it flooded.
And this could open up a whole new world. The media's
going crazy. National Geographic has about ten camera
people and journalists here. More soon.

Love,
Mark

The girls and I will be at the beach for my birthday, so Alyssa and
I celebrate early—she-crab soup at Jimbo's, an old "single house"
built to take advantage of very little street frontage. The short side
of the building faces the street, and the longer front, which is a
covered porch, faces an oak-shaded lawn, creating a kind of court-
yard. On the porch, tables are set with yellow and white tapestry
cloths and centered with yellow roses mixed with ivy. It looks like a
wonderful place to eat, but invisible heat transforms this cozy spot
into a mirage.

"I had that packing dream again last night," she says, after we're
seated at an inside table. "Again?"

"Yeah, I just kept moving from room to room, trying to find the stuff I needed to pack, which I never could, and I was supposed to be leaving for the airport. On and on and on. I was so happy to wake up."

"I usually don't have dreams, or don't remember them," I say. "But I had a stupid one a few nights ago. I was running through a thick fog looking for something, and I didn't know what it was. I just knew that when I found it, I'd be safe forever."

"That's not stupid," Alyssa says.

"It's stupid because it's not *my* dream."

"What do you mean 'not *your* dream'?"

"It's Scarlett O'Hara's dream. You know, the one she has over and over again."

Alyssa laughs and hits the table with her hand. "But that's not stupid. It's funny."

"It's embarrassing."

"But seriously," she says, wiping her eyes with her napkin, "having *any* dream is a good sign you're trying to figure yourself out. Even if it was somebody else's dream." And she starts laughing again.

One month into summer, and the heat is constant and stifling. In just the short amount of time it takes to walk to the end of the driveway, the humidity molds itself to every inch of my body, a weight against me. The sun jabs needle-like rays into my skin, actually hurting. Even the girls are lethargic, the excitement of summer replaced by the boredom of being trapped inside by the unrelenting heat. I pull my sticky clothes away from my body as sweat drips between my shoulder blades.

We're all excited about our vacation. Wild Dunes, on the Isle of

Palms, is only about twenty minutes outside the city, but we have a place right on the beach. Before we even unpack, we open our door to the ocean and the girls are in the sand with buckets and shovels.

On June 29th—Elizabeth's third birthday and my thirty-seventh—the three of us sit on the sofa to look at Elizabeth's baby pictures, something I do with each of the girls on their birthdays. The pictures of Elizabeth's short red hair and round, pudgy face make it hard to trace her to the little girl with long, blonde hair sitting beside me. But if I look closely at the pictures, I can see the blonde highlights that have since taken over, and if I look closely at the real girl, I can see a few red highlights that link her to the baby she was. Both in the picture and beside me, her sparkling brown eyes and her emotions are right out there for all to see.

When we come to the picture of Elizabeth in the grocery cart, I repeat the story of the time I was loading groceries into the car and the cart started rolling away—with Elizabeth in it.

"Mothers came from everywhere!" Elizabeth says before I can. She knows my favorite line by heart.

"Tell a story with me in it, Mom," Caroline says.

"Once upon a time there was another little girl who was three years old. Her name was Caroline. One day, her mother, who loved her very much and who was very pregnant with her little sister—"

"That was me!" Elizabeth shouts.

I pat Elizabeth's leg, smiling. "The mother took Caroline to the dentist, and since it was her first trip, the dentist said Caroline could sit in her mother's lap to get her teeth cleaned. And that worked for about three minutes. When the dentist put the metal toothbrush in her mouth, Caroline jumped up and ran out the door of the room.

By the time the mother could get her pregnant body out of the tilted back chair, Caroline was out the door of the office and headed for the street!"

These stories are funny now, I think, because those dangers have passed. They were not at all funny at the time. I close the album and stand. We each take a bottle of bubbles to the patio so we can listen to the waves as we blow the afternoon away. Then we eat an early supper at The Boathouse at Breach Inlet. The three of us sit at a corner table, and I keep looking at the fourth chair—the empty chair. There's something I've been meaning to do, ever since that day at the eye doctor.

"I wish Mark were here," I say. "Doesn't it feel like somebody's missing?"

Caroline looks at me. "You said we were fine by ourselves."

"We are fine, but don't you think it would be even better if Mark were here?"

"Mark plays with me," Elizabeth says, her mouth full.

"I think it's good to have time to yourself. I also think it's important to be with the people you love. I miss Mark. I wish he were here."

Caroline looks down at her plate. "I miss Mark, too."

"Me too," Elizabeth says, looking at Caroline.

After supper, the waiters bring three bowls of ice cream, each with a lit candle.

I tell Elizabeth to make a wish, and Caroline whispers in her ear. Then Elizabeth says, "I wish Mark would come back."

"Dummy," Caroline says. "You're not supposed to say it out loud." Caroline stares at the flame in front of her. "Now it won't come true."

"Caroline, be nice."

To Elizabeth, I say, "Close your eyes and think your wish in your head. Try not to say it out loud."

Both Caroline and I watch her.

She opens her eyes, grinning. "Can I eat now?" she asks.

"Blow out your candle," I say.

"Mom, you have to make a wish too," Caroline says, looking at me, her eyes wide.

I close my eyes. *I wish Mark would call. I wish he would come back. I wish I could have another chance.*

I open my eyes to two little girls, ignoring melting ice cream, who look as if they expect my wish to come true right before their eyes. I blow out my candle.

"Sometimes wishes take a while to come true," I say, picking up my spoon. Elizabeth digs into the vanilla ice cream. Caroline watches me for a second longer. I imagine she's trying to decide if she can trust me with her wishes.

I blow her a kiss. She smiles, blowing out her candle.

Back at the condo, I go to the bathroom again. I seem to be going all the time. I let Caroline and Elizabeth fall asleep with their iPads. In my room, I flip on the TV to connect with something bigger than me, than us, and the movie *Breakfast at Tiffany's* is playing. I open the window wide to the waves and fall into bed with a case of the "mean reds," when you're afraid and you don't know what you're afraid of. I finish an entire bottle of wine.

Re-entry. The girls are so excited to see their toys that I am unnecessary. The sun has set, although it's not yet dark. Shaking out a trash bag, I head down the rocky path to the car. When the lights come on, I see jackets and lunches and toy bags on top of candy wrappers, half-empty, decaying drinks, and a few stray chicken nuggets, some missing a bite. I usually take time at the end of each day to scan the car and respond. A trip makes car vigilance more challenging, but even so, I'm usually able to discard some trash along the way. Not this trip.

These days I'm unable to stay on top of the unceasing, gurgling up of stuff that appears everywhere, including my car. "Things" are winning, and I'm losing. I start each day behind. And, worst of all, I have little interest in digging myself out.

I lean against the car. Everywhere I go, I feel the absence of Mark—the silence. I let my head fall back—mistake, mistake, mistake.

"Get a hold of yourself," I say, straightening up and swinging the car door shut. I just need to make it through the summer—until the girls are back in school. Then I'll have some extra energy and be able to take charge.

June 22
Dear Emily,

Ballard is gone for a week, and we've decided to do a little sightseeing. In the museum here is a statue of the third century philosopher, Diogenes the Cynic. Apparently he was born in Sinop. Last week Tommy left for Istanbul, where he's meeting some friends to travel for two weeks.

Yesterday I bought a small wooden rowboat, simple lines, but with tiny, intricate coloring. You would like it.

Anna and I are taking advantage of the black sand beaches, reading and swimming. We're planning to travel in the fall during our time off. Italy first. She wants to end up in Paris.

I hope all three of you are well.

Love,
Mark

Mark too will be in Paris. Mark and Anna. I imagine small bags, newspapers, hands being held, exotic food and plush train compartments, a life so different from mine that it's like reading a book. It's not real; it's a story—about people I don't know.

In *The Red Studio*, color is no longer expressive; it's just itself. Red covers the walls, the floor, the table, the chair. Matisse's own paintings hang on the wall and are stacked on the floor. A grandfather clock stands among them, and on the table, a vine encircles a small statue of a woman. *"Matisse's paintings usually avoid a single 'focal point' because they are organized in such a way that one thing usually acts as a foil for something else. Wherever you look, you should also be looking somewhere else at the same time."*

"Your abdomen does feel distended," Jack says.

"Well I think it's probably just too much ice cream and pizza. But I thought I'd mention the pain. Since I was here anyway for the blood test."

"Any indigestion?"

"Yeah, but like I said, we've been eating out a lot lately. And I've had a little more wine than usual. I assumed that's why I felt bloated."

Jack presses near the middle of my abdomen, and then slowly moves his fingers to the side, continuing to press. It hurts. He stops abruptly.

"What?" I ask.

"Well, I'm not sure." He presses again on the right side and grimaces.

"You can sit up now." Jack puts his hand on my shoulder and before I can wonder why, he says, "I feel some kind of small mass near your ovaries."

I hear his next words from some far-off place, as if he's not talking to me, but to a woman I don't know.

"I want you to get dressed and wait in my office. We need to schedule an ultrasound." He puts his hand on my knee and asks if I'm okay. I move my head up and down. Then he leaves.

My mouth tastes sour. I touch my bare foot to the floor, trying to feel the solid surface of cold linoleum, trying to trust that it will support me. I make my way to the corner, step inside, draw the curtain. Staring at the underwear, the jeans, the white linen top, I wonder who these clothes belong to.

Holding onto the wall, I gag emptiness into the trashcan. When I take off the gown, I don't know what to do with it.

I get my clothes on my body and reach for the doorknob. Then I retract my hand. Maybe. Maybe if I just stay in this room, nothing will change. I face the table, the stool, the light, the sterile instruments, the magazine from last year. And then I step into the hall, wondering if I can sneak by the crowd waiting to see the woman with a mass near her ovaries.

A nurse—I knew her name before—takes me to Jack's office. She pushes me toward the couch.

"We're going to rush the CA125," he says, as he opens the door. "So we can have the results first thing in the morning. And I've scheduled an ultrasound for 2:00."

Not good for the woman.

"I'll meet you at the hospital. Try not to worry until we know what we're dealing with."

I move my head up and down again.

When I step outside, the sun is bearing down, and with the larger space and different light, it feels as if I've crossed into a foreign country. I stop beside my unfamiliar car.

Inside, I grip the steering wheel. Then my head falls forward. Don't think about it. Think about something else. Henri. Soothe me. The images that appear are the two sequences of paintings. *Lorette in a Green Robe, Black Background* is a painting of Lorette, and *The Painter in His Studio* is a painting of Matisse *painting* Lorette in the green robe. It's about me, but then it's not. Distance. *Lorette Reclining* is another painting of Lorette, but in *The Studio, quai Saint-Michel*, Lorette reclining is only a small part of the whole. When life zooms in, I will float above. Distracted, I start the car.

For too long it seems, I circle the hospital. And then I turn in, find the place I'm supposed to wait, and tell the nurse I remember it from before. When was before—six months ago, seven maybe? The nurse tells me I'm an hour early.

I begin to drink the water, staring into space, unable to catch a thought or a feeling. A nurse calls my name and walks me to a room, where I take off my clothes from the waist down. Then I wrap a sheet around myself and lie on the table. I do everything they tell me to.

Despite the warmth of the room, I shiver. The technician comes in, and then Jack and the radiologist. Nobody speaks. Everyone must be afraid of the words. Jack watches the screen, his hand on my leg. I look away. I don't have a good feeling about this. I don't have any feeling about this.

"I'll be right back," Jack says. "Go ahead and get dressed."

Everyone leaves.

When I come out of the bathroom, Jack is standing there. "Emily, it's not good," he says.

"Tell me," I say, sitting in a gray chair.

Jack sits beside me. "We found two areas that appear to be solid on your ovaries, a larger one on the right and a smaller one on the left. You—we need to remove them right away."

"Is it cancer?" I ask, looking into the air.

"It might be, but we won't know for sure until we operate. We'll have your CA125 in the morning."

"Ovarian cancer?" I ask.

"Maybe."

I try to focus, but I can't. I try to speak, but no sound comes out.

"Emily?"

I blink, shake my head, and then moan. I'm not supposed to moan, but I can't make my body do what it's supposed to. "How could this happen? We've been monitoring the CA125. Wasn't it normal the last time?"

Jack looks at his notes. "It was 72 the first time when your sonogram was clean. Then it went down to 35. Then it was 47, 54, 64."

72, 35, 47, 54, 64. The numbers are real, concrete, and they bring me back.

"What kind of surgery?" I ask.

"A hysterectomy, removing the ovaries and uterus, in order to remove the growths. I recommend Dr. Mason. She's a gynecologic oncologist, the best around here in my opinion."

"But we're not even sure it's bad, right?"

"Emily, you want a doctor who's trained in ovarian cancer so she can try to get it all out and do an accurate staging. To know what kind of treatment you need. To avoid another surgery."

Visions swirl—Victor Hugo's nightmarish world of ink drawings, where mysterious black fluid spreads into unnamed shadows and gradually takes the shape of a road going nowhere, an anguished being, a hanged man, a skeleton head—*cancer*. I think I might pass out. I lean my head back against the wall, close my eyes, and drift upward.

"Emily, is there someone I can call for you?"

Mark.

Then I remember. Turkey. Anna.

But Mark.

I slip out of my sandals and place my feet on the cold hard floor. I bury my feelings and start a new layer. I need to think.

Jack scoots his chair from beside me to in front of me, staring at my face with a worried expression.

"I'm okay," I say, taking my appointment book and a pen out of my purse. "What's the doctor's name again?"

"Dr. Mason. Her office is across the street. Do you want to talk to her?"

"Yes," I say, and I quickly add, "as soon as possible," so I don't have to hear him say it.

He calls from the phone in the ultrasound room. I go straight over, where I have to wait because they're working me in. When they finally call my name, they take me to her office. She comes in after only minutes.

"Dr. Kathleen Mason," she says as she looks at my eyes, shakes my hand, and takes the envelope, all in one concise motion.

I watch her, trying to focus on something I can see, something real. She's thin. Her brown hair is pulled back in a ponytail and fastened with a silver barrette.

"Dr. Matthew tells me you need a second opinion," she says, as she sits down at her desk and opens the envelope.

"A better one," I say.

She looks up from the papers and gives me a contained smile. Then she looks back at the sonogram. "I'm afraid I agree with the radiologist and with Dr. Matthew that the masses seem to be solid. This does look like cancer, but we won't know for sure until we operate. Jack said you wanted me to perform the surgery. Is that right?"

Again I move my head up and down.

"I recommend we move swiftly. Are you ready, or do you need some time?"

"I'm ready," I hear myself say, digging my nails into my palm to feel the pain, to block other feelings so I can think.

"Do you have any questions?"

"What exactly will you be doing?"

"I'll make a vertical incision on your abdomen, and I'll remove as much of the tumors as possible, taking tissue samples of the lymph nodes and other areas in the pelvis and abdomen. We need to be aggressive in the tumor debulking if it's ovarian cancer. From what I find out, we'll be able to accurately stage the disease. Do you know what that means?"

"Sort of."

"Well, stage refers to how far the disease has advanced. Ovarian cancer has four stages. Successful treatment of the disease depends on accurate staging."

"How long will I be in the hospital?"

"At least three nights. Maybe more."

"When will you do the surgery?"

She rolls her chair to the other side of her desk and takes hold of the mouse. "Today is Tuesday. So Thursday if I have an opening." The mouse moves in circles. "I don't have anything, but it looks like I can move an elective surgery to next week and do you second on Thursday. They'll have to double check out front."

I nod, holding tight to my purse.

She makes some notes on her computer and then turns to face me. "This is bound to feel like you've stepped on a moving sidewalk and you can't get off. I'm telling you, that if you feel you need to, you can get off. You can take some time."

"But don't we need to do it as quickly as possible?"

"Yes, but you need to be ready. A few days won't matter."

"I don't like not knowing," I say. "And I want it out of me, whatever it is." My last few words trail off as I start to float away again. I'm not focusing.

"Okay, Emily," she says, using my name for the first time and leaning down, trying to find my eyes, "here's what's going to happen."

I'm back.

"Right now," she says, "we'll get a chest x-ray. Then, I'll do a pelvic exam. After that, you'll meet with my nurse for some pre-op paperwork and instructions. She'll set an appointment for you at the hospital tomorrow for some blood work and to meet with the anesthesiologist. I'll see you Thursday morning for surgery. Since things are moving fast, I'm going to give you my cell in case you need to talk to me before Thursday."

Steel yourself, I think.

In the parking lot, I look up at the sky, the sun slipping away, the day gone. I pick up Caroline and Elizabeth from camp at the Little Red Schoolhouse and drive home, concentrating on the sturdiness of the steering wheel, the clicking of the turn signal, the accelerator. Inside, I put on a movie for them to watch. My first feeling is a thought. I don't think I can do this by myself. In my study I sit down and pick up my cell to call Alyssa, but I can't punch the numbers.

I did everything Jack told me to do, and still I got cancer. I should have insisted on a hysterectomy right from the start. Instead, I listened to words like "radical response," "unnecessary surgery," "hormones," and "more children."

It can't possibly be true. That's the explanation.

I stare at the phone in my hand. I can't have cancer. I have children to take care of. It's a false positive. Of course, it is. I let go of the phone.

131

Caroline comes to the door of the room, and I try to reach her, but as I stand, I feel as if I'm being swirled away.

I hear the TV. Then I hear Caroline's voice at intervals, as if in a slow rhythm. "Alyssa?—Something's wrong with my mom.—She's on the floor.— Crying.—I'm okay. —She's watching *Tarzan*.—Yeah. It's not.—Yeah.—Okay.—Okay."

Then just the TV.

Alyssa's voice. I see her reach out to me, but I don't feel the touch. I close my eyes. I hear Alyssa call Martha, the doorbell, and the door close. Then I don't hear anything.

The hallmark of this disease is no warning. By the time you have any clue, it has spread so far that there's nothing to do. But I had warnings. I had time. Now I have nothing.

I turn over and become vaguely aware of hardness. I open my eyes and feel the instantaneous relief of waking from a nightmare. I sit up on the sofa—I don't remember moving to the sofa—and I see Alyssa sitting in the chair beside me. "Oh God," I say, as I slide back down, squeezing my eyes shut. I know, of course, as soon as I see her that my relief is the illusion.

All she says is "Emily" as she puts her arms around me. I don't think we've ever touched before, but neither one of us hesitates or is unsure. It's at the same time a physical expression, as well as a deepening, of our friendship.

After a while, I try to sit up again, to get control of myself.

"When Caroline called, I thought something had happened to Mark. But I found all your papers from the doctor and the hospital." She hands me a glass of something. "Do you feel like talking?"

I take a sip, and my mouth and throat burn. I manage to swallow. "Is this scotch?"

Alyssa nods.

I laugh, taken so by surprise, remembering the bitter taste from the summer I turned eighteen and discovered I preferred beer and wine. "Where did you get this?"

"I asked Martha to bring it when she came to pick up the girls."

The girls. I make myself take another sip, as if the scotch were something good for me. "They think I have ovarian cancer."

"Emily, I'm so sorry. That's what I was afraid of, looking at your papers."

More scotch. "I'm having surgery. Thursday morning."

"Shouldn't they make sure you have it before they operate?"

"That's how they know for sure, by operating."

"Should you get a second opinion?"

"I already did."

The next day I pick the girls up from camp and take them to get ice cream. We sit in the park, and I explain that I'm sick and need to have an operation. That's why I was upset. And that the doctors are going to help me get well. I tell them they'll stay with Martha for a couple more days, and then their grandparents will arrive from Hawaii and they'll be able to stay at home. We name all the people who love them. We talk about how there will always be someone to take care of them.

Of course, we name Mark, whom I have not called. I know he was being kind not to call after he and Anna got together. But I should call to tell him about the surgery. About the cancer.

I count our blessings having the money Frank left for the girls, and good medical insurance from the museum. And my parents will be glad to help. We'll be fine.

Martha brings supper and the four of us eat together at the kitchen table. We talk about the days ahead. Caroline is quiet. She's probably miserable at Martha's with all those people. Just as I would be. But she gives nothing away. Elizabeth talks nonstop and can barely finish her supper. She's excited about going back to Martha's, where she's not limited to one sibling, but has her choice of four. I help them repack their bags while Martha cleans up. I tell her it doesn't feel right to let her clean up my kitchen. She says I better get used to receiving help, that it's one of the perks of being sick. And already I feel weak.

With surgery mere hours away, I sling my shirt on top of the other clothes on the armchair, and in that motion, I *feel* how I discarded my feelings for Mark. Lightning flashes, and I can hear the wind picking up. It was so hot all day. Now a storm is coming. I crawl into bed but turn facing the pile of accumulated clothes, which grows bigger and bigger until I get up.

The shirt I wore today—dirty and into the hamper. The jeans, I can wear again, *after*. One at a time, I sort through the clothes until the pile is gone and the chair is empty and I remember. Mark used to sit there.

I leave the bedroom and wander the empty house—wanting to check on the girls who aren't here, pausing at the door to their darkened room, thinking how all this might affect them. My mind goes blank. It's too much for now.

Back in the bedroom, I pick up my book on Matisse. At forty-two, he *"was extremely well-dressed, carried himself with great composure, and during our conversations his white teeth flashed through his neat, full, reddish blond beard... His voice was handsome, sonorous and penetrating."*

I imagine his red hair. I want to hear his voice.

Again, I rummage through the drawer until I find the scrap of paper. I leave another message asking Mark to call me—no extra words this time—and then I lie down, staring at my phone and waiting for nothing.

An hour later when the phone vibrates, my heart kicks.

I sit up, look at all the strange numbers, put the phone to my ear, and say hello, leaning against the headboard.

"Hey, Emily."

I hear him grin, and I relax. For one second, it's as if everything's okay. As if he'll be over in a minute with pizza. "Thanks for calling me back."

"Nothing's wrong, I hope." I hear concern in his voice, and it reminds me why I'm calling.

"Actually, I'm sick. I'm having surgery in a few hours."

"A few hours?"

"They think I have ovarian cancer."

"Oh, my god," he whispers. "That can't be right. The numbers on that test came down."

At the sound of his voice mixed with mine, tears.

"Oh Emily, I'm too far away."

"Mark, I miss you." Stay in control, I tell myself. More lightning and wind. The lights flicker.

"Emily—"

"I know you're in a relationship with Anna and way involved in the work there. I struggled with whether or not to call again. But I figured you would want to know about the surgery."

"Of course, I want to know. Wait a minute. What do you mean *again*? You called before?"

My heart catches, like a piece of cloth on a nail. "You didn't get the message?"

"When did you call?"

My mind can't work fast enough to figure out what I should say and what I shouldn't. "The night of the announcement of the paintings. I left a message. Asking you to call."

"I never got a message. I would have called."

"I don't know if you would have or not." Tell him. "It was when you and Anna got together."

"I would have called. You know that."

"But I asked the man to tell you something from me. *Yes*. That's what I said. To please tell you I said *yes*." I breathe out, and it feels like the fullest breath I've ever released.

"Oh Emily."

"All this time, I thought you were being kind not to mention it."

"God, you're going to be okay, right? It might not be cancer?"

"They're pretty sure already."

"But maybe—"

"Mark, I do need you. I just want you to know I know that."

"I wish I could be with you."

I knew he wasn't going to come back just because I called. I knew that, and I didn't expect it, and yet it appears that somewhere deep inside, I thought he would.

"Hold on a minute," I say, not waiting for an answer. I put my phone down. I tense my entire body to make the tears disappear. I take some short little breaths, blowing out. Then I pick up the phone again.

"I'm back," I say, choking out the words. "And it's my fault you're not here so..."

"Emily, forget about all that. It's done. Tell—"

"Mark, I realized I made a bad decision letting you go. That's why I called before. I wanted you to know. And then Anna. And I'd lost my chance. And I don't expect you to drop everything and come home just because I'm sick."

"Emily, I wish I could be there for you now, but I don't know how I can."

Finally, the rain against the window. I exhale.

"How are the girls?"

"They're okay. With Martha until my parents get here. They miss you."

"I miss them."

My heart is swelling, fluid pouring in around the break. I swallow.

"I'll be thinking about you. I'll call tomorrow after the surgery."

"Thanks, Mark."

"Take care of yourself."

I hang up and tilt my head back, squeezing my eyes tightly to keep from overflowing with sadness.

The Invalid

The warm color of the terra cotta tiled floor, the red-and-white striped cloth, and vases and vases of flowers. A viridian vase with muted crimson poppies and two tall irises, the color of blue ink. A small lavender-gray vase with flowers of white, red, rust, and celadon. With the flax-colored walls, it feels as if sunshine is coming straight through from outside.

And then there he goes, dipping his brush into the midnight blue of need. Then into the magenta of want, into the dark golden-rod of regret. Must he add the ochre of fear? And what of missing him? I admit to seashell white.

Tired of lying still on the other side of the canvas, I drift in search of the one force that can center me, hold me, soothe me. His voice, sonorous and penetrating.

I feel a draft, hear a steady beeping.

"Open your eyes," Jack says.

I see his white shirt, his rust-colored hair.

"You have more flowers," Mark says.

Two cerise-colored roses in a Persian green vase.

"I'll put them on this table with the striped cloth," Henri says.

As he comes close, the floor creaks. He finds my feet under the covers and dips them into slippers of midnight blue.

"We will shrink the red, change the pointed fingers to hearts. I'm sending a horse and carriage."

"To take me to you?"

"To take the red away. I will take the red from you. Cover a room in red."

"You see how it takes over everything," I say.

"Like ivy. Like nasturtium. Like a clock."

He's arranging cracked dishes of dirt on the hospital table, draping scraps of colorful fabric on the bed. *"Against a deep blue,"* he says, *"I feel the desire of the line. I feel it, fighting against the red. Where does it wish to enter?"*

"You're going to paint with your trowel?"

"I will use bright yellow to attack the red. But the black also is reaching for you, surrounding, intruding." He grumbles. Then he lights up. *"A blue star."*

He turns toward me. Those dark eyes, the full red beard. Such a warm smile. "Is that you?" I ask.

"And the line," he says, *"where does it wish to die away?"*

"Call me Anna," I say. "I am young and healthy."

"I'm painting," he says. Then he throws the canvas on the floor. *"There it is again. I'm letting reason lead my emotion astray. I must use reason only for control."*

"Open the window so we can hear the sea, smell the salt in the air."

"I can still be your muse," I say.

He reaches through the open window and picks an orange from the tree. He peels it and places a section in his mouth. *"Circle your arms over your head, Emily. Raise your left knee."*

I try to do as he asks, but the pain prevents me.

The muse with the hole in her stomach.

"How do you feel?" Jack asks.

"I can't breathe."

"What do you feel?" Mark asks.

"Pressure."

"Use the colors," Henri says.

"I feel red fingers."

"Yes?"

"Reaching into my body. Sharp and pointed, wing-like. And there's black out there."

"Anything else?"

"At the edges, shadows—of yellow and blue."

"You see, feeling is an enemy only when you don't know how to express it."

Exhausted, I close my eyes.

My gown is open. I smell antiseptic.

He places his hand on my stomach. "I feel emptiness," he says.

"Heal me," I say.

He withdraws his hand and takes up his brush and palette.

Something's tight around my arm. When I reach for it, it's gone.

"You're supposed to walk a little," he says.

I might throw up and lean against him, turning my face to his chest and inhaling the smell of the garden. I shuffle a few steps to the armchair.

"Let me put this cushion underneath you."

I sink into the softness, a little dizzy after so much lying down, but the warmth of the sunshine feels nourishing.

He places my right arm at an angle on the chair and stretches my left arm around my hips. I hear a creak as he sits in the straight-backed chair he loves.

"I knew you would come," I say.

He turns, and I see the hospital bed.

"How much longer will I be here?" I ask.

"It's only been two days," Jack says. "Are you anxious to leave?"

"The girls," I say. And I hear beyond. Beyond the blue. Beyond but limited?

"Beyond the ovary and the pelvis but limited to the abdominal cavity."

"I brought you four goldfish," Henri says. *"Watch them swim. It will train your eyes to remain open."*

My body is burning, itching, on fire.

"In every picture I paint," he says, *"my whole life is at stake."*

"Cut it out of me," I say, my nails scraping skin.

"She's having an allergic reaction."

"A reaction?" I say.

"Open your eyes."

"They are open."

"Stage three."

"Is that you?"

"There are four stages."

"I knew you would come."

"I will always come for you."

My parents take me home from the hospital. Caroline and Elizabeth wear lace dresses I don't recognize. I sink into my own bed. Swallow pills. The girls watch me race around the clocks that hold up the house. Be careful, they say. Don't go so fast.

I lie in a room with an empty armchair. Heavy, somber colors surround me.

You are my Invalid.

The beginning of dusk. The end of my first day home.

Sweet sounds float in from out there.

But I'm in the world of the bedroom. Cut off from normal. Separate.

Out there, Caroline and Elizabeth exist without me. How can they, at only six and three?

In here, it is the gradual lessening of light.

I watch him mark off a square around me. They begin to dig. A man and a woman. And lots of red-headed little girls in a circle. They're all digging, spraying dirt up onto me. Wait, it's not dirt. It's yellow, red, sapphire, white, magenta.

Scissors. I will cut Anna out of the picture.

I lean on my elbow to swallow a pill. Then I lie back down, glad to be waking in my own bed this morning. I move my body as little as possible. My eyes drift to the hazy blue sky, framed by the floor-length gauze drapes that lie still against the closed windows.

I think of Henri with a white beard, sitting up in bed, a cluttered table across his lap, an extra plaid quilt across his feet, a ladder against the wall in the corner, and a chest at the foot of the bed. Some of his cutouts are pinned on the wall. A bird cage sits on the floor. He's drawing with what looks like a long stick. Being in bed doesn't stop him from anything.

I roll to my right toward the door, pulling the white sheet as best I can up over my shoulder and closing my eyes. I already feel as if I'm healing so much faster in my own house than at the hospital, where I was constantly disturbed for something, never allowed to sleep through the night or finish a dream.

Alyssa is making lunch for Caroline and Elizabeth, relieving my parents for a couple of hours. I hear voices and giggles, her soft footsteps in the hall. Then I hear, and feel, the door open and close back, slowly and carefully, with almost no sound.

My body is paper. Henri will take scissors and cut the red out. But the cages are open. Colors are flying. Landing on the armchair. On the dresser. On the chest at the foot of the bed. Blue, yellow, and still red.

Boil a life down to its essence. Freeze it and see what rises.

They're playing hide and seek. Mark with his trowel, Caroline with her hair bow, and Elizabeth with her ice cream. I'm in here, I say. They don't hear me. I insist. In here—look in the painting.

Alyssa brings me two soft journals, leather bound, small, five by seven maybe. Holding them under my nose, I inhale the rich smell of the leather. "Two just alike," she says, "so you'll feel comfortable writing in one, knowing that if you mess it up, you can throw it away and start over." Someone in the world knows me this well.

Being sick has taken away the busy surface of my life. Gone are the errands and the superficial, the insubstantial, the time-wasting. Being still forces me to reflect on what remains.

It's Thanksgiving. I'm home, Mark is with me, and I smile a lot. My father says Mark is his favorite. I explain the "just friends" part, remind him about Frank, but my father insists. "Maybe he's the one, Emily Jane." "The one for what?" I reply, wishing I were being as sincere as he is being earnest.

Frank is dead. Mark is gone. I have cancer.

The night I found out I was sick, Alyssa stayed with me. But this isn't her house, or her life. When she left the next morning, I was alone again. What's missing is a person in the same stratum as me, not in the past below me like my parents, or above me like the girls pushing up out of the here and now into the future, or off to the side like Alyssa, but someone in the same circle as me, someone right beside me. What's missing is someone whose life is concentric with mine.

In Woolworth's I look over all the pads and pens. Glass partitions are stuck into metal holders. Tiny "leather" notebooks. Three little rings. Stacks of plain white pads glued together one on top of the other. The metal globe pencil sharpener fits in my small hand, covers my whole palm. My sister Susan is in hair supplies. She gives me barrettes and ponytail holders for Christmas. I give her a pen and a pad.

In my bedroom, all three windows, one to my right and the two in front of me, are closed against the summer heat. A tall palm stands in the corner between the windows to soften the effect of the TV beside it. A framed poster of a Whitney Museum exhibit of Edward Hopper paintings highlights his *Cape Cod Afternoon*—no people, just a sprawling house, shuttered windows, long shadows, and a crumbling shed. Across the room, Matisse's *Landscape Viewed from a Window,* with its deep blues announcing a Paris exhibit, adds another window to the room, the white drapes from the poster a link to the white gauze drapes of this room. Looking straight ahead, my dresser shows no sign of clutter. Nothing of anyone else's. I take a quick look. Nothing of anyone else's anywhere. And no one. Only the empty blue armchair.

My body is weak and anchored to the bed, but my mind wanders. Afraid of where it will take me, I sit up, fluffing two pillows behind me. I need something concrete to latch on to, and I glance over my faded blue-gray comforter that used to match the darker walls to my art books and the leather journals from Alyssa stacked on the old chest at the foot of the bed. What I reach for is *Matisse on Art.*

I lean my head on the headboard and hold the thick paperback to my chest, thinking of the story I know by heart. When Matisse was twenty and sick in bed, his mother brought him a paint box with two pictures in the lid to copy. She was trying to distract him from feeling bad. *"From the moment I held the box of colors in my hand, I knew this was my life."*

That was the key for Matisse, the way he discovered who he was and how to express himself. My eyes are pulled to the window, but the muted light is mere background for my thoughts. A box of colors—could it be that easy for me?

On my way back to bed from the bathroom, I hit my knee on the corner of the chest. I stop and sit, holding my leg for the few seconds that it hurts, checking for blood. That's all I need, somewhere else for blood to come from. Sticking out of a book is a postcard of *The Thousand and One Nights,* with its white background and colorful blocks filled with shapes, symbols, and words. One day in high school, we were studying this long, rectangular cut-out. I loved all the little hearts. My art teacher mentioned that it was completed in 1950. And I realized I had just missed him. Matisse and I are a part of the same century. Henri Matisse was here. Now he's gone.

The third day home and already—too quickly it seems—I'm taking less pain medication. Susan arrived yesterday. My parents left an hour ago.

I stay awake longer and am less groggy. I have time to think, and to feel, too much time and too much space. It's a disorienting feeling, not being able to take care of myself. Accepting help is the only way. I close my eyes. I'm not yet ready to isolate and follow any feeling to its source. I need it all to stay a jumble.

A sudden pain, and all I am is body. I change positions, taking a long time to turn over. Facing the picture I took on our dig at the park, I reach out to touch it, but my fingers hit glass. I remember feeling especially tired that day—I wonder if that was a sign I missed.

The girls come in to tell me goodnight. Whenever I've seen them since the surgery, they're together. As they get closer, I smell soap and feel the warmth from their damp bodies.

"Are you well yet?" Elizabeth asks. She's wearing one of my t-shirts and looks shiny pink.

"Not yet. But I feel better. How was camp?"

She jumps on the end of the bed.

Caroline's eyes follow my hand, which goes to my stomach.

"Elizabeth," she says. "Aunt Susan said not to do that."

"Sorry," Elizabeth says, jostling the bed as she slides off and leans against it.

"No problem," I say. "How are *you*, Caroline?"

"Fine."

"Is that what Aunt Susan told you to say?" I ask, smiling.

Caroline glances at the door and fingers her hair behind her ear. The sleeves of her nightgown are too short. She stands there, not touching anything, a few feet from the bed, from me.

"We should go to bed now, Elizabeth," Caroline says.

"Goodnight, Mom," Elizabeth says, and turns to leave.

"Come give me a hug," I say.

Elizabeth looks at Caroline, who looks at me as if I had suggested they could stay up all night.

"Really, both of you, come over here and give me a hug. I don't care what Aunt Susan said. I'm not going to break."

Elizabeth grins and comes rolling over. Caroline follows slowly. I reach to hug Elizabeth, the pain mitigated by the feel of her healthy body against mine.

"Thank you for letting Aunt Susan sleep in your bed," I say, keeping hold of her squishiness.

"I only let her have one of my animals, though. I hid the rest under the bed."

"Good thinking," I say, giving her a kiss on her forehead.

Caroline hugs me, holding back. I lower one hand and scoop her tense body closer to me.

"Thank you for letting Elizabeth sleep with you."

"Caroline makes me put my head by her stinky feet," Elizabeth says, lingering by my bed, periodically bumping it, full of energy even at the end of the day. At first, I think she's trying to delay leaving *me*, and then I realize she's waiting for her sister.

"You're the one with the stinky feet," Caroline says. "Mom, Aunt Susan said to ask if you need anything. Do you?"

"No thanks. Do you need anything?"

She finally looks me in the eyes, shaking her head. But I don't think I broke the surface. She knows she's not supposed to "bother" me. I don't think she would tell me even if she did have a problem. I watch them race out the door together. Then I turn out my light and fall asleep to the muffled voices of my children and my sister floating in from across the hall.

According to the surgeon, today, my fourth day home, is the day I'm supposed to start walking. I'm counting the days as if I were on a trip, to slow them down, to appreciate each single one. I pick up the letter I got today from Mark, the first one since I've had cancer—since I've known about the cancer—but written before he knew about it. I hold it in my hand and look around the room, as if trying to figure out who the letter is for. Who was this person he was writing to? Has the illness so changed me that I'm unrecognizable to myself?

> June 29
> Dear Emily,
>
> Happy Birthday! I hope you have a good day today. Obviously you won't get this letter on your birthday, but know that I was thinking about you. I can't believe it's been six months since I've seen you. I'm thinking about a visit back to North Carolina to see my parents, and to Charleston, at the end of August. I don't know if it will work out though.
>
> I hope y'all are having a good summer. Here, the excitement continues. After obtaining permission from the Turkish government, Anna and I began to sample and test some of our observations. You'll never believe this— the samples are in my refrigerator at the pension right now while I'm getting everything ready to mail off for analysis.

Apparently, the people in the past who used to live where the water is now built their homes from stone and wood. Tell the girls about the highly scientific "Three Little Pigs Concept." People used many types of building techniques, depending on the situation.

Love,
Mark
P.S. It's been a while since I've heard from you.

He doesn't know who I am anymore. I tried to tell him on the phone that I've changed. If he comes for a visit, will he recognize me?

Preparing for my walk, I change into a bathing suit cover-up that comes to my knees and is not tight around my waist. It's not exactly getting dressed, but it's a start. I lie back down to rest for a minute. Then Susan knocks and sticks her head into the bedroom to say she's ready.

Walking out the front door is like diving into a pool of warm air.

Susan says, "See, it's not so bad."

I roll my eyes at her relentless positive attitude.

On the porch, I pause at the top of the steps, watching the heat shimmer in front of me. I wipe a trickle of sweat off the side of my face. Susan takes my elbow firmly, treating me like an old person. I shake her off.

"You don't have to actually touch me," I say. "Just be a spotter."

"Doesn't it look nice out here?"

Susan, too, knows how to avoid a conflict.

"The yard service came yesterday, and last night I had Caroline and Elizabeth put their bikes in the garage and pick up all the yard toys."

"Now that you mention it, it does look strange." It's also quiet with the girls at camp during the day.

"I think it looks nice," she says.

We reach the mailbox. I lean on it for a second, looking back at my little one-story house, which reminds me of a beach house, with its white clapboard, dark green shutters and door, and the wide front porch.

"Let's go," Susan says.

"I hope I'm going to be okay," I say.

"Of course, you are. You're going to be fine. You just need to get your strength back."

"I mean really okay," I say, noticing that the crepe myrtle tree to the side of the house is full and blooming.

"Don't think about it," she says. "Just walk."

We can sometimes be very much alike.

After the walk, I'm breathing heavily and sweating. Of course, no sweat on Susan. Even when we were little, she always looked perfect, not a hair out of place no matter what. Actually, in that way, Caroline reminds me of her.

In my bathroom, I sit on the edge of the tub, then slide to the floor to get as much of me as possible against the cold tile.

After another day of successfully walking to the mailbox, I read about Matisse. At forty-three, he said, *"Oh, do tell the American people that I am a normal man; that I am a devoted husband and father, that I have three fine children, that I go to the theatre, ride horseback, have a comfortable home, a fine garden that I love, flowers, etc., just like any man."*

Just like any man.

I shut my eyes, but I still see a single line on a blank sheet of paper. The emptiness around it. The nothingness it creates.

At the close of my fifth day in the bedroom, I crawl under the covers, thinking again of the man who created the painting that means a whole world to me. Looking at him on the front of *Matisse on Art*, it feels as if he's here with me now. I've always kept this book at home, instead of at the office. It's soft and pliable, and I'm continually drawn to this self-portrait of him at forty-nine, with that red beard and olive green suit, sitting in a straight-backed chair, a brush in one hand and his palette in the other, the rug underneath a deep rose. I always go back to his eyes, staring forward with such intensity at his subject. I fall asleep, the book in my hands, imagining the one he's staring at is me.

But I wake alone, missing Mark, not understanding who the person was who sent him away. I want his hands on me, his breath mixing with mine.

I should leave the bedroom for more than just a walk. But Susan is doing everything for me, and for Caroline and Elizabeth, as efficiently as if she were running a business. I hardly even see the girls, except to say goodnight.

Really, there's no need for me to go out there. And in here, it feels safe.

Susan and I walk again, our daily ritual. We go even farther today, up the street and back. I fall on my bed, out of breath.

"Hop up," she says, bursting into my bedroom.

"I'm not getting up."

"Yes, you are," she says, pulling the comforter off the bed. "I need to change the sheets, and you need a bath." My official week of convalescence is over tomorrow, and Susan returns home. Good news, bad news.

"I can't take a bath," I say. "You know that."

"Take a sponge bath with that peppermint-rosemary body wash I brought you."

Now she's tugging at the sheet underneath me. I get up.

"You know you can wash your hair just fine in the sink," she says, handing me a clean t-shirt.

Coming out of the bathroom, I was exhausted, but now that I'm propped up in the middle of the bed with two pillows behind me and one on each side, I feel my energy returning. Although I'm savoring my last day in the bedroom, I'm ready to move forward, out of reflection, back to life. Right this minute, though, I sit without moving, relishing the feeling of the clean cotton sheets against my faintly scented skin. A perfect still life.

On her way back to Atlanta this afternoon, Susan dropped Caroline and Elizabeth at Alyssa's to spend the night—so I could make sure I could take care of myself before I was also responsible for the girls. I open the bedroom door and wander through the empty house, the floor creaking as I take small steps through the dining room to the kitchen, into the den. I gaze at the front porch and into the girls' room, seeing how it feels to be me again. These places look the same, but I feel different—farther away, yet at the same time more present. In my study, I pick up an old black and white postcard from my desk of a woman in front of the Eiffel Tower. When we were talking about the trip to Paris, I'd copied Matisse's words from his essay on travel on the back. It's good to *"stop the usual mental routine and take a voyage that will let parts of the mind rest while other parts have free rein—especially those parts repressed by the will. This respite permits a withdrawal and consequently an examination of the past."*

Ever since Frank, that's what I've been doing—repressing parts of myself. I've been using my will instead of my heart. Well, not anymore. I miss the girls. I miss Mark. I'm ready to lead with my heart, to hurl myself into life.

As I crawl under the covers, I see that picture of Mark and the girls on the far night table—he's smiling right at me and yet he's so far away. Then, as I lean back in bed, I look at the picture of *Breakfast* beside me.

Matisse on one side, Mark on the other.

I turn out the light and dream of my life as a painting, an incomplete painting. I spend the long, dark hours of the night searching for, but never finding, the missing color.

Blue Nudes

I look out my bedroom window to see a moonless, starless dark. Although I don't see it or feel it, I know the heat is there too, invisible. The girls are asleep in their beds. The proper order has been restored in this little house.

It was almost three weeks ago that I woke up in the hospital after surgery—ovarian cancer, Stage III, beyond the ovary and the pelvis but limited to the abdominal cavity. Mark called, as promised, to check on me. Alyssa talked to him. He said to tell me he had called and that he would be thinking about me.

Once I got over the pain from the surgery, the hot flashes of menopause set in. Which would have been shocking except that cancer had already hurled me beyond shock. Now I have moments when this whole thing is so unreal it seems like a movie I saw, or a book I read—something happening to someone else.

As for the minutes of the day, I fill them with little girl kisses and tangles, the smell of grape jelly and crayons, the sound of doll voices. It's the three of us against the world.

I tiptoe into their room. As usual, Elizabeth has kicked her covers to the bottom of the bed. I pull them back over her and return Caroline's book to the shelf. Her black waves look just brushed, even in sleep.

In my bed, I reread the letter that came from Mark today.

July 4
Dear Emily,

I just hung up from talking to you—I feel terrible, crushed that you're having to go through this. I'm so sorry. I wish there was something I could do. Even though I'm over here, I'm thinking about you and wish I could be there with you and the girls. Call me any time, and I'll also check on you.

Love,
Mark

It's the night before my first cycle of chemo, and I'm trying to latch on to my fears. I'm trying to stop the swirling. I put my book down and retrieve my journal. Back in bed, I pull the covers close. *Matisse wrote, "I do not think exactly the way I thought yesterday...I do not repudiate any of my paintings but there is not one of them that I would not redo differently, if I had it to redo."*

Looking at the sketches Matisse did for the Blue Nudes, I recognize how I feel—empty, flat, nothing but a black outline. When I compare these sketches to the finished nudes—complete, full of heart and soul, luminous—I wonder if I'll ever be finished.

A month or so ago, before cancer, I noticed that every time I walked into the garage, this bird—I assumed it was the same one—zoomed past me, taking me by surprise. I finally did a little investigating. Without touching anything, I discovered a nest inside an old wicker basket I'd left on a shelf. It made me happy to think about the safe place this bird had found. I told Caroline and Elizabeth.

A few days after that, the bird perched near my car long enough for me to notice her short little tail sticking up. She appeared to have her eye on me. I stood still while I observed her small, round body, a dull brown on top and grayish white underneath, with bars of white on her tail and wings. This was a house wren. My mother loves birds and was always pointing them out to me when I was little. I didn't realize, though, that I was listening.

I forgot about the bird until I heard a whiny, chirpy chorus. Suspecting baby birds, I stood on my car to peer into the nest. Sure enough, it was filled with tiny, wet-looking little beaks, opening and shutting. I told the girls the babies were here. Then I helped them stand on my car to see. Over the next week or so, sitting on the front porch to watch the girls play in the yard, I would also watch the mother bird fly in and out.

Today, walking into the garage to drive myself to chemo, I remember the birds. Very carefully I stand on my car, but when I peer into the nest, it's empty. I concentrate on finding my keys, opening my car door.

I back out. Alyssa wanted to drive me today, but I told her I needed to do as much as I could by myself in this sea of needing help, to feel like the old me, somebody who could take herself to the doctor.

After I arrive at the hospital, a nurse calls my name before I've even relaxed enough for my head to rest on the wall behind my chair. She takes my blood and shows me into an examination room where a doctor does a pelvic exam. I close my eyes only to recall the routine of monthly visits when I was pregnant.

In the chemo room, there are four recliners against the wall. Curtains can be pulled, but none are. We each have our own TV and remote, giving us an illusory sense of control. I'm the second to arrive. The other woman is holding hands with a husband or male friend. I lean back and close my eyes. The IV starts. I imagine the Platinum and the Taxol destroying the cancer cells, just as I have read that others do.

If Mark were here, would I have told *him* not to come? I don't think so. And I imagine him next to me, my hand in his.

I intend to put the TV on the news, but as I pass a gardening show, I stop there. Any form of nature would be more the state of mind I seek. Five more times I have to do this, and then I'll be well. Five more times I have to do this, and then I'll be well. Five…

I take Zofran for nausea.

I open my eyes to the dark. For a second, I don't know where I am. My eyes adjust. I'm in the den, on the couch. I hear something. The girls. Jumping up, I rush toward the sounds coming from their room. I open the door, and my hand goes to my eyes to shield them from the blast of light.

"Mom," Caroline says, looking up, "do you feel better?"

I can make out both girls—in no danger. I lean back against the door jamb and slide to the floor. My heart hurts; it's beating so hard. Against my will, almost reflexively, I begin sobbing. I lean my head over my knees to hide it from the girls. A useless exercise—I'm making so much noise.

I feel both girls beside me, one on each side, and I smell peanut butter.

"What's the matter, Mom?" Caroline says. "Are you okay? Do you want me to call Alyssa?"

I wipe my face with my shirt and take a deep breath. I lean my head back and put an arm around each one. I smile as I try to breathe normally. "I'm fine. I was just really scared for a minute. I woke up and didn't know where you were."

"We were here," Elizabeth says, patting me on the head, her hand sticking to my hair as she pats.

"You were sleeping," Caroline says. "So when it got dark, I got stuff from the kitchen for our supper."

"You did?"

"See," Caroline says, pointing to where they were sitting on the floor.

"See," Elizabeth says.

The red-and-white striped cloth lies on the floor. On top of it are small boxes of apple juice, the jar of peanut butter with a spoon stuck in the middle, the open loaf of bread, the jar of grape jelly on its side, a bag of chips, the box of fruit snacks, chocolate chip cookies, and a melting tub of ice cream.

"I fixed our supper so you didn't have to wake up," Caroline says.

I look at her and start sobbing again.

"What's wrong, Mom?" she says. "We'll clean up the mess."

"I'm just so proud of you. That's all. I don't know why I'm crying." I hug them both; for too long, I'm sure. I feel them fidgeting and let them go. "What time is it anyway?" I ask, looking at my watch. After eight. I remember Alyssa calling to check on me around five and then lying down on the couch. Three hours ago.

Elizabeth licks ice cream from the tub. She even has grape jelly in her hair.

"Here's what we'll do," I say. "I'll clean up while you two get a bath. Elizabeth, I'll be in in two seconds to help you wash your hair."

"Is it Sunday?" she says, continuing to lick.

"No, but I think we'll wash it anyway. And listen, I know what everyone's telling you, about not bothering me and letting me rest. But when I'm the only grown-up here, my job is to take care of you. You're supposed to wake me up for things like supper or darkness or somebody getting hurt or a fire."

"A fire?" Caroline says.

"Caroline told me not to wake you up," Elizabeth says.

Caroline turns to look at me.

"And I'm very proud of her for being so grown up and taking such good care of you."

Caroline smiles and sits on her bed.

"From now on, though, it will not be bothering me to wake me up. *Your* job is to wake me up. *My* job is to take care of you. And I can. Otherwise, I'll be afraid to go to sleep. Deal?"

"Deal," they say together.

August 1
Dear Emily,

I don't know what to say to you in my letters anymore. Nothing seems interesting or important compared to what you're going through. Let me know how the chemo is and how you're feeling. Tell the girls hello. I'm thinking about you.

Love,
Mark

Although Caroline and I come home from her soccer practice the same way we did in the spring, I feel as if I'm driving somewhere I've never driven, as if my life is trying to locate its previous frenetic pace but is unable to do so. Stopped at a red light I watch some men putting stakes in the ground on a corner lot full of grass. I put a wintergreen lifesaver in my mouth.

"Hey, Mom, that grass is for sale."

"It looks that way."

On our street now, I notice trees and green everywhere—next to the curb, between houses, on side yards, and in back yards. Our neighbor, Suzanne, waves to us as we drive by. She's also a single mother with a daughter a couple of years older than Caroline.

I pull into the garage and turn off the car. "Pick up all your trash," I remind her. "And your soccer bag."

"I can't carry it all."

"My hands are full already. You'll just have to make two trips like me."

"Mom…" she says, drawing it out.

"Caroline…" I say, shutting the car door.

She looks up at me with a big grin on her face, and we walk together along the short rock path to the house.

I think about Frank and wonder what it was like not to take care of your own children. To be separated from them. I wonder if he knew he was about to die, if he had time to be afraid.

With the girls in school again, time speeds up. I shut the front door and the tiny mirror on the hat stand catches my eye. Yesterday Elizabeth told me my head looked like the baby birds we had in the garage. She's right, I think, as I look in the mirror to adjust my tufts. I had my hair cut even shorter than normal before my first chemo, and shorter still afterwards. Somebody told me to do this so I would feel as if I were in control.

I hope Caroline and Elizabeth won't be afraid of me when I don't have any hair. I hope *I* won't be afraid of me. When they come in to see me in the mornings, they do a hair check. They seem to understand that I'm sick. That I'm taking "medicine" to make me better. That the medicine makes my hair fall out.

I remember to wear loose clothes for this next cycle of chemo. Monochrome seems appropriate somehow, varying shades of gray. My Lamaze breathing helps to keep the fear away. If it's like last time, I'll be okay until the day after.

August 27
Dear Mark,

My second round of chemo was a week ago. The first day, I was okay. So Alyssa came the morning after to take the girls for donuts and then to school. She kept them for one night and then Martha had them for two. Kari and Victoria took turns helping me. Day 4 was the worst. Who could imagine I could throw up for two days and then have the worst day? I started feeling a little better on Day 5, although I couldn't take care of the girls yet. Martha brought them home the next day after

168

school, along with some chicken noodle soup she made that all three of us ate at the kitchen table.

I hope your work is going well.

The girls say hi.

love, Emily

On the porch steps, on a bright, warm, fall day, the good kind of warm because you know cooler days are in the forecast, I see that the magic transformation has begun—green to color and fullness to sparseness. The sky is an undiluted blue, and I think of Mark. I imagine him bending over in a perfectly hollowed out square, marked off with twine, using his trowel and then his small brush to examine a handful of dirt. As I broaden my view, I see Anna working in the square beside him.

September 15
Dear Emily,

A miniature boat artisan from Dubai was in Sinop today. He told me that his family has carved boats for as far back as he knows, to at least his great grandfather—and he was old enough to be a great grandfather himself. I bought a tiny pearling boat, made out of "saj" wood, the same wood the regular pearling boats are made from. When I was talking to him about how he acquired his expertise, he patted his chest and said, "It all comes from within."

Hope you're feeling okay.

Love,
Mark

I sit up and turn on the light by my bed, my heart racing. I was trapped in a painting—Matisse's *Studio Under the Eaves*. The brown, slanting walls and darker brown, overwhelmingly low ceiling were pressing in on me. I glance at my ceiling and around at my familiar walls to convince myself that I'm really in my own bedroom. I take slow, deep breaths to fill my lungs. In the nightmare, there was no door out of the room. And there was nothing in the room except an easel, a canvas, my brushes, and palette. But there were no colors on the palette. I could do what I loved all day—paint, but without any colors. I climbed on the ledge of the open window to escape, ready to jump into the light.

October 2
Dear Mark,

Elizabeth wants me to take the rocking chair out of their room. She thinks three is too old to be rocked, even though it's not like I rock her to sleep. I just never broke the habit of going into their room and letting her sit with me for a few minutes in the rocking chair. But I have promised to move the chair tomorrow. I wish I could rock her one last time, but my stomach is still too sore for her to sit in my lap. Otherwise, I feel okay.

While she fell asleep in her bed tonight, I rocked, remembering rocking her when she was a baby. Remember back then, once I thought she was asleep, I would make myself count to 100 before I tried to put her in bed because if she woke up, I would have to start the process all over again? Tonight, I would have been glad to start over. It was hard to leave the room—it felt too much like an ending. I left the door open.

The house is quiet as I write to you.

I miss you.

love, Emily

The three of us get out of the car at home after Elizabeth's karate lesson and an early supper at the Mexican place. Karate. Self-defense. One more step toward her being able to take care of herself. Of course, someone will always be there to take care of her, until she's old enough to do it herself. My sister Susan is named in my will as their guardian. Even a healthy person should have a plan.

"I can't believe it's dark already," I say, shutting my door.

Caroline continues to collect her stuff from the car, while Elizabeth and I start toward the house. I take a deep breath of the fresh, cold air and look up to see a star. Elizabeth looks up at me as I look down at her. Bending to pick her up, I lose my balance and just sit down on the ground in an effort to reclaim some sort of control over the motion I began. She looks afraid, but I pull her onto my crossed legs, as if sitting down was a better idea I had in the middle of picking her up. The world is not supposed to be a scary place.

"Star light, Star bright," I say, as Caroline comes to stand behind us, leaning against my shoulders, her hands full.

Together, they finish what I started, "First star I've seen tonight, I wish I may, I wish I might, Have the wish, I wish tonight."

On the cold grass of our yard, we listen to the silent wishes and watch them float to the stars.

> October 16
> Dear Emily,
>
> Write to me more often like that.
>
> Love,
> Mark

I stare out the window in the den, holding Mark's letter. I have no idea what he wants. I try to remember what I said in my letter, the words I used. It was something about rocking Elizabeth, and I wrote it without thinking. After a while, I add this letter to the others. Then I take them back out, to hold all of them together. I rub my hand. Everything about me is dry—my eyes, my skin, inside of me. I itch; I burn. On the table by my bed are drops and lotions, lip balms.

Later, when I try to write Mark, I can't. I reread his letter, hoping his words will pull forth some of my own. I even sit in front of an empty sheet of paper. But nothing.

Take the girls to school. Buy two cases of Fresca. Go to the hospital for chemo, round five. Pick up the cleaning. Pick up the girls.

Somehow the tart, bitter taste of Fresca counteracts the metallic taste I get in my mouth during the bad days right after. The carbonation helps my stomach.

I wake up around five, feeling funny. Then I remember. I have cancer; I had chemo. I am Mademoiselle Yvonne Landsberg in her portrait by Matisse, all black, a touch of orange around my nose and mouth and my body coming out of itself, but glowing white at its core. I throw up. I get back in bed. Alyssa comes around seven to help the girls get ready for school and to take them for donuts. I hear her shut my door and I relax a little, knowing I'm all I have to worry about for a while.

> November 4
> Dear Emily,
>
> Thanks for my birthday card. You always remember to mail it so I'll have it <u>on</u> my birthday. That's nice. Things are quiet here and I'm catching up on paperwork. I'm ready for a break.
>
> I hope you got my last letter. I can't tell you how much your letter about rocking Elizabeth meant to me. It was as if I could see right inside you, as if I could see how you felt—as if you were here beside me.
>
> I hope you're feeling good.
>
> Write again.
>
> Love,
> Mark

Since my surgery, I've only been able to go to work for three or four hours at a time. And only during the two weeks each month I'm not having chemo or recovering from it. Later this month I'm scheduled to talk to a museum group on Matisse, to commemorate his birthday. Sam is concerned that I might not feel up to it, but I've assured him that it will require no extra anything for me to give a talk on Matisse, and that talking about a subject I love is bound to make me feel better, not worse.

But right this minute, I have a cough and my stomach hurts. I hope it's just a twenty-four hour thing, but that's what everybody with cancer hopes. I'm secretly, buried-very-deep, scared. When I cough, it's hard to catch my breath, and my chest feels heavy. I visualize Michelangelo's finger of God reaching out, touching me, curing me.

One of my large, full color books of Matisse's paintings is open on my bed, and as I flip through, I imagine being in *My Room at the Beau Rivage*, painted right after Matisse moved to Nice. With the view of the ocean from my bed, I look around at the peach carpet, the lace curtains, the violets on the ceiling and the green armchair with the lace doily. I imagine sitting in the armchair. Matisse went to Nice in search of peace and tranquility and in search of light. His paintings of this period reflect the soothing atmosphere he found there. I wonder if moving to Nice would work for me.

I lean back on my pillows and close my eyes. Matisse was the master of the use of color and form to convey emotion. I remember his words when he was asked why he painted. *"Why, to translate my emotions, the feelings and the reactions of my sensibility through color and drawing..."* I sit up. That's what Mark wanted—for me to translate my emotions into words on paper. In a letter meant for him.

December 2
Dear Mark,

I'm sorry it's taken me so long to write another letter. When I wrote last time, I didn't even think about it. But when you mentioned it, I couldn't remember what I said, so I froze.

I was just going over a talk I'm going to give on Matisse later this month. I wasn't thinking—I was just over-flowing. I plan to mention the mural he created for the Barnes Foundation. I've probably told you this before. The theme of the mural is dance, but he only shows us part of the drawing. Matisse explained, "I permitted the observer to see a much larger dance, because I used fragments." And then we use our imagination to com-plete the drawing. Even though it's not there, we can see it, and hold it in our minds. It's as if the dancers leap and turn, moving beyond the mural. Every time I think of this, it takes my breath away. It also reminds me of some-thing you wrote in one of your letters—how finding fragments can be just as revealing as finding the whole object, maybe more.

Everywhere I look I see fragments of you—you digging and smiling, a million miles away from me—and I use my imagination to complete the picture.

I realize now I should have been looking at my life in a different way because no matter how full it may have been, with you not in it, there's a distinct empty place.

love, Emily

This morning was hopefully my last round of chemo, and I'm not sure whether to focus on being hopeful or on being prepared for more. But Christmas is just the thing to focus me on two little girls, aged six—actually almost seven—and three. That's where I direct my energy. Both still believe in the magic, but this may be the last year that's true.

We'll have Christmas here this year, the three of us together in our cozy little house—the simplicity of the holiday, the rituals, and no packing. Susan and her family will ski in Colorado. Our parents are staying in Hawaii.

Last week, I helped Caroline and Elizabeth make a list. Then I took each one separately to shop and to lunch. Yesterday, the three of us picked out a tree, which was delivered, already in a stand, an hour ago. The girls carry little bucket after bucket to water the tree. I rest, watching them and inhaling the smell of evergreen. I try not to think about my chemo this morning or how bad I'll feel for the next few days.

Caroline helps Elizabeth get ready for bed. I put in eye drops and rub lotion on my itching fingers. I go in to kiss them good night and fall asleep quickly. Around seven, Alyssa will be here to wake the girls and take them for donuts, a soothing ritual, despite the reason for it. I think they're going to make Christmas cookies too. By day eight, I should feel good enough, and have enough energy, to decorate the tree. December 18th is a little late, but that's the best I can do this year. Alyssa and I have tickets for the four of us to see the Nutcracker on the twenty-third.

A couple of years ago, I remember seeing a woman who had cancer sitting and chatting with other women, waiting for her daughter to return from a Brownie field trip. It seemed odd to me then that she wasn't doing something more important. Now I realize the significance of being the one to be there when the bus pulls into the parking lot. Not Paris or Rome or a candlelight dinner, not finishing *Anna*

Karenina—just living an ordinary life and being there, the privilege of being there for the people you love, and who love you.

The night before the planned tree decorating, I feel well enough for a glass of wine. I put it on my bedside table, crawl under the covers, and pick up a book on Matisse. As the words flow through me, Matisse becomes alive, his gray-blue eyes peering at me. *"His round beard, which bears a hint of its earlier reddish-brown and is carefully and closely trimmed, was tinged with gray, with clean, dry curls, darker and closer to its original color under the chin. His mustache was almost completely flecked with gray; it covered his sullen lips, pale and wrinkled...."* I slide under the covers, closing my eyes. Henri lies beside me. My fingers move through his beard, my mouth against his mustache, his lips on mine. His penetrating, sonorous voice whispers in my ear, along with the nighttime creaking of the old house.

On the 18th, around five, after resting all day, I pick up the girls from The Little Red Schoolhouse, which thankfully stays open until the 24th. Neil Diamond fills the car with "Alleluias." Once home, we get ready to decorate the tree. First, I give them each a box to open. Striped PJs—red and gray for Elizabeth and green and gray for Caroline. They run to take a quick bath together before putting them on. I start Handel's "Messiah," and then I change into something Christmassy that I can also sleep in—a sleep shirt with the word *Believe* across the front. I adjust a red scarf, which hides my lack of hair. My clothes hang on me, but my stomach is still a little bloated and sore. I pull on black sweatpants and slippers. It's cold enough for a fire so I check on the girls, and then I bring in one log, which is all I can carry. I turn on the gas starter and light a match, standing up slowly to take in the tree, the cozy den, the fire. The darkness outside. I inhale a deep breath of Christmas tree. This is good.

At the same moment that Caroline and Elizabeth come giggling and sliding through the dining room into the den, the doorbell rings. I let the UPS man wait while I catch them and kneel, all three of us laughing and knocking our heads together, as if we were trying to cement our little trio for all time.

When I finally get to the door, it's not the UPS man. It's Mark, standing in front of me and grinning through a dark red beard. My hand goes to the scarf on my head.

"Merry Christmas," he says.

I fall into him, and he catches me, wrapping his arms around me. I feel his head on top of mine. I breathe in sweat and travel, and as I burrow deeper, the earth.

Then I remember Anna and step back.

When he comes into the house, Caroline squeals "Mark," and Elizabeth copies her. He reaches down to them, but Elizabeth runs into the den. It's bizarre to see Elizabeth being the shy one. He keeps one arm around Caroline while he follows after Elizabeth.

"Where is that red-headed baby?" he teases. "Who is this little girl with blonde hair?"

When he turns back to me, he looks right in my eyes. He cups his hand around the back of my head. "God, it's great to see your face."

I feel my heart coming up out of my chest. I swallow to make it stay in its place. "I'm so happy to see you," I say. Then I feel dizzy.

What is it about him that gives me permission to fall apart? Half of me wants to run and hide like Elizabeth, and the other half wants to ask a million questions. Is he home for the holidays? Is Anna here with him? I want to take cover in his chest, but instead I say, "I was about to pour a glass of wine. Would you like one too?"

"And a gallon of water," he says. "I've been traveling for days."

Caroline jumps between us. "Mark, are you going to help us decorate the tree?"

"Let's wait just a minute for that," I say to Caroline and Elizabeth. I put *The Greatest Christmas Ever* DVD on for them to watch. They each grab a blanket and hop up on opposite ends of the couch.

Mark and I wander to the kitchen, and despite all the times he's been here before, it's weird for him to be here now. He leans against the counter, and I feel self-conscious as I get the wine out of the fridge.

"Is Anna here with you?" I ask, taking two wine glasses out of the cabinet.

"She's still in Turkey."

I pour the water and then the wine.

"How long are you here for?" I ask, without looking at him. And as I set the bottle down, I feel his hands on my shoulders. I turn around.

"Forever I hope."

I stare at his chest, unable to believe.

He tilts my head so my eyes look into his.

"I love you, Emily," he says.

"Please," I say, "hold me forever."

After Mark takes a quick shower, we hang ornaments on the tree, bumping into each other so often Caroline and Elizabeth start bumping into each other, copying us, laughing and saying, "Sorry," "No, I'm sorry" and "Excuse me." Each year, I give them a new ornament and write the date on the back. This year's is a flat, wooden cream-colored pony, with cream-colored dried flowers instead of a saddle, a yellow satin ribbon on Caroline's and a red satin ribbon on Elizabeth's. I keep thinking about having a scarf instead of hair, but I don't feel weird. I feel like me. So I stop thinking about it. It's hard to believe it's been a year since we've seen Mark, since he's been in this house. By the time the tree is decorated, it's as if he never left.

We have our traditional tree-decorating meal of cheese fondue with chocolate fondue for dessert. It's after nine thirty before I get the girls in bed and when I come back to the den, Mark is sitting at one end of the couch with his head to the side, asleep. I put up a few things in the kitchen and turn out the light. Then I turn out the lamps in the den so I can fully enjoy the twinkling white lights on the tree and the light of the fire, which Mark must have worked on before he fell asleep. I sit down and study him.

He has lines around his eyes and his skin looks rough, from being outside so much, I guess. I want to reach out and touch his dark red hair, full and wavy. Then I notice some gray, and my hand goes to my heart. His beard is close to his face, and dark red. He has on a dark green t-shirt and a plaid, green, white, and black flannel shirt I've never seen before, but which looks as if it's been worn a lot. He stirs and his hand slides to the sofa. I reach out to put mine in his, and he opens his eyes. That's his only movement, the opening of his eyes, no jerking from sleep at the touch.

Then he smiles. "It's nice to be back," he says, sitting up and brushing his hair off his forehead.

"It's nice for you to be here."

He turns toward me.

"Mark, I—"

"How are you really?"

"With you here, surely I'm cured." I smile.

"I hated not being with you."

"I go back for tests in January," I say, "to find out if I have to have more chemo." I look away. And then, a tightening in my stomach and chest pushes the words to my lips, "Mark, I'm sorry I let you go to Turkey. I don't know what I was thinking. I mean, I loved you before, but now I also know how if you're not here, a part of my life is missing. And—but," I pause, "What about Anna? And work?"

He angles one leg on the couch so his whole body faces me. "The work was amazing until you got sick. Then it was just work. I felt like I had to stay until the end of the summer. Then, with all the discoveries, it took me longer than I expected to wrap things up. And I care about Anna—she loved being with me and I needed that—but Emily, it was easy. When I saw her after you called to tell me you were sick, I knew how I really felt. All I could think about was you. Then I got that letter about rocking Elizabeth, and there you were on the page, the woman I loved. I didn't want to be in Turkey anymore. When I got the letter about the fragments, I just left."

The next morning, the girls are delighted to find Mark in my bed and climb in with us. Whatever shyness Elizabeth had the night before has evaporated. I persuade Caroline to fix them both some cereal—I keep the milk on a low shelf—and Mark and I stay in bed a little longer.

In the kitchen, we have trouble finishing a subject, with one of us interrupting the other to ask a question. I find myself watching him, the way one watches a newborn, amazed at the fact that he's here in front of me, making sure he's breathing, wondering what he's going to do next.

After lunch, we all bundle up and head outside. Mark and I pause on the wide front porch, which has always been one of my favorite places, like another room only outside, running the entire length of the front of the house. The girls head on to the swing set, angled into the side yard—the backyard is only a narrow strip of grass. Behind the swings, the trees and empty lot next door add the space my father always talked about when we were little. "A house must have sufficient space to breathe," he would say.

As Mark is about to head down the steps, I put my hand on his arm. "Will you live with us?" I ask.

He puts his hands on my waist and looks hard into my eyes. "I've been waiting years to hear you want that. Yes. Will you marry me?"

"Yes," I say.

On December 21st, at eleven o'clock, we get married in the chapel of the neighborhood church, a satin scarf on my head and two sweet flower girls by my side. I give myself away, as the saying goes, but Mark says for me not to take that literally. Susan flies in for the day so she is my family representative. Mark's parents drive down from North Carolina. Alyssa, Martha, Victoria, and Kari are all there. After a small celebratory luncheon at The Mills House Hotel downtown, Mark and I have a one-night honeymoon at The Inn at Middleton Place. I picked this spot, remembering being here with him the night of the Spoleto Finale, right before he left for Turkey. We stroll in the gardens overlooking the Ashley River, talking about how it was before and how we hope it will be now, a new beginning. After dinner we have a slow carriage ride through the plantation. The next day, breakfast in bed, and then we return to real life and Christmas, full of hope for the future. That night, Alyssa cedes her ticket to the Nutcracker to Mark, and all four of us together go see the Sugar Plum Fairy.

On the Monday after Christmas, Mark goes out into the world to make a few job connections. He has a meeting with Ferrell and Sam to talk about continuing the work he was doing at the museum before he left. They, of course, are anxious to set a date for a special exhibit on the Black Sea and the work Mark was doing in Turkey. Mark also wants to do some teaching at the College of Charleston and some more field work in this general area for the State of South Carolina.

When he gets back that afternoon, I'm reading on the sofa and the girls are playing with new toys in their room. He comes in carrying a cardboard box with his computer on top.

"I went by the storage unit and picked up a few things," he says, grinning and putting the box on the coffee table.

"How did the meeting go?

"Great," he says. "I just need to answer a few emails, and I'll be done for today. These are my boats—mine and my grandfather's."

He sits next to me and opens his computer. I peer into the box, inhaling the pine, and then I look around the room. While he works, I get a stepladder and, starting with the top shelves, I push the books to the back. I'll put his grandfather's boats on these higher shelves away from small hands.

He stretches. "I'm going to say hey to the girls."

As I lift a boat out of the box, I notice his computer on the sofa and a photo of a woman with long blond hair and strong legs. I look closer. She's crouched in the dirt, holding some sort of rock.

He comes back in.

"Is that Anna?" I ask.

"Oh, yeah," he says, closing the photo. "She just sent that." He starts typing again. "Every once in a while, I miss the work. You know, my hands in the dirt."

I stand there holding the old boat. "I never asked how Anna felt about your leaving."

He closes his computer and puts it to the side. "She's having a hard time. I'm trying to be nice."

"You're always nice. That's who you are."

He doesn't smile.

"You told her we got married, right?"

He doesn't say anything.

I put the boat back in the box. "Why not?"

"I was trying to slow it down for her."

I tell myself it doesn't matter and lift the boat out again. "One of your grandfather's?"

He nods.

"It's beautiful."

He stands up and takes the boat and puts his arms around me. "I love you. I want to be here. And I'm going to tell her." Then he goes back to his computer, and I carry the fragile boat to a high shelf. As I come back for another one, he closes the computer again.

"I like what you're doing with the den," he says, taking out two smaller boats.

"Do you remember your grandfather?" I ask.

He nods as he places the boats on a shelf. "He would never just sit, but would always sit forward, with a piece of wood and a knife in his hands. He carved other stuff too, and bigger things—birds and ducks, and blowguns."

"Did you ever try the other stuff?"

"I only ever wanted to make boats—little boats."

When he goes to get another box from his car, I hear the girls laughing.

"What about your brother?" I ask when he comes back in. "Did he carve too?"

"No interest—too slow a process."

"I wish I could have known him."

"You two are a lot alike. I think you would have liked each other."

"These are my favorite," I say, holding out two rowboats. One is painted and then "weathered" to look old and loved. The wood on the other one is not painted but natural. "They smell good."

I hand them over. "These are made out of wood from some old window frames," he says, inhaling. "Old cypress planks." He adds them to a shelf.

When we stand back to look around us, there's a new depth to the den.

I'm kind of awake, aware that Mark is already up, but probably not the girls because it's still quiet. Hearing the door open, I turn over.

"Good morning, Mrs. Hudson," Marks says, grinning.

And despite my dislike of the morning, I smile at this handsome man bringing me tea in bed. I lean forward and pile up the pillows behind my back.

He hands me the mug of tea and a muffin on a napkin. "Breakfast," he says, kissing me. At the door, he says, "Enjoy your *time to yourself* in *our* bed." I smile again, and he closes the door behind him.

But the tingling caused by his beard lingers. I touch my face and realize how easy it's been to accustom myself to his beard, to his being here, to him.

Our bed. I wait, wondering if I'll have any negative feelings. *Mrs. Hudson.* Still nothing.

Mark kept the picture of him and the girls on his bedside table. The framed note card of my painting still sits on mine. My favorite pen lies next to marbleized index cards looking like a yellow, brown, and rust abstract painting, which reminds me of fall. On Mark's night table, there's a pad from the Holiday Inn Express. My dictionary and *The Runaway Bunny* are on my bottom shelf in a basket. Issues of *Archaeology* and his work notebooks, plain spiral ones in harsh colors, are spilling from his bottom shelf onto the floor, along with yesterday's paper. His faded, dark green work vest with all the pockets lies across the armchair.

Feet hit the ground, and there's running, and then the girls' laughter and Mark's voice mingling with theirs. I imagine them jumping into his lap on top of the paper he was reading. I don't know if it's the foundation of Mark's presence when they were little, their memories—conscious or unconscious—of him before he left, or just his easy-going presence, but they have adjusted to having a father as if they have always had one.

But they thought it would be weird to call Mark "Dad," so he will remain "Mark," or "Markie," as Elizabeth likes to throw in every now and then.

I slide down in the bed and close my eyes, just for a minute more.

That afternoon, sitting in my study, I google "ovarian cancer" for the hundredth time and finally register with the Gilda Radner Familial Ovarian Cancer website. Just like that, I now have an automatic connection to thousands of other women—some alive, some dead. The hotline number in case I need it is 1-800-OVARIAN. I save cancer. net as one of my favorite places.

A pain in my side reminds me of all my weird, unexplained pains and illnesses over the years. My periods were always irregular, and I often had spotting in between. When I was twenty, I had non-stop bleeding. They did a bunch of tests and then put me on the pill. That seemed to handle it. Once they thought my thyroid was enlarged. The ultrasound was clear. Then I had a swollen lymph node on my neck, which required more than one round of antibiotics. Periodically, it feels as if there's a knot in my throat when I swallow. Stress was the explanation for that. I had one weird Pap smear, but when they retested, it was fine. An endometrial biopsy for erratic bleeding showed I had cystic hyperplasia.

I took something for that, and the condition seemed to go away. Oh yeah, and that "spot" on my low back. I wonder how long something has been wrong with me. Was my body trying to let me know?

I stand and stretch gently. I was one of the ones who had no increased risk for ovarian cancer because I had no first-degree relative—mother, sister, daughter—who had uterine, breast, or colon cancer. I had no fear to follow me around, no spot on my record. But now, when my mother, my sisters, and my daughters are asked this question, they have the spot. I have done this. I have given my three-year-old daughter and my six-year-old daughter an increased risk of ovarian cancer, a scary shadow that will follow them for the rest of their lives. There is nothing they can do to make it go away. On every form they fill out, in the back of their minds and in the center of their hearts, "my mother had ovarian cancer." I started a cycle. I put the red paint in the middle of the canvas. I'll never know how far out it spreads.

Even though we're touching, huddled close to keep out the cold wind, Mark's silence and his faraway eyes make me feel apart from him. It's New Year's Eve and freezing outside the Pomodoro, our favorite Italian restaurant. We left our coats in the car because the restaurant's ten tables are crammed so close together that not only is there no room to take a coat off once inside, there's no place to put the coat after you take it off. When a small table finally separates us, and we're sitting in our own chairs waiting to order something to drink, I ask, "What's the matter?"

"Nothing," he says.

That sounds like my line, not his. "Well, you look like something's the matter."

"Actually, you're right." Then he smiles. "I'm not sure you ever noticed before when something was bothering me." He pauses, as if to hold onto the moment. Then he frowns. "I'm having a hard time because I don't feel like I ought to bring it up. It's just a small thing."

The Pomodoro is a one-woman operation, and the owner stops by our table. "Red or white?"

"White," I say.

"Red," he says.

"We talked about this. You promised you would treat me like a regular person not a sick person."

"I know but—"

He pauses as our wine is delivered and we order.

"It's hard to be normal," he says, continuing. "What's normal?"

"Normal is the way we were together before you went to Turkey."

"That was *not* normal," he says, laughing.

And I laugh too.

"Anyway, that was eons ago." He pauses again as a basket of bread is plopped on the table. "That *is* what's bothering me though. Yesterday and today, a few times, I've felt like I did before, like you're not saying everything you're thinking—as if I'm still on the outside trying to get in."

He has some wine. I look at him. He doesn't seem mad. I try to take in what he's saying. I may have been doing this with small things—

"Emily, say something please."

"But I don't know what to say yet."

"For Pete's sake, Emily, that's what I'm talking about. Just say the first thing you think of. Include me."

I look at him.

"I'm afraid, sometimes," he says, "that it's going to be the way it was. I know I need to trust you. But it's hard to forget how I felt before."

The wine is cold, but it warms me going down. "Before, I felt as if I were trapped inside a chest. And I couldn't get out because too many people were sitting on the top. So I let you leave. But—"

I pause, and he starts to say something but stops.

"You know, I wondered, worried a little, that if I could have my wish and you came back, what was going to make it different this time."

"I assumed it would be different," he says, "because my being gone had made you see how much you loved me."

"Mark, I knew I loved you before." I look at him. "What I discovered, though, as people have gotten up off the chest is that all along, the chest was locked from the inside. *I* had to find a way to let myself out. When Matisse first held a paint box—*a box of colors*, he called it—in his hands, he knew it was the way he could finally express himself. I've known this story forever, but after the surgery, I thought, that's what I need—a box of colors." I pause, feeling my cheeks getting red and feeling ridiculous. But when I look at Mark's face, he's looking right in my eyes, waiting for my next words.

Our table is in the front corner of the room, up against the wall. I'm facing the window, where thick lines of people pass in front of the restaurant, some with party hats and blowers. Inside, however, despite it being New Year's Eve, it feels safe and manageable—ten tables, two kinds of wine, one server.

"I had a conversation with Alyssa," I say, circling back, hoping to

190

sneak up on myself. "We were talking about how impossible it was to be strong enough to take care of yourself, to stay yourself—to stay intact—*and also* pliable enough to have a relationship with another person. I started wondering why I cared so much about staying 'intact.' I realized that worrying about remaining myself came from not knowing myself. I didn't know what I should fight to keep and what it would be better to lose."

Mark puts his hand next to mine, on top of the table—only the inner edges touch.

I start to feel comfortable with the words. "I thought I needed to stay separate, like a single line. Actually, I often thought we were like parallel lines, together yet separate. I loved that."

"Always distance between the lines," Mark says.

"Exactly."

"No wonder I wasn't happy," he says.

"Maybe the secret has something to do with the volume Matisse was talking about. 'Do remember,' he said, 'that one line does nothing; it is only in relation to another that it creates a volume.'"

I pause again, feeling as if I'm saying too much, going too far. I look at Mark. He's completely at ease with this conversation. It reminds me of the way he was when he was helping Caroline on that dig.

I play with his fingers, and I keep going. "You always seem to know what's going on inside you. But I need a way to get the inside out. I needed time—I have to quit saying that. It wasn't time I needed; it was something else. And it's still happening. I feel more of myself seeping out of the chest every day. Not like I've found a key to open the top, but like the boards are shrinking. I'm able to emerge, little by little, between the cracks."

"Since I've been home," he says, "you seem more present, more here, more confident. I guess, instead of being happy with that, it made me greedy. I can see how much more there is—and I want it—you—all of you." He looks down for a minute, then back into my eyes.

"I keep coming back to that quote," I say. "What creates the relationship, or the painting, is the way the lines intersect, bounce off each other and come back. The pattern they make as they entwine."

"And yet each line stays separate," he says.

We look at each other.

Plates of food appear in front of us, but we don't move.

"I'm ready to do my part," I say, thinking I've been meaning to tell him this since he got back. "That's what you said in that first letter from Turkey, that you had been doing all the work. I see that now." And then I add, "I don't know how I could have thought the goal was a single line."

I taste the grapes in the wine and smell the garlic in the pasta. I notice the shadows between the tables and the other couples sitting in candlelight. The sounds of clinking, talk, and laughter link our table of two to the rest of the world. We order champagne and toast a new year, a new life. Then we walk to the Battery, where music and darkness conceal the continuous sound of the waves and the endlessness of the sea.

For Caroline's seventh birthday, we have a tea party. All the little girls come dressed in their mother's clothes. That's the best part, Caroline going through my clothes. She spends one long afternoon, taking each dress from my closet to hold in front of her, tilting her head to the right and then to the left for effect, and finally choosing my black slip dress—short on me, long on her—with a black sheer over-dress of gold flowers. Standing in front of the bathroom mirror the day of the party, I pull her hair back from her face in a grown-up looking ponytail, which makes me notice her round lips and long, thin face. I stand behind her as she adds "pearls" and an old, black straw hat with a wide brim. Her brown eyes look to my mirror image for approval. I smile and she smiles. Caroline says it's "her best birthday ever."

I spend the morning in my study ignoring all the bright yellow sticky notes of new year's resolutions and instead turning about half the stuff in my basket into piles before ignoring the rest of the stuff in the basket in favor of looking at paintings in books. I think of an art project for the girls and call them from the den to the kitchen. The TV stays on, but in a minute they both appear around the table, looking at the book in my hand and picking up scissors and construction paper. Elizabeth opens the paint box.

"Wait a minute," I say. "First I want to show you something Matisse made."

"The King of Color?" Elizabeth says. Her hair is short now, in a little bob with bangs. It suits her. It can swing free, with no barrette or bow to hold it back.

"Yes," I say. "The King of Color." I point to a picture but cover up the title. "What do you think it is?"

"I don't know," Elizabeth says. "A bunch of pieces of color?"

I look at Caroline who shrugs her shoulders.

"Matisse called the picture *The Snail*. Now can you find him?"

I hand the painting to Caroline, and she stares and stares. Then she hands the picture to Elizabeth, who turns it upside down, right side up, close to her nose, and then as far away as her arms will reach. "I see it," she says.

"Where?" Caroline asks, standing behind her sister.

"The green square is his head. Then go to the orange rectangle and start around. It makes a curve, like for his shell." She traces the spiral with her finger.

"I see it," Caroline says. "But maybe the blue is his body and the curvy part is the shell on his back. So what is the violet green piece at the top corner?"

"Maybe a building," Elizabeth says.

"A snail is tiny, dummy," Caroline says. "Those aren't going to be buildings."

"Caroline," I say.

"Oh yeah," Elizabeth says.

"Maybe a flower?" Caroline says.

"And the lighter green at the bottom is grass then," Elizabeth says.

"What about the orange border around the whole picture?" I ask.

Caroline says, "That's the frame."

"It could be a frame," I say. "Elizabeth, what do you think?"

"I don't—maybe it's a window somebody's looking out of," she says.

"Maybe," I say.

"And the white looks like light," she adds.

"It does. Matisse said he put the white patches there so the colors could breathe."

"I'm going to breathe," Elizabeth says, taking a long breath.

"Matisse said, 'First of all I drew the snail from nature, holding it between two fingers…'"

"Ooh, gross," Caroline says.

"Listen, he says he drew and redrew it. Then he picked up the scissors. It was important that 'the end should always be contained in the beginning.'"

"That's why there are so many greens," Caroline says. "One for his head at the beginning and one for the end of the curl of his shell."

"Yeah," Elizabeth says, looking at Caroline.

"Okay," I say, standing up. "I'm going to find the glue."

As I pass through the den, I turn off the TV and turn up the heat, thinking of Matisse at eighty-four creating the shape of the snail and the sensation of movement out of color and form, all from his bed.

Back in the kitchen, I say, "Now let's each make our own picture. Matisse called this 'drawing with scissors.' It's also called making a collage. And we can either cut up construction paper or if we can't find the color we want, we can paint a piece of white paper the right color and then cut it the shape we want."

"What do we put it on?" Caroline asks.

"I forgot the poster board." When I come back, I take the scissors and cut the poster board in half, giving one piece to each.

"What about you?" Caroline asks.

"I'm going to watch and help if you need it."

Caroline works on hers for over an hour, making a flower with all pastel colors, except for one square of black at the top. She takes her time using the paints to come up with many shades of yellow and washing her hands every few minutes so that they never have glue or paint on them for more than a second. At the end, she adds a green-yellow border with slim patches of white. She includes everything she is "supposed to." Elizabeth finishes in about twenty minutes. She makes a ball, using lots of glue and only choosing colors available in the construction paper, the texture of which gives her picture a kind of rough feel. "No black and no border," she says. "I want lots of white places to breathe."

Today, while the girls are at school, I go in to the museum for an hour or two. Sam has given Mark an office and his being here feels like reinforcement. The exhibit on the Black Sea is tentatively set for a year after the "Our Favorite Paintings" exhibit, roughly a year and a half from now. Mark will work outside the museum too. He'll be teaching a course this spring at the College of Charleston. He won't know about the job he wants with the state for a few months. An element of excitement surrounds his work now. Perhaps it was there all along.

We walk to lunch, pushing against the cold wind—Mark's been craving a turkey cheese steak. He tells me he talked to Anna and Tommy this morning and that he has a telephone conference with Robert Ballard next week. He's receiving requests for talks and articles and interviews, and his assistant is beginning to book lectures. The first one will be next month at The High Museum of Art in Atlanta.

Outside again, the wind has died. As we walk back, not having to fight it, I'm less tense but also tired. The busyness of the world seems to be over there, while I'm over here. At the museum, I get straight in my car to drive home, to rest and have some time before I pick the girls up from school. They're going to spend the night at Martha's. Her oldest daughter Charlotte is babysitting, trying to earn money for a ski trip. Caroline and Elizabeth are excited at the thought of sleeping bags on the floor of her room, just like when I was having chemo. I drop them off while Mark is still at work. When I get back, he's watching a soccer game. I flop next to him on the sofa.

"What do you want to do for supper?" he asks, when the game goes to a commercial. "Eat here or go somewhere?"

"Eat here," I say. I'm reading an old *Art & Antiques* magazine, an essay on "Endangered Art."

"I'm going to take a shower," he says, as if that were a choice we mentioned, only we hadn't. I look up but he's already on his way to the bedroom.

On the coffee table, his phone vibrates. A text from Anna. I look down at the pages of art in front of me. His phone vibrates again as if insisting that someone—anyone—look at it. I can hear the shower, so I pick up his phone.

When he comes back in, I'm flipping pages of the magazine. He just stands there. I look at him.

"Did it ever occur to you to ask me what *I* wanted to do for supper?" he says.

"Did it ever occur to you to tell me you and Anna still have a relationship?"

"We don't still have a relationship," he says, rolling his eyes as if I were boring him.

"She wants you to call her back, by the way. She has something else to tell you."

He sits on the sofa but farther away than he was before the shower. "She's having a hard time."

"So you said."

"I thought if we talked, it would help her process things. So I called her."

I look at him.

"She's called me back a few times."

"You're stringing her along," I say, "giving her hope."

"I guess you would know about that."

I close the magazine and start to get up.

"Sorry, sorry." He reaches for my hand and pulls me back. "Come on, I didn't mean that."

"You did mean it."

"Well, I'm sorry I used it like ammunition. I don't know how to help her."

"Did you tell her we got married?"

"That seemed to make things worse."

"Jeez. Hard things happen."

And it's as if the electricity goes out except it's bigger than that. Everything around me stops. The scene is frozen. And then I hear the grunts and kicks and cheering of the soccer game. I see the ball fly across the screen.

"I'll tell her to stop," he says.

"Whatever."

He rubs my shoulders and arms. He kisses my neck and turns me toward him. But instead of putting my arms around him, I tuck my arms between us and stay small. He just keeps kissing and rubbing as if to get the blood flowing, and eventually I'm all here again. Eventually, I uncurl and reach for him.

"So, about supper," he says.

"Let's eat here," I say again, sitting up.

"Emily." He's buttoning his shirt.

"What?"

"I don't just want an answer. I want a conversation. And I think *I* might want to go out."

"Why didn't you say that?"

"I thought asking you first would be nicer."

"Well, there's another way being nice causes problems." I pick up my magazine from the floor and toss it on the coffee table.

He sighs and sits down across from me. "You're right. I could have just said what I wanted to do. I should have. I guess I set things up that way to involve you more."

"I'm not used to saying every little thing. Saying something out loud makes it seem more important than I mean it to be."

"When you don't share what you think, though, if feels like you're trying to shut me out. But maybe that's my problem. Not yours."

"I'm not trying to shut you out. I'm just doing a little work on my own before I open my mouth. It's automatic. I've done it forever. I decide what I want, and then I speak." I look at the boats on the shelves. "But I can work on thinking out loud," I say, "because I don't want you to think I'm trying to shut you out."

He looks over at the boats too. "Maybe this is still about my not truly believing you want me around all the time. I guess deep down I keep expecting you to want me to leave again."

And I wonder if that's what Anna is about too.

When Henri Matisse was sixty-nine, he became seriously ill with the flu. While he was recuperating, he said, "I thought I was about to die. I was sure of it. It's not fair. I did all that I could not to become ill, but to no avail. No, it just isn't fair…I should have liked to finish."

I also wanted to finish. But we just met with my doctors, and, according to them, I won't be able to. The tests show that the chemo didn't work. The cancer is spreading like paint seeping into the canvas.

There will be no happy ending, no happily ever after.

A series of paintings, six. In the first one, a woman by herself, wearing black, takes her black clothes off. In the second, the woman is still by herself but wearing blue and holding her hand to her mouth, as if to cough. In the third one, she wears white and there's a man with her. They each hold a book, his open to the first page, hers to the last. The woman continues to smile but the man looks sad. In the fourth painting, two young children sit with the woman in a room with two open doors. Another woman stands at the first open door, while the man stands at the second. In the fifth painting, the woman is with the man but slumped in a chair, the black clothes like weights around her. The final painting shows the woman dressed in black lying still in a bed, the man and two children by her side.

What is it those "Make Your Life Better" seminars always ask? What three things would you want to do if you found out you only had six months to live? The question is supposed to make you focus, to help you cut through the crap, to help you see what's important in your life before it's too late. After you answer the question, you're not really supposed to have only six months to live.

A little tired, some indigestion, a cough, and some weird pains. I don't feel that bad. It doesn't feel true. It can't be right. I pinch myself, and I don't feel anything.

I still have cancer, I say out loud in the bedroom, my breath condensing on the cold windowpane as I stare at an imaginary family next door. The young mother, dying of cancer, just married to a wonderful man. Two young children.

Marriage is supposed to be the beginning, not the end. But I knew when I got married that I had cancer. And Mark knew I was sick when he came back from Turkey to be with me. And now—now he's going to have a life without me.

I'm the isolated swimmer in *Jazz*, the red fingers of cancer on all sides now, and I'm falling into the black.

How can my heart and mind comprehend "only six months"? How can I take that in? And then, what can I really do with six months?

I ball my hands up in fists, unfurling my fingers as I count February, March, April, May, June, July. No more too-hot Augusts for me. No more falls.

Then I hurl myself back against the wall. Six months will not get me to Matisse.

My heart beats too fast. All that effort to see my painting again, and now *dying* will keep me from it.

Six months is just a guess. I have to make it longer. I will see that painting again—one last time. And then my skin tingles with guilt. Shouldn't I want to live longer for every moment I could be with Caroline and Elizabeth, and with Mark?

I still have cancer, I say to the person in the bathroom mirror. Why me? Why not me? I shiver. I have goose bumps too. I don't know how to do this. It's not supposed to be too bad until the end. I grip the sink with both hands. I don't want to leave everybody.

What's going to happen to Caroline and Elizabeth? Right now is all the time I have to get them ready for the rest of their lives. I can't put anything off.

I still have cancer, I say as I walk through the house, pausing in front of the mirror on the hat stand. I could try painful intra-abdominal chemo or bone marrow transplants, but the doctors don't recommend either. So I've decided to be done with curative treatment. Now I will concentrate on living my life, enjoying the time that I have, something I should have been doing since the day I was born. Still, it's hard for me to give up.

I did used to think about the what-three-things question. I would write my children a letter, something they could keep forever. Only I never got so far as to imagine what I would say in the letter. I remember thinking I should write it at the beginning, before I felt bad. I need to do that now, I guess. But I don't believe I'm dying. How can I act like I do when I don't? I'm going to have to feel worse to believe it, and then I won't feel like doing what I want to do to prepare. I've got to get a grip on this. After the letters, do I work on my things—what I want the girls to keep?

Mark makes a fire in the fireplace, but it doesn't help. As we wait for Caroline and Elizabeth, I want to float away. I lock onto the floor littered with crumbs and onto the three cups scattered around the den. The pillows on the couch need washing. The cleaning service has been coming once a week, but maybe it's time to see if they can come more often.

Caroline is so thin. Hardly any fat to protect her. I'm afraid she'll break before she arrives at the couch to sit beside me. Elizabeth is losing the fat she had just when she needs it. She leans into Mark, who puts her in his lap across from us on the big chair.

I can't do it. I feel my eyes get too wide. Mark. I latch onto him, right here with me.

"Sick," I say. "I'm still sick, girls."

"You still have cancer?" Caroline looks at me, then at Mark who nods, then back to me.

"Yes," I say looking into her face one last time before life changes her.

"So you have to do more chemo, then?" she asks, trying to hang on to logic as I would in her place. She looks at the floor, then finally back at me.

"No," I say as I glance at Mark. Still with me. Elizabeth is watching Caroline.

"Well, that's good, right?" Caroline asks, looking over at Mark. She turned seven just weeks ago. Now I'm about to ruin seven forever. I swallow.

Mark brings Elizabeth and they sit on the other side of Caroline. He puts one arm behind her and rests his hand on my shoulder. I curve my arm back to grasp his hand. I put my other hand on Caroline's knee.

"Mark and I want the two of you to understand what's going on. We want you to have all the time there is. It's good that I don't have to have any more chemo, but it's bad because I'm not going to get well."

I have to be the strong one, the parent. I have to say it first. I have to use the word.

"You girls are lucky to have so many people who love you. Mark. Susan. Alyssa. Martha. We all know when we were born. Usually, we don't know when it will be our time to die." I take a breath. My stomach is all knots. I don't stop to feel any more than that, though;

I have to keep going or I won't make it. "But I know my turn will be soon. Nobody lives forever. Some people die because they're sick."

"You're going to die?" Caroline whispers, the brown of her eyes shrinking to nothing. "You can't die," she moans and moves off the sofa. "You're our mom."

"Caroline, come back," I say, my hands pushing against my thighs. "You can't die."

I move to her as tears stream down her face. My arms surround her small body, but she fights to free herself. I hold tighter. She fights harder. She catches me off balance and pulls us to the floor. I roll on top of her.

"Caroline," I say, rocking from side to side with her. If we were still, we wouldn't be able to bear it. "Angel, it's going to be okay. I love you and I'm sorry I'm sick. But you're going to be okay."

"I hate you," Caroline says, again in a whisper.

"No, you don't," I say. "You're mad that I'm sick, and I'm mad too. It's not fair. I tried to make it go away, but it didn't. I'm sorry. I did the best I could. The good thing is I have time to make sure you're taken care of before—"

Caroline stops struggling. I look up at Mark. Elizabeth, always the loud one, lies with her head on his shoulder crying quietly. *I can't do this*, my eyes tell him. And I feel them both as they lie down beside us. I reach one arm around Elizabeth and Mark puts his arms around all of us.

Elizabeth raises her head and asks, "If I don't hit Caroline anymore, can you not die?"

That night, I cry and Mark holds me. He cries and he still holds me. I don't float away, because he doesn't let go. We slide to the floor. He keeps on holding me. I wake in the middle of the night, and he's holding me. He holds onto me all night. He never lets me go.

A couple of weeks later, after taking the girls to school, I go back home to change clothes, intending to get the last visit to the museum over with. So much for being curator, I think, sitting down in the kitchen. And then, oddly, I wonder what Frank left unfinished, if he had any plans for the future.

I roll tight the inside bag of the cereal left on the table from breakfast and get up to put it back on the shelf. Then I try to raise the window shade, but it sticks. I turn back to the table, only to face a bowl of milk and mushy flakes, which I should put in the sink. A pain jabs through my back. Instinctively, I hold my breath, then remember to breathe out. I sit again, resting my head on the table next to the mush, giving in to the pains and lethargy I've been fighting all morning. I'm not going to work; I'm going to the bedroom.

I put my coffee by the bed and open the drapes. Light streams in. I raise the window a crack, letting the cold breeze blow energy into the warm room and onto my face. From my small frame of glass, the sky is a far-away winter blue. The trees, closer to me, look either black or dark green. The most vivid ones are the ones without leaves.

After stepping out of my shoes, I crawl under the covers with the pillows propped up so I can drink my coffee, which finally tastes good again. I feel better in this room, in my bed, more relaxed, safe. Surely Cancer wouldn't come in here.

I reach for the bottle of pain meds, swallowing one with room temperature coffee so I don't have to get up for water. Bad decision. I try to generate some saliva to rid my mouth of the grains. Mark will be here in a couple of hours for lunch. I slide further under the covers.

When I open my eyes, Mark is sitting in the dark blue armchair, holding the newspaper but watching me.

"How long have you been here?" I ask, sitting up, feeling better.

"About thirty minutes. Can I warm some soup for you?"

"That sounds good." I put my feet on the floor.

"Why don't I bring it to you in here?"

"Thanks," I say, not looking at him. "I want to go to the kitchen."

Sitting at the kitchen table, we eat milky tomato soup and toast because we're out of crackers. I'm almost finished when I put my hand down on the table harder than I meant to.

"Emily?"

He looks panicked, which in this small moment that I can control actually calms me. I reassure him. "Just a wave of pain. Gone now. Do you have time to walk to the end of the street before you go back?"

"I'll get our jackets."

Mark offered to cancel his lecture at the High Museum, but he's been looking forward to it, and I encourage him to go. This morning, in the pouring rain, he left for Atlanta. Tonight will be the first night we've been apart since he returned from Turkey. I miss him already.

We need milk, so after I pick Caroline up, we stop by the grocery store. Parking in a no-parking zone by the curb, we walk the short distance from the car without the umbrella, which seemed like too much trouble. I can hardly move one foot in front of the other, yet I want to hurry so I can get home to rest before Elizabeth gets home from her friend Lily's house.

"Can I pick out a treat?" Caroline asks.

"Like what?"

"Some kind of candy, like what they keep where you pay."

"Okay, but first grab a loaf of the bread you like off the shelf right there. I'll pick up the milk and some bananas and meet you back here at the front."

I head to the back of the store, repeating in my mind, *milk and bananas*. I grab a jug of two percent and head for the produce. Most of the bananas are green, but I find some of the small ones that are almost yellow.

As I'm rounding the aisle to the front of the store, I glance at the magazine section to my right. My eyes go to the top row, resting on the *People* magazine cover of Caroline Kennedy. Despite the ache in my legs, I lift the magazine to read the blurb on the cover. I remember my Caroline, and, looking up from the magazine, stand on my toes to try to see her. She's standing with her back to me, looking at the cashier, who's talking to a customer. Then she puts some sort of candy in her pocket. There's a pain in my heart and a little explosion in my brain as what I just saw clashes against what I know about my daughter. I feel hot.

While I'm trying to figure out what to do, I watch Caroline reach for the loaf of bread she must have momentarily put on the floor.

Then she flicks her hair behind her shoulders and looks around. I come down off my toes and look at the strange magazine in my hand, then place it back on the rack. I move slowly around the display. Caroline smiles at me. Who is this child?

"I picked out some M&Ms," she says, holding up a pack, her long black curls looking fake, her pink bow out of place.

I think I might throw up.

"I forgot something," I say. "Stay right here. Don't move."

I go down the first aisle where she can't see me and lean my head against a shelf. I close my eyes to think. Then I grab a bottle of ketchup from in front of me, hoping she has had a change of personality and returned the stolen goods.

She has not moved. We put the five visible items on the conveyor belt. Caroline picks up the M&Ms I paid for, I pick up the paper bag, and we walk out of the store. I want the act to be complete. I don't want any possible way around what she did.

At the car, she climbs in the back, and I put the bag on the floor. After I get in the front, I turn to look at her, really look at her. "What's in your pocket?" I ask.

"What do you mean?" she asks, her serious brown eyes giving nothing away.

"Don't play games with me. I saw you put something in your pocket. Now pull it out this minute."

She reaches in and brings out another bag of M&Ms, which she holds out to me.

"One wasn't enough for you?" I ask. Then I burst into tears, resting my head on the steering wheel. The clarity of a child's world breaks my heart.

We go back into the store so Caroline can return the extra package of M&Ms. I confiscate the legitimate pack. We begin a longer than usual drive home.

"You have to think about what kind of person you want to be," I say. She has to see how important this is. Now. "Do you want to be the kind of person who would steal?"

"No," she says, slammed up against the door, as far away from me as possible, staring out the window.

"Well, just because you stole something once, it doesn't mean you're a bad person. It just means you made a mistake. It's okay to make mistakes."

She doesn't say anything.

"You're probably angry because I'm sick. I would be if my mother were sick." As I brake for the light, I glance at her. She has her right hand balled into a little fist. I pull into a convenience store parking lot, turn the car off, and crawl in the back with her.

I reach over to give her a hug, but her body is stiff and my body feels prickly, the energy draining from my head, my chest, my arms. Slowly, I move back to the front, leaning my head against the seat. Already it's about me again. Home is not far, and I put the car in drive. As I pull to a stop in the garage, she jumps out and runs toward the house. My back aches. I can't do anything about anything. I turn the car off and lean against the seat, closing my eyes.

The next morning when it's still dark outside, I'm up for about two hours, sick to my stomach. At breakfast, I manage to eat a little oatmeal, holding a bite in my mouth until it disintegrates, and then

210

letting it slide down my throat. At lunchtime, that doesn't work. I try a spoonful of the applesauce Elizabeth likes. Then I start throwing up. I haven't had much appetite recently, but, at least until today, I've been able to eat and keep it down.

Oblivious, I had only little hints from my body. Knowing I'm dying, every pain hits me full force. I wonder if I would feel worse anyway now or whether it's the knowing that makes it worse, makes me feel every discomfort.

I call Mark who's on his way home from Atlanta. He calls the doctor and then picks up another prescription from the drugstore, something stronger. I don't even look at the label—I just pour a white oblong pill into my hand.

My eyes are open when he comes into the bedroom bringing tea. I sit up slowly. "How long have I been asleep?"

"Almost two hours. Do you feel better?"

He puts the tea on my bedside table, but the smell of the milk and sugar overpower me, and I swallow so I won't gag. Turning away from the tea, I wonder what's wrong with me before I remember I'm dying. I curl up and the tears fall onto the pillow.

He sits on the edge of the bed. Minutes later, he says, "Maybe it's just a twenty-four hour virus."

I hear in his voice the struggle to find some way to help me, the fear that he won't be able to, the fear that he doesn't know what to do. But I can't help him. I'm sunk in and tensed up against the nausea. I have cancer, for life—actually death—I think.

He rubs my back and shoulders in a large circular motion, and I relax a little. I hear Caroline and Elizabeth talking above the TV. His circles get smaller. I close my eyes and sleep.

When I'm able to push myself outside, I'm shocked to see our crepe myrtle tree. All the leaves are gone. Nothing is left but stubs of bare bark—bone. It must have been our neighbor on the other side of the empty lot. I know he thought he was doing us a favor, but the last time I looked, it was so full and healthy.

Mark and I sit on the porch wrapped in coats, gloves, and blankets. He tells me about the article he's writing for *National Geographic* with Robert Ballard. The red wine he heated with spices makes me feel good way down inside. We rock back and forth, and sip. Neither of us says anything about the tree.

"I had such a good day," I say, staring straight ahead. "Taking the girls to school, going to the grocery store, taking Elizabeth and Lily to soccer practice, fixing supper. I don't feel sick at all. Maybe they're wrong."

I feel him glance sideways at me.

"You know they were wrong about Matisse?" I say.

"What are you talking about?"

"When he was seventy-two, Matisse had some kind of stomach or intestinal cancer. He had surgery. Then he had complications. They told him he was going to die, but he didn't."

"Emily."

"Well, I don't feel sick, and I don't want to be sick. So I'm deciding not to be." The street is empty for as far as I can see—no cars, no kids, no dogs. "You don't have anything to say?" I ask, finally turning to look at him.

"Not if you're going to pretend you're not sick."

"But I could get better too."

"You're not being honest with yourself."

"What if I'd had a hysterectomy back when I was first having all the problems?"

He stops rocking and looks at me. But I don't want to look at him now. He comes over and bends down in front of me, putting his hands on my knees, forcing me to see him.

"I had such a good day," I say again.

"Emily, we need to concentrate on adjusting to your being sick. It won't help to pretend you're not."

"Since we're not supposed to be pretending, we shouldn't use the word *sick*," I say, spitting the words at him.

His head collapses into my lap.

"I'm sorry," I say, putting my hands in his thick hair and bending over him. When I straighten up, he lifts his head to look in my eyes.

"Emily, I know it's hard to—"

"I don't know how to act," I say, interrupting him. "Am I supposed to remember every second? Or am I supposed to try to forget about it?"

"I don't have any answers. I just know we shouldn't try to act like nothing's wrong. We can't make it like it was before." He pauses. "I don't know whether we're supposed to try to remember you're sick—"

"Say it."

Mark takes a deep breath, looks at the floor, and then looks me straight in the eyes. "I don't know whether we're supposed to remember you're dying or try to forget you're dying." He says this holding my hands and with tears running down his face. "Somehow—at the end, I hope the words 'if only' don't even think about crossing our lips, because we will have lived the best we could with the time we were given."

I don't have any desire to read. Imagine that. I don't want to sleep anymore. I don't want to watch TV. I want to be with people. No, that's not true. I want to be with Mark and Caroline and Elizabeth. I used to think it was a waste of time to just sit and talk. I would have rather read or accomplished something. *Before* I never wanted to *be*; I always wanted to *do*.

And—I hate to admit it—I want to see *Breakfast* again. I thought that maybe this last desire would drop off, give way to the more important ones about the people I love; but it remains, clinging like flesh to the bone.

My eyes spring open to darkness. I turn over. Mark is still reading with only a small light.

"What is it?" he asks.

"Who's going to take care of Caroline and Elizabeth?" Of course it's not the first time I've thought about this. But it's the first time the future's been real enough and I've been afraid enough, and brave enough, to push the words out.

Mark closes his book and turns on his side. "I was thinking it would be me."

I wonder if he feels obligated to say this. "I don't want to tie you down. And Susan is family."

"I'm not family?"

I reach my hand out to touch his arm. "You know what I mean." I close my eyes again. What if Mark remarries? Somebody I don't know will be taking care of my daughters. Somebody like Anna.

He threads his fingers through my hair. I feel him looking at me, wanting to say more. After a while, I hear the light click off.

The next day, I call Susan. "What about the girls?"

"What about them?"

"You know, the rest of their lives."

"I'm still the guardian in your will, right?"

"Yes, but things are different now." Out the window, the fullness of green gives me goosebumps.

"Because of Mark?"

"Because I'm actually dying."

"Jeez, Emily."

"Well."

"There *was* always that chance. Even though nobody wants to think about it. Of course, we want the girls to come here. Really. Peter and I have already talked about it."

"Where would they sleep for example?"

"I was thinking the guest room."

I'm not sure if the fact that she already has a room in mind makes me feel better or worse.

"I thought the girls could redecorate it, make it theirs, however they want. There's also Beth's room. She'll be leaving for college in September."

"Exactly. Aren't you looking forward to that, to not having any children at home?"

"Actually, having the girls would be great. Take my mind off Beth being gone."

"And you haven't driven a carpool in years."

"Emily, really. It's just a few extra years of parenting. And we often wished we'd had more children. Don't give it another thought."

After we hang up, I sit there, staring out the window rubbing my arms until I'm okay with the tiny dots of white, pink, and yellow, until I'm okay that the azaleas are starting to bloom.

I want to write to Caroline and Elizabeth, but I don't know what to say. How do I make a place for me in their lives when I'm not actually here anymore?

And then, just like that, I know what to do.

When Mark gets home from work, we drive to the antiques' mall. I pick out a dark mahogany chest for Caroline and a lighter pine one for Elizabeth.

Although I want to start filling the chests, I'm only able to run my fingers along the top of Caroline's and take a deep breath of pine from inside Elizabeth's before I have to rest. As my body sinks part by part onto the bed, I let out a buried breath. *Memory chests.* The girls can open them and remember me. When my head reaches the pillow, I'm peaceful.

Today I wake early and feel rested. This time I'm able to dress for work, choosing black linen pants, a sleeveless top, and a light sweater. I wish I didn't have to go back to a world already functioning without me, but I don't like the picture in my head of someone else carrying a box of my stuff out of my office. I think I have two memos to read and send out. Sam said if I felt like it, he had a few things to ask me. I know I shouldn't look in the mirror, but I do. My clothes don't fit, and naturally my next thought is of buying new ones.

I turn out the light and leave the bedroom. From the museum, I'll go straight to the doctor. My circle is shrinking.

When I come into the kitchen, Mark has the coffee ready. I pour a cup and start to sit. The material on the chair is torn. The chair next to it is losing its stuffing. I look at Mark. He goes to wake the girls.

We're almost to the museum when his cell rings. Her name flashes onto the screen, and I have nowhere to go. Trapped in the car with the two of them, I feel like the outsider. Mark silences the phone.

"Turns out it was a good idea to string her along," I say, knocking my head against the window. "When I'm dead, you can pick up right where you left off."

"Emily," he says, reaching his arm around my shoulder.

"Don't touch me."

"I didn't call her. She called me."

"I guess you're still being nice to her. Of course, you are."

He pulls over to the curb and puts the car in park.

I open the door to get out. I need air, my own space.

He reaches for my arm and holds onto me. "I asked her not to call or text anymore. Emily, listen. She's been calling every day for the last week. I'm not picking up. Will you close the door?"

I feel it now, the wet heat pouring in, even this early in the morning. And I wonder why it's worse now, this idea of Anna. The open door angles onto the sidewalk and reminds me of Matisse. It *is* all one space. I close the door and look at Mark who's holding my hand, twirling the gold band on my finger, and I have a vision of time after I'm not here anymore, and it's okay. "Sorry," I say, and I reach to touch his face.

When Mark gets home from work, his cheeks are more flushed than usual. He sits and then stands. Some guy who drives a backhoe called right before he left work because he'd found something that looked to be very old in a place about four hours from here.

"I might go look at it," he says. "No, I can't go, but from what he described, I just know it's a hearth."

"That's your favorite thing, hearths. You have to go."

"But I've seen a million. I don't need to see any more. And I've got stuff I need to do tomorrow at the museum." He gets a beer out of the fridge.

"Well, why don't you go the next day then?"

"The construction crew is under a deadline. It's a salvage situation."

"What does that mean, *salvage situation*? Do you just go in there grabbing stuff?"

Laughing, he comes to sit beside me on the couch. "It means we can't approach the site in the normal, civilized way we usually do. We don't go 'grabbing stuff.'" He grins. "It's just that we try to learn as much as we can about the site in a short amount of time. Actually, before I went to Turkey, most of my work was salvage work." He looks at me. "You don't remember me talking about going somewhere in a hurry because a road had to be built, or there was a sink hole in Florida where I only had a few hours."

I shake my head. I don't remember much about what he did

before he went to Turkey, but I know I don't remember him ever using the word *salvage* before.

He looks over my head out the window. "Here we only have two days if somebody's going to save anything." He stands again. "I'm still not used to so much sitting. Anyway, it's no big deal. I can't believe the guy even took the time to call somebody, and that he found the right person to talk to. And if the hearth is partially exposed, it may already be in danger of disintegrating. We're fighting time on both fronts."

Now I turn to look out the window, trying to figure out how I feel about all this.

"I told him I didn't think I could do it," he says, sitting down again and picking up his beer. "How are you today? Did you see Alyssa?"

"Mark, I can tell you want to go. Don't not go because of me. I'll be here when you get back."

He looks away.

I know what he's thinking—I'm thinking it too.

"I've heard you talk about discovering a hearth before. I know you love each one you find. You love reconstructing the dwelling. You're just not going because of me. I bet there's nothing at work that couldn't wait. I feel fine. It would only be one night, right?"

"Just one night."

"Mark, one night. I like to be by myself, remember?"

He laughs, but says, "What if I asked Alyssa to come stay?"

"I don't want, or need, Alyssa to come. We'll be fine."

"I don't want to go, and I do want to go."

"Go."

"Are you sure?"

"Positive."

When Alyssa brings Caroline home from their afternoon at the library, Mark tells her he'll be gone. She tries to insist on coming to spend the night. "Save yourself for later," I whisper, "when it's worse."

Tonight is nice, just the girls and me, like it was before, but I need to rest after supper and homework and bedtime. I pick up a book of paintings, pull down the covers, and stretch my legs between the sheets, closing my eyes for a second.

When I open them, I look around. The residue of Mark's pockets lies abandoned on the dresser—pennies and a crumpled yellow receipt. Green and brown clothes are draped across the armchair—not dirty, but not clean either. Yesterday's newspaper lies on the dark blue ottoman; the sports read, the rest untouched.

I reach for the book of paintings again. Looking at pictures doesn't seem to take me away from myself like reading does. I peer at the paintings one after another, Renoir's *The Promenade*, a woman and a child out for a walk, the child oblivious, the woman looking straight at me; Toulouse-Lautrec's *The Laundress*, the woman leaning on the table, her expression resigned; and Monet's *Train in the Snow*, the chilling whites and grays, and the two train headlights shining through the darkness. Instead of being soothed, however, I get upset. I keep turning pages, but I feel more and more agitated. I almost close the book, but now I *need* to look at the pictures. I wipe my nose on my sleeve.

As a little girl, I would stay in my butter-colored room for hours, lying in bed reading. When I would take a break and look up, my eyes would go straight to the painting taped by my bed. When I grew up, I planned to have my mornings to myself. I would not wake up and be thrust into a group of people like my family, all loud and fighting and asking me questions.

One Christmas my mother gave me a red-and-white striped tablecloth, like the one in the painting, for a table I had in my room—one of those round, unfinished wooden tables, where the top circle fits into grooves cut into a base. The tablecloths for these kinds of tables extend all the way to the floor because nobody is supposed to see what's underneath. I realize now that the table in *Breakfast* is square. Back then I didn't notice the differences, just the similarities.

I remember turning to my painting when I was embarrassed or when I hadn't lived up to someone's expectations—or my own. I would crash into my room, full of feeling but not knowing what to do with it, throwing myself face down on the bed. When I would turn over moments later, my eyes were drawn to the grays and reds and whites. The colors would absorb the feelings and create order.

But now, each page I turn to stirs up feelings, the red and the black and the blue rushing out of the paintings. I try to take myself out of the bed and away, but my foot becomes tangled in the sheets, and I fall to the floor. My cell rings. I refuse to answer it. I'm the one with cancer. I'm the one who's not going to be here same time next year. I don't want things to go on without me. I don't want Mark to fall in love with someone else. I don't want the girls to love another mother.

I'm alone in my room as I'll be alone in the end. Nobody can help me. Nobody can go with me. I have to do this all by myself. All by myself—it's what I wanted and now I have it.

Not wanting to wake the girls, I crawl, sobbing tears I didn't know I had, into my closet. I crouch under my clothes and pull the door shut. With my nose running and my chest sore from heaving and cancer, I curl into a ball on top of my shoes and cry until all the tears are gone. I'm so scared.

In the middle of the night, I wake up with a shoe digging into my cheek. My face is caked with dried mucous. My throat is sore and my eyes itch. I crawl out of the closet. Trying to stand, I'm stiff and have to lean on a chair. Three fifteen. I take a pain pill and go back to sleep.

In the morning, I stay in bed. Caroline tells Elizabeth what to do to get ready for school. Then she calls Suzanne, our neighbor, to drive them.

Around ten, my cell vibrates. I stick it under a pillow. It vibrates again, then again, and again. I answer, my eyes stuck together. It's Alyssa, who says Mark called her because he was worried when I didn't pick up. She's calling from her car on the way here.

"Don't come," I say. "I'm fine."

"You don't sound fine. I'm coming, and I'll pick up some lunch for us."

"No. I'm serious. Don't come. I need some time by myself."

"Please, Emily. Let me come just for a minute." I hear the panic trying to be normal. But we're way past normal.

"No," I say. And I turn the phone off and roll over. After a minute, I slide further under the covers and put a pillow over my head.

The wisteria is blooming from its strong, twisted bark. The clusters of grape-like blooms hang heavy, as if ready to pick. All that remains of winter is a refreshing breeze. A cream-colored throw rests over my legs while I wait on the front porch for the girls to come home from school. I probably look like an old woman, but I feel good today.

I've put off writing to the girls because I couldn't decide on the most important things—how to condense into a letter what should have taken the rest of my life to say. Then I decided it wouldn't just be one grand finale. I would write often, to give them random pieces of me and them and our life—what they wore to school, what we ate for breakfast, how proud I am of them. This morning I wrote Caroline a letter on yellow paper, put it in a yellow envelope, and then in her chest. For Elizabeth, red paper and a red envelope.

I want to find a small wooden box to hold the letters or maybe just an old cigar box, like the ones that hold the treasures of children in books. Temporarily I hope, I put them in zip-lock bags in the corners of the chests.

Last week I bought two white gift boxes, sprinkled baby powder in the bottom of each and then lined them with brand new, white tissue paper. In one box, I carefully folded the baby blanket I wrapped Caroline in when I brought her home from the hospital, and on top of that, the clothes she wore home. In the other box, I did the same for Elizabeth. I put the box tops on and put the boxes in the chests. The day before yesterday, I washed my two favorite sweaters, a chestnut brown cashmere and a black angora. I wore each one around for a day and then placed the brown one in Caroline's chest and the black one in Elizabeth's. To keep them warm, later.

I lean my head back in the rocking chair, look up at the sky, and take a breath. For now, I have my appetite back, although I can't eat much at a time. About ten minutes ago, I sliced some cookie dough and slid the pan into the oven. Before I came out here, I could smell the chocolate, and, so far, it smells just like it's supposed to.

"Are you ready?" I say, as loud as I can from the porch.

Caroline and Elizabeth come running.

"I love to finger paint," I say, on the floor with the plastic tub of art supplies.

"So do I," Elizabeth says, sitting down right beside me.

Caroline just stands there staring.

"Come on," I say. "I'll get a bucket of water, and we can rinse our hands whenever we want to. It'll be fun."

She turns around and runs back in the house, slamming the door. I'm surprised but shouldn't be.

"Elizabeth, let's wait on this. Come back inside for a minute."

"What's wrong with Caroline?"

"Hop up and watch your show, and I'll go find out."

I knock on the door to their room before I go in. Caroline is sitting squeezed into a corner, her knees pulled up, and her arms wrapped around them. "It's not fair," the words stomp out of her mouth. "I'm supposed to have a mother."

I step toward her, and she picks up a book and throws it at me and then another one before I can get to her and get my arms around her.

We try again in the afternoon—Caroline has been glued to my side since the morning. I give them each an oversized piece of white construction paper, and I set out the red, blue, and yellow paint. "It's cool," I say, "that each of your favorite colors is a primary color. Caroline, hand me that color wheel out of the container, please."

She hands it over and scoots right back next to me.

"You see the primary colors, right? And you know that the secondary colors are orange, green, and violet. Now *related* colors are right next to each other on the wheel. So what would they be?"

"Yellow, yellow-orange and orange," Caroline says.

"Red, red-violet and violet," Elizabeth answers. "It's kind of like me and Caroline are related colors 'cause we were born next to each other, right?"

"Kind of," I say, grinning.

"I want red," Elizabeth says.

"Duh," Caroline says. "Violet for me."

"Just pick a primary color," I say. Then I stop myself. I don't have time to be lazy. "Actually, whatever color you want."

"Violet."

"Elizabeth, get a blob of the red out. Okay, Caroline, you get a little red out too. Smear it on the paper. With a different finger, get some blue and blend it into the red." I inhale the paint, smelling my third-grade art class, and seeing the basement room next to the cafeteria, the long tables.

Caroline looks worried.

"Okay, you can rinse your hands," I say to her. "Now we're going to see what we can do with *complementary* colors."

"What's that?" Elizabeth asks.

"A complementary color is the color opposite from another color on the color wheel. Elizabeth, you picked red. What's the complement of red?"

"Why aren't they just called opposites?" Caroline asks.

"Because they work together, not against each other. You'll see. What's the complement of violet?"

"Yellow," she says, smiling.

"Green is the complement of red," Elizabeth says.

"But that's Christmas colors," Caroline says.

"Christmas colors are opposites?" Elizabeth says.

"Put your complementary color on the paper right next to the color we started with."

"This is fun," Elizabeth says.

"Caroline, what do you think about your violet now?"

"I don't know. It seems brighter, maybe more violet."

"Yeah," Elizabeth says. "My red is even redder."

"So the colors are stronger side by side than they would be by themselves. Now let's see what happens when we mix them together. Try it."

"Yuk," Caroline says. "Mine is kind of gray."

"So is mine," Elizabeth says.

"Get another piece of paper and put two blobs of the color you started with on it." I'm trying to do too much, I know. I'm trying to do it all, everything, now. "Put just a *dot* of the complementary color into the second blob and mix it up. Compare the two."

"The second one is a little less—violet," Caroline says.

"That's right. So to tone your color down, just add a little of its complementary color. I need to take a pill."

"Are you coming back?" Caroline asks, looking up.

"Yes," I say, looking at her, and then at Elizabeth, who has stopped what she's doing. Both are watching me. "I'll be right back."

The next day, I sit in my study, looking through a stack of postcards of Matisse paintings and smelling the hamburgers on the grill, eyeing my essay journal that I haven't had any desire to open in so long. I open it now and add to it.

"What is striking about Matisse when one knows him slightly, is the extreme interest he shows, in conversation, about trivia as well as about important matters. Under a nonchalant exterior, one feels that his keenness pierces the secret of things." *This description of him makes me wonder if I could learn something from the superficial, if I could work with the surface of life in an effort to pierce through to the essential. With Matisse I have developed a habit of reflection, but I'm still seeking clarity. Which is why I have to see that painting again.*

I put my pen down, thinking I'm finished, and reread what I've written. *Odd that I still think—*

Mark sticks his head in the door to tell me supper's almost ready.

"I'll be right there," I say. As I write, I wonder if I'll feel this pull until the end.

Odd that I still think of my life in terms of possibilities, as if there were things worth learning for the short amount of time I have left.

Today was Mark's first day of teaching. He loved it. The kids had a thousand questions about the Black Sea Study. Several of them had copies of articles he had written while he was over there and wanted him to sign them. The girls are playing in the front yard. Mark brings me a blanket and a glass of wine out to the porch. Just my feet are cold, but I drape the blanket over my legs and wrap the bottom around my feet. "Wine still tastes good," I say.

"I put it in the freezer right when I got home," he says.

On the porch, I'm outside yet protected. Elizabeth and Caroline are doing somersaults. A bluebird makes a noise, and I look up to see her perched in the tree.

"Mom, look at me do two in a row," Elizabeth says.

"I'm watching."

"Mark, will you watch too?"

"Already am." He smiles.

Caroline is lying on her stomach with her head propped in her hands, her eyes on Elizabeth, who does not two but three in a row.

I stand, letting the blanket fall.

"Mom, where are you going?" Caroline asks.

"Just to the bathroom." Mark reaches for my hand as I go by. I bend down to give him a kiss, the roughness of his beard mixing with the gentleness of his lips.

"Mom, will you watch me try to do three when you get back?" Caroline asks.

I tell her I will, but I walk slowly, needing a break from life proceeding without me. From people wanting me to be there. From my wanting too much. Sitting on the toilet, I lean my head against the counter. It's okay to get smaller while everything around me gets larger. It's okay.

On my way out of the bathroom, I turn on the lamp on my bedside table, illuminating the stacks of books and magazines, the clothes draped across chairs. As I go through the kitchen, I ignore the still unfixed shade and pour another glass of wine. I pick up my wallet to put it back in my purse.

And then I stop, staring at the wallet in my hand and then at my purse. I have to sit down with the question of how much longer I'll need a purse, a driver's license, credit cards. I haven't been out of the house in a week. The last time was for my doctor's appointment. I feel myself sinking into the unknown.

Somersaults.

As I step onto the porch, both girls are watching me. "Let's see what you can do, Caroline."

She grins at Elizabeth and curls into a ball. "Ready?" she calls, turning her head toward us.

"Ready," we answer, and she actually does three somersaults in a row.

"Hey, good job," Mark says, clapping.

The pizza arrives, and we pile into the house to watch *Chitty Chitty Bang Bang*. Mark uses paper plates that Elizabeth delivers. Caroline is on the floor with the remote, fast forwarding through the previews. Mark refills his wine glass and starts to put the bottle in the fridge.

"Can I have some before you put it up?" I ask from the couch.

He empties the bottle into my glass and says softly, "You haven't been drinking much wine lately."

I take a large swallow.

He puts the empty bottle in the recycling and another in the freezer.

I wake up to Caroline hugging me and telling me good night. Mark is carrying a sleeping Elizabeth to her room. I try to remember when I fell asleep but can't. I fall into bed and pull the covers up.

Sometime later, I wake to go to the bathroom. Mark is still reading in bed.

Coming out of the bathroom, I head to the den. Mark asks where I'm going.

"I'm looking for a room that's not spinning. And don't say anything." I get a glass of water in the kitchen, come back to bed, and take three Advil along with my regular pain pills.

In the morning, I look in the mirror, and I don't look so good. I have dark circles under my eyes, and my very short hair is dull and sparse. My skin is dry. Rubbing moisturizer into my cheeks, I notice in the mirror how old my hand looks. I pick up some foundation and start to take the top off. Instead, I put it back in the drawer. If someone didn't know me, would they know I have cancer?

"I don't care!" I scream, as I slam our bedroom door, my peacefulness evaporated. I feel stuck again, and unable to work *with* the dailiness of life. I fall onto the bed. Then I sit up, leaning against the headboard and crossing my arms. I try to slow my breathing, but every time I sort through it, I'm mad all over again. I can't be mad at Mark, but I am. He's doing the best he can. I know that.

Last night I fell asleep before the girls, so I didn't get to tell them good night. And I've asked Mark to please wake me up before they go to bed. "But you were so tired," he said. And now I've missed them this morning. They're already gone to school. I've said over and over to wake me up so I can tell them good-bye.

I can't sit still. I lock the door. Which I shouldn't because it's his room too. So I unlock it. *His room, too.* And I'm soothed by this thought. I'm not alone.

I hear a crash and open the door. In the kitchen, the table is on its side, the breakfast dishes in pieces, milk everywhere.

"God dammit, Emily," he says, and then he turns his back to me.

I step around the broken bits and when I reach him, he's sobbing. I wrap my arms around him and hold him as tightly as I can. After a while, he turns and leans over me, and we slide into the mess.

"I'm sorry," I say. "I know you're doing everything for me."

"I didn't hear the alarm, and they wouldn't get dressed and wouldn't hurry and when you were asleep, I was glad. It made the morning the tiniest bit less complicated, a tiny bit easier. And I took it. So *I'm* sorry."

"I know this isn't what you signed on for—"

"But it is. I mean, I wish it weren't happening, but it's exactly what I signed on for. There's no place I'd rather be than sitting with you on your kitchen floor in a puddle of spilled milk and broken dishes."

In Matisse's *Jazz*, I'm the black figure with a red heart, reaching high and floating in a blue world sprinkled with bright yellow stars— black because I'm clear about what's coming but soaring because I'm living my life. I'm grateful for the luminous stars.

My doctor is trying a new pain medicine, but the dosage isn't right yet. Since midnight the pain has been so constant that I've had to move around to stand it. Finally, I crawl into my closet to try not to wake Mark or the girls, and I rock back and forth, hugging my knees just like Caroline. The closet door opens. I feel Mark reach for me, putting his arms around me and his body beside me. He doesn't say anything. I moan, the feeling coming from deep inside.

"This is great," Elizabeth says the next day about Matisse's painting *Harmony in Red*. As a girl I had loved this scene of domestic order, believing the woman in the black top and white skirt to be the mother. Elizabeth, of course, loves all the red—a red tablecloth and a red wall taking up the whole painting except for a square in the left corner where a window shows the fresh blues and greens of nature. The girls are propped up on our bed, looking through art books for their favorite paintings. "I pick this one," she says. "I can either be inside all red or playing outside."

Caroline has more trouble. She stops for a while on *Harmony in Yellow*. Loving, I imagine, its bright, enveloping yellow drapery and the sleeping girl who is so much a part of the painting that she's almost invisible. This one, with the sleeping girl in her own little corner, was also one of my early favorites. It's similar to *Breakfast*—the table, the tray, the curved woman/girl. Caroline loves the paintings of girls reading and narrows her choices to *Interior with a Young Girl/Girl Reading* and *The Painting Session*, both of which show a girl mesmerized by a book, and both of which include a patch of yellow. Black and sadness predominate in *The Painting Session*, but in the end she chooses *Interior with a Young Girl/Girl Reading*, with its richness and fullness and its jumble of color, light, and life.

When we finally close the book, Caroline asks if I'll get them each a note card of their favorite paintings.

The fullness of the yard shocks me, as if I'd forgotten how green *green* could be. The new leaves on the short branches of our crepe myrtle appear bigger and healthier than when they were cut off. The fragrant magnolias, bursts of white against dark green, are blooming and will continue to bloom through the summer and into fall. I try to visualize being here, lasting into September, when Matisse will be here to see me.

I gravitate toward the porch well before the girls are due home from school. Even if I've been buried in my bed, I feel a pull. My perspective begins to shift from me to them. My face is drawn upward and outward. On the porch I rock slowly and breathe fully. I listen to the sounds of birds, and the light, running sound of the wind as it rustles the new leaves. I see the clouds in the sky and watch them float forward. In the winter, I seemed to be in sync with nature, yet fighting it. Now nature and I seem to be headed in opposite directions, but peacefully.

While the girls are at school, I pull their baby books off the shelf in the hall closet. To add them to the chests—which is impossible to do without looking at them. My two tiny babies. And even as I fight against the thought, I know it to be true. *This will be the last time I'll ever look at their little toes and fingers.* I'm relieved to hear my cell.

"So?" Susan says, when I answer.

"What?"

"The girls?"

"I don't know yet."

"Emily."

"What? I don't know. This isn't easy. Mark wants to keep them here, keep our family together."

"What if he remarries? Who knows who'll be taking care of them?"

"I thought of that."

"We want them here."

"I know, and I appreciate it."

"Emily, this is not just about you. You have to figure this out. They're old enough to be worried about what's going to happen to them even if they're not talking about it."

"Well, I can't talk about this right now."

"Emily."

"Susan, I got it."

She will not bully me into a decision. In the world of the living, she may be right to pressure me, but this decision exists somewhere else, in a place only I have access to and it will come in its own time.

"What?" I say, confused, sitting up in bed in the dark, my hand going to my wet forehead.

"You were screaming," Mark says, sitting up too, his eyes wide. "You're soaking wet. What should I do?"

"I'll just change shirts," I say, wiping the sweat off the back of my neck. I put one foot on the floor at a time. In the bathroom, I turn on the light so I can see to find my drawer and a t-shirt. Finally, I turn off the bathroom light. It feels as if it takes a long time to do all this.

Mark is watching me. "Were you dreaming?"

"I was running," I say. "No, I was looking in the mirror, and it wasn't me looking back. It was a wraith, all wavy and gray, and floating. Then there wasn't anything looking back." I slide closer to Mark.

He takes his hand from my back and stretches his arm around me, pulling me to him. "I can't seem to get close enough to you," he says.

I slide my hand inside his and settle down, but my mind continues to beat. That's the third nightmare this week. I don't usually have nightmares, but I'm not usually dying either. I settle back into Mark, remembering that I used to prefer sleeping by myself. That seems like another life, another me, the me before, so empty. Then I remember one of my other nightmares, which jolts me out of the fall to sleep. Despite opening my eyes, I still see inside the cabinet to the breathing but unmoving mouse, the dying mouse—the dying mouse whose eyes glow large with fear.

"Mark?"

"Yeah?"

"I'm afraid."

He tightens his arms around me. "I am too, but—" He pauses. "I've been thinking about that. And I think it'll be okay. If we have each other to reach for, I don't think it'll be more than we can bear."

I fold my arms over his and relax a little. I think about Matisse and his palette, and I breathe slower, eventually drifting to sleep amidst the many colors.

"They want the painting story," Mark says, coming into the bedroom. "I tried to tell it, but they said I wasn't using 'the right words.' Do you feel like going in there?"

"I do," I say, momentarily happy to be the only one who can tell this story.

In their room, Elizabeth is sitting very close to Caroline on Caroline's bed. When she sees me, she jumps back into her bed.

"Mom," she says looking straight at me, "Who's going to tell us the painting story after you die?"

Her question and her facility with the words are everything I could have hoped for, and yet, knock the breath out of me. Caroline looks as if she has no idea what might happen next, glancing at me, then at Elizabeth, then back to me.

"I'll write it down," I say, "and make a copy for each of you."

I can do it on the computer and make it like a little book. And I'll put a copy in each of their chests.

"Why don't I start the bath water?" Mark says, when he comes home for lunch. "And I could help you wash your hair." But I don't want to be distracted from feeling bad. This morning, when the doctor changed my pain medication again, he said no more driving. Just like that. As if it were only for two weeks while I recuperate from something. No more driving, he said. What that means is *ever again*.

I hear Mark going around the room, opening drapes, and picking stuff up.

I burrow deeper under the sheet, under the blanket, under the quilt. I would crawl into the mattress if I could, to be smothered by all the padding inside. Quick and easy.

"Emily?"

Please don't let him ask me if I want to get up, enjoy the day, participate in life.

"Emily?" he says, softer this time.

I feel his weight on the bed and his hand searching for me. Afraid he'll try to pull the covers off, I hold tight. But when his hand finds my body, it rests on my shoulder. And I relax.

Sometime later, I feel his body next to mine, then covering mine, with his legs on top of my legs, his chest on my back, his mouth above my head.

Later that afternoon, it rains for the first time in two weeks. The day becomes gray instead of its usual green. I stay in bed as long as I can stand it, then I do take a bath. As I get ready to step into the tub, I catch sight of myself in the full-length mirror. All I can see is the black outline of a woman, and I'm reminded of Matisse's nude with the fern, just a minimal number of brush strokes of black ink to create the most desolate-looking woman, and the black fern taking over, seeming to push the woman out of the picture.

I've come into my study but can't remember why. Everything looks frozen—the piles, the books, my laptop. Picking up my cell, I call Alyssa to talk to someone who isn't mired down in all this. To find a new perspective.

"I was just about to call you," she says.

"You were?"

"No, I've been avoiding calling you. I have no idea what to say, how to be helpful."

"Tell me something interesting."

"Well, how about something funny. On the way to work this morning, I was on the interstate, and this woman—maybe thirty—comes up on my left in some kind of jeep. As she goes by, I notice white writing on the back windshield and tin cans trailing off the back of the car. Guess what the writing said?"

"What?"

"'Just divorced' and 'freedom.' Isn't that great?"

"Yeah." I lean my chin against the windowpane.

"Emily, what's wrong?"

"Why does everybody keep asking me that? You all know what's wrong with me."

"See," she says. "I was right not to call."

And I laugh. A large, blue butterfly floats by. "Sorry," I say. "I don't know what's wrong with me. What happened to that other person who worked at the museum, who had a life out in the world? I miss her, me, you."

"Maybe we could go out for dinner or something?"

"I'd like that."

"I would have suggested it earlier, but I mean, you told your parents not to come. I thought the four of you wanted time to yourselves."

"Which is true, but all I've been doing lately is going to the doctor and resting and I feel as if I'm starting to slip away. And I'm not ready yet. And I miss being a part of the world, a part of the rushing and doing. But now that I'm talking to you, I think I was missing you—"

"I'll pick you up around six."

"We don't have to do anything today. It's not *that* bad. Don't change your—"

"I'm not changing anything. Rest up. I'll see you soon."

I find Mark working at the kitchen table and ask if he's able to watch the girls while I'm out with Alyssa. He stretches and exhales. "You know, maybe we all need a break from this. I'll take the girls to play putt-putt."

And I just stare at him.

He stands. "Emily, I didn't mean it the way it sounded."

"I know," I say. "It's okay. I don't think they've ever played putt-putt. They will love that." And I turn toward the bedroom. He's right of course. And I try to imagine "this" as being something separate from me that I can get away from too.

A few days after my dinner with Alyssa, I'm sitting in a comfortable chair that Mark brought into the kitchen for me, and I'm watching him at the stove making supper, his cheeks bright red. He's going to treat us, he says, to a dish he learned how to make in Turkey. Caroline is working on her leaf report. Elizabeth is coloring. They sit on opposite ends of the table. James Taylor is singing "How Sweet It Is" in the background, with Mark singing in the foreground. I have that weird feeling of not being in the picture, of being up above everything, watching life go by.

Be present, I say to myself. "Mark, what are you making again?"

"Two things, *kofte*, which is meatballs in a stew with vegetables, and *ayran*, which is a yogurt drink, which the girls are sipping on right now, which they are liking. Right, girls?"

"What did you say?" Caroline asks, looking up from her book.

"You like the drink, right?"

"It's good," she says.

"Elizabeth, you like the *ayran* too, right?"

"Yep," she says, and then takes a loud slurp.

She's using what's left of her Christmas box of sixty-four Crayola crayons, which is not much. Caroline, of course, has all sixty-four, none broken, which she is guarding at her end of the table.

"Emily, how about a sip for you?" he asks, holding the blender in one hand and an empty glass in the other.

"Not tonight," I say, as if there will be a million other nights when I might.

He puts the blender and glass down and takes a big gulp of his *ayran*. Then he stirs the meatballs in the skillet and the stew in our biggest pot.

"You were in Sinop, right, when you learned how to make this?" I ask, making another effort.

He nods.

"I have a postcard you sent me from Sinop," Elizabeth says. "It's near some water."

"That's right," he says. "The Black Sea."

"Wasn't that the name of your job?" Caroline asks.

"Yeah," Mark answers, smiling. "The Black Sea Study." He appears to wait for more questions, which don't come. Then he adds, "We had the *kofte* the first night after we started working on the field survey of the Akliman delta. A bunch of us eating together outside."

"What's a field survey?" Caroline asks.

"It's where we walk through fields collecting and taking pictures

240

of pottery, stone tools, anything we find that could be evidence that people lived there a long time ago."

"Like those wheels we found on the dig." Caroline says. "The ones on the bookshelf in my room."

"Exactly," he says.

"Cool."

We're quiet for a while, listening to "Fire and Rain."

"I don't understand this," Caroline says.

"Bring it to me," I say.

She huffs but brings the book over, showing me the paragraph where she needs help.

"Let me look at it."

"I'm going to the bathroom then," she says.

I read about how the true colors of the leaf are hidden by the more powerful green pigment called chlorophyll. About how when the shorter days and cooler nights of fall break down the chlorophyll, the true colors of the leaf are exposed. At the same time, the leaf begins to die. I read about tiny pipelines between the leaf and the stem, and about an abscission zone. Even after the leaf is gone, a mark remains on the twig where the leaf stalk was attached. It's called a leaf scar. A scar is permanent. It's there forever.

"Have you read it?" she asks.

"Yep," I answer.

"What is that word right there?" she asks, pointing to *chlorophyll.*

I tell her how to pronounce it and answer her other questions. She goes back to the table to write some more.

Mark says, "Supper in fifteen minutes. Girls, take five minutes to finish up. Then we're going to set the table." He walks into the den.

I close my eyes and lean my head back, thinking of the power of everyday life to cover and hide my true thoughts and feelings. I see the arrival of my cancer, breaking down my life and exposing my deepest thoughts and feelings, those that were there all along, just buried. My true colors.

I wake in the middle of the night and try to go back to sleep, but it eludes me. I still have no idea what would be best for Caroline and Elizabeth, whether they should live with Mark or Susan. He's doing an amazingly good job, especially for him, of not pressuring me. And it's comforting that both Susan and Mark want them. But I go back and forth.

"Who will take care of the girls?" I wonder silently. And then over and over again. I go to the bathroom, but the words follow me in there. I turn on the TV in the den, hoping that its words will be louder than my own. The light flickers in shadows against the darkness. And then I see it, there in the shadows—the fear. The fear that if I make this decision—choose Mark or Susan—I will speed the girls on their way without me. I will become unnecessary.

Two small children need me. Why should they have to grow up without their mother? But these feelings of anger and sadness seem disconnected from me, as if they were patches of color on a palette I could reach out and touch. It's April, and I'm finally starting to believe what they said. I actually feel the slowing down. I feel myself entering another rhythm, one that is separate from this world.

Rocking on the porch, I close my eyes to better smell the honeysuckle. I open them in the direction of the vines coming up on the left side of the house. Only a little is visible, but there must be more under the porch because the scent is so strong. I try to remember pulling the stem out of the flower and sucking the nectar.

Mark and I met with someone from Hospice yesterday. So now, no more trips to the doctor. I feel the squeeze of the circle shrinking again.

The goal of Hospice is to comfort, but it makes my heart jolt to think about the visit. Mark and I couldn't look at each other while the woman was here; we kept our eyes focused on her. She'd already spoken to my doctor, and after we talked for a while I went ahead and signed the consent and insurance forms. She suggested we order the hospital bed right away. Mark called after she left; it will be here Tuesday. Our family is meant to make friends with it before I need it.

I don't know if it's good to have this much time to watch, inch by inch, as one's circle of life is circumscribed. Driving and then never driving again. In our bed one night, and then one night not ever again. I can't believe how fast time—life—is going. My body is losing now. Last week I looked forward to walking to the mailbox once a day. Now walking to the porch is my goal.

I thought we would put the hospital bed in our bedroom, but the hospice person suggested the den. So when I can't move around, I'll be in the center of things and not feel isolated. Mark joked that isolated is something I've never felt. I laughed. Then I began to understand another reason to put the bed in the den. It will make death—my death—a part of life, not a separate event that takes place somewhere else.

"I could help you a lot more," Mark says, later that night on the porch, the candle between us illuminating our little space. It's after midnight. The girls have been asleep for hours. Our entire street is asleep. When we first came out here, it was so dark I had to stop for a minute to let my eyes adjust before I could see the rocking chairs.

"But I need so much help," I say. "I feel like I should do what I can by myself, so I won't flood you."

"Flood me," he says.

And I get up and sit in his lap. We rock for a while, not speaking. Our one little flickering light, all by itself, is pushing the darkness into the street, keeping it away from us.

"I can help with all these decisions you have to make," he says, rubbing my back. "I don't want to make it harder for you, but I want to do this *with* you."

"And I want your help. I just didn't know it was okay to ask for so much."

The hospice person has become Meg, and her phone numbers are on a pad in the kitchen. She'll come every Tuesday. But she also came today to help us prepare for the arrival of the bed tomorrow. Meg and Mark moved furniture around so that the bed could be next to the window. They put one of the sofa end tables near where the bed would go to act as a night table, but we need to look for something taller. Meg suggested we move the sofa so I would be able to see the people sitting on it. Finally, we moved the TV closer to the door so we could see it from the bed and the sofa. I thought it looked okay after the vacuuming was done, and all the lost toys, old food, and wrappers were picked up.

I find *Matisse on Art* and my journal in a stack of books piled on top of other books on a shelf in the den. Meg must have moved them. My journal. I used to have so many, and now I'm down to one, the one with my essay in it. I get off my knees and sit against the wall, spreading my legs in front of me. I lean my head back for a minute until my breathing slows.

Putting my journal beside me, I open the book. When Matisse was diagnosed with abdominal cancer, the doctors told him he was going to die. Instead, he lived many more years, and he called that time afterwards something I can't remember. Which is what I'm looking for. I thumb through my underlinings until I find it. "…the time that you live from now on is a gift from life itself—each year, each month, each day…."

A gift from life itself. That's what I want—July and August. I close the book and pick up my journal, holding both in my lap. Why is seeing this painting again so important? And is it important now for the same reason as before? Opening my journal, I look through my essay.

I believe the power of this painting lies in its ability to allow me to see things about myself that I otherwise cannot see. Over the years, it feels as if I've lost something. To discover what it is, I need to see this painting again. Here. To look at it, as Matisse said, as though I were seeing it for the first time.

And I did want to look at the painting with fresh eyes.

I should be one unity—no separation between the interior and the exterior. It is Breakfast *that will be my passageway.* And so it was.

Yet, looking back over what I wrote then, it doesn't read like the voice of reason, but instead, the voice of desire.

Could it be that in this one instance I led with emotion?

Desire. To see it *one last time.* To have an ending. To complete the circle.

It turns out Meg was right about the bed. The first day it was here, everybody looked at it, but nobody, including me, went near it—as if there were a force field around it. The second day Elizabeth asked if she could sit on it. The next thing I knew Caroline was moving Elizabeth's head and feet up and down. Then Elizabeth was doing the same for Caroline. After a few days, the bed lost its ominous quality. Yesterday Caroline was reading on it. This morning I rested my hand there.

"Mark should be home soon," I say to Bobby Thomas, Mark's friend, the reporter, who's doing a story for the paper on Mark's work in Turkey. "Come on in."

I get a beer for him and a sparkling water for me. We go out to the porch to wait for Mark.

"I don't want to take up your time," he says. "I'll be glad to sit out here and let you get back to what you were doing."

"I wasn't doing anything," I say. And I wasn't—just lying on the couch listening to the girls play with dolls in their room. It's been so long since I had to make conversation. I notice the light breeze. "It's nice out here, isn't it?"

"It is."

I feel him looking at me.

"I'm real sorry about your cancer."

"Thanks," I say, noticing how that felt. Then I speak. "It felt good to me that you said that—that you didn't try not to mention it."

"You know, Mark and I met last week for lunch so I could explain to him about my idea for the article."

"He's looking forward to it."

"Mark told me that the 'Our Favorite Paintings' Exhibit was really your idea, that you had mentioned it to him years ago."

I nod.

Our neighbor Suzanne drives by and waves.

"When Mark told me about your cancer, I suggested we put this article off, but Mark said now would be fine, that he was specifically trying not to set things up as before and after, that he didn't want to fracture time like that, that he wanted to work with time and not against it."

I look at Bobby, and he smiles. I remember his wonderful smile.

"That's an amazing perspective to have. It says a lot about how he feels about you and your family."

I smile and lean my head back, as a breeze lights up the leaves around us.

It's two in the morning and I'm having trouble sleeping. Mark forgot to close the drapes again. The full moon floats above the trees, illuminating a portion of the darkness. It seems like just yesterday there was no moon at all.

Three o'clock. I look for the stars. I wonder if I'm afraid to go to sleep.

Four twenty-five. I sit up in bed, my heart racing, my nightgown drenched.

Mark turns over, and then sits up. "What is it?"

"Another nightmare. I was having my picture painted. The first time I looked at the painting, I didn't have any face. I said I wanted a face. The next time I was just a face—no, a skull—and I said to try again, that I wanted to be all there. Then the artist couldn't see me, and I was yelling that I was right here."

Mark puts his hand on my arm and asks if he can get me anything.

"I'm going to change my nightgown. And take some more pain medicine since it's after four."

"You want me to write it down?"

"I will."

"Is your breathing okay?"

"Yeah, you go back to sleep." I decide to take a sleeping pill too. What the hell. I write down what I take and turn off the bathroom light.

Mark is at work; the girls are at school. I'm home alone, just getting out of bed at ten. My bare feet act like adhesive, picking up little crumbs and things on the floor. Coming out of the bathroom, I no longer have the energy to get dressed. But I don't want another line to be crossed, so I try to make myself do it anyway. Opening a drawer, I can't decide what to put on. I don't know what still fits. I've lost so much weight, but my stomach is bloated. I concentrate. Underwear, shirt, sweatpants. I sit down on the bed. My arms hang by my side. I give in and go back to sleep.

Around eleven thirty, I wake up, and I really should get dressed because Kari will be here soon with lunch. But when I notice what a beautiful day it is outside, I'm distressed for the second time this morning—I have no desire to go out in it.

Still in my nightgown, I make tea and put it on the table beside the hospital bed, where someone, probably Meg, has put the remote and an unopened bottle of water. I pick up the art magazine that Sam and his wife brought yesterday when they came to visit and crawl into the bed. The back is already raised to the perfect height.

I close my eyes for a minute.

A knock at the door. I didn't even hear footsteps. As I glance out the window, I see Kari's car.

"Come in," I say, not sure my voice is loud enough to reach her.

She opens the door. "Hey," she says, "When did you move out here?"

"I haven't. At least, I don't think I have." I look around the room and notice the mess. Then I look down at my nightgown. "I didn't feel like getting dressed today, the first time—" She puts our lunch on the coffee table and comes to give me a hug. We never used to hug.

"It's okay. Who needs clothes anyway?"

I clear my throat.

"Alyssa told me to bring some candy to refill your candy drawer. I'm just going to put it in the kitchen. Can I bring you anything?"

I shake my head and pick up the magazine, opening it to the feature on outdoor sculpture. When Kari comes back, I show her the picture of the *Walking Wall* by Andy Goldsworthy.

"I love this," she says.

"I do too. Can you believe they actually moved the wall?"

She reads, "'The final stage of *Walking Wall* will see it move south into the Donald J. Hall Sculpture Park and, ultimately, into the Bloch Building.'"

"Turn the page and look at *The Fountain of the Muses* with the five life-size figures—painting, architecture, sculpture, and I forget what else."

"Poetry and music," she says. That one's at Brookgreen Gardens, only an hour and a half away.

I cough and take a sip of my cold tea.

"I'm glad Alyssa called me," she says, closing the magazine and sitting down. "Honestly, I'm ashamed to say I've had a hard time with this. I should have just bolted right over instead of disappearing. I'm sorry for that and this creepy, selfish thing I'm about to say. I've never known anyone who was dying before."

"Neither have I," I say.

She smiles. "I'm so glad to see you. How are you really?"

"I'm okay really. Today I have less energy. It's like water going out of a tub with the drain clogged a little. For days I stay the same, and then one day for no reason, I'm much weaker. I had a little trouble breathing last night. Mark said he'd check with the doctor. How are you?"

"Oh, you know, the usual, trivial concerns. I can't seem to lose this weight I gained at Christmas, and it's already May."

"At least I don't have to worry about that anymore." I grin.

"And if I read another one of those makeover stories, where some woman loses sixty pounds by walking around the block every day, I'm going to scream."

Meg is here again, the second time this week. I always expect her to look more special, like an angel maybe, but she just looks like a regular person, with her light brown hair clean and straight. She wears long, comfortable, colorful clothes that remind me of a kindergarten teacher. Today, she brings brownies, along with some papers I asked for—a "Do Not Resuscitate" order. When I close my eyes, I see us sitting in a row, all dressed up, facing forward, on a pew—Elizabeth, Caroline, me, Mark; Mark, Elizabeth, Caroline, me; Mark, Elizabeth, Caroline.

She helps me take a bath and changes the hospital bed, which I use for naps now. She checks my blood pressure and listens to my heart. I tell her that the pain in my back is worse and so is my cough. She adjusts the dosage of my medication, explaining that my cough is worse due to the fluid buildup in my lungs. Then she heats some vegetable soup for my lunch.

"I found the last corner piece," Caroline says. The three of them are fluttering around the coffee table in the den. I'm on the hospital bed—unmoving and out of the picture.

"Okay," Mark says, "now let's look for the border. Try to find all the pieces that have a straight edge."

"What do we do with them?" Elizabeth asks.

"Let's make a pile over here. Are you sure you don't want to help, Emily?"

"I'm too comfortable."

"Mom," Caroline says, "that bird is back, the one that makes a nest in the garage."

"It is?" I say. "Could it be the same one? How long do birds live anyway?"

"What bird?" Mark asks.

"Doesn't it have to be the same one?" Elizabeth asks. "How would it know about the place otherwise? Do birds talk to each other?"

"We have a bird that makes nests in the garage and has babies there," Caroline says.

"Yeah," Elizabeth says. "We saw the babies. We never saw the daddy bird though. Did we, Caroline?"

"Mark, here's a bunch of the border," Caroline says. "I'm going to start hooking them together."

"Mom told us you knew our dad," Elizabeth says, looking at Mark and holding a puzzle piece in her hand.

"That's right. I did. We were all in college together."

"Did you like him?" she asks.

"I did. The three of us were always together."

The TV is on low.

"Can you tell us something about him?" Caroline asks.

"Everybody liked your dad," he says. "He was the captain of the football team."

"Did you play football too?" she asks.

"I played soccer. And your dad was also good in Spanish. We

were in the same class. Look, Caroline, see if this is the last piece of the side you're working on."

"It is," she says, with a big smile.

"Can you tell us a Spanish word?" Elizabeth asks.

"I don't know if I remember any—wait, I remember some colors. *Rojo* is red and *verde* is green. Oh yeah, and brown is *café*."

"*Rojo*," she repeats.

"I have a postcard he sent me when he got to New Mexico," Caroline says. "On the front it's all yellow except in the middle is a red sun. On the back it says the yellow field with the red sun is the flag of New Mexico, the Land of Enchantment."

"I'd like to see that sometime," he says.

"He didn't know about me then," Elizabeth says.

"I'm sure if he had," Mark says, "he would have sent you a postcard of the flag too."

"Yeah, that's what I think," Elizabeth says.

"Do you know how to say *father* in Spanish?" Caroline asks.

"*Padre*," Mark says.

A few days later, I'm resting on the hospital bed. Mark is making me a cup of tea. We're going to talk about the girls. I've put it off for too long. I don't think I can decide by myself, and it occurred to me this morning I don't have to.

Looking out the window, I see and hear lots of birds, not staying anywhere for more than a second or two. I wonder if one of them is our bird from the garage. Several butterflies, a large blue one in particular, hover by the rocking chairs on the porch. And then they're gone.

I turn away, back to the inside. My eyes rest on the little pot of ivy that Mark brought home for me last night. It reminded me of a painting by Matisse, which I found in one of my books this morning, *Ivy in Flower*, a beautifully balanced painting, mostly in neutral tones. I'd forgotten that the woman in the painting was merely a rectangle of gray behind the ivy, merely a drawing on the wall.

This relegation, this absence, brings me back to Caroline and Elizabeth, who will be living here, like the ivy.

They've been a part of my illness. We didn't want to shield them. We wanted them to have the benefit of my gradual deterioration, in order to come to terms with my eventual death. We wanted death to follow naturally, not jump out and surprise them. Mark and I talked about this. And now we'll talk about the rest of their lives.

He comes in from the kitchen with the tea.

I sit up.

He doesn't sit down. "It's been hard for me, not knowing and not talking about it, but I kept telling myself to give you time and you'd come to the right decision."

"Is there a right decision?"

"I think there is. You know, as much as I love you, it's always been about the girls too. They weren't something I had to accept. They're like, more of you."

I feel a cool breeze and look toward the window.

"I was there when Elizabeth was born. And I never thought about you not being here. But when I had to, I assumed we would just keep going, the girls and me." He moves back and forth. "And that was a good feeling in the middle of a bad one."

"You knew Susan was the guardian."

"I guess I was thinking you'd change that before it mattered."

"But I don't want to tie you down."

He stops. "Emily. I'm thirty-eight years old. The three of you are my life. I only just made it through Turkey. I don't know how I'll bear it if all of you disappear again." He crosses to the bookshelf and leans against it. "But if you really think the girls would be better off with your sister, then that's what you should do."

"It's not that I think they'd be better off with Susan; it's that you'll probably get married again. And then who'll be taking care of them?"

"Me, and somebody who loves them as much as me. Damn it. I meant to start by talking about the girls." He sits down on the bed. "See, if they stay with me, their lives keep going. This family keeps going. If they go live with Susan, they'll have to leave what they know. They'll have to become part of another family. Not only will they lose you, but all of this, all these spaces filled with you, and filled with all of us together."

I get scared again. But it's time now. Their future is as clear to me as my own. I don't know why it always takes me so long to see the obvious.

"You're right. Even without me, it's *our family*. Caroline and Elizabeth stay the same people. And I trust you—I do. I want them to have that sense of belonging, of feeling safe in the world."

Mark's body rounds at the edges. He comes to hold me. I relax my vision of the future. It's safe now.

When we tell the girls, they look at each other and then back at us. Caroline says, "Of course we're staying here with Mark. What else would we do?" And Elizabeth adds, "Yeah."

Again, the next morning I'm aware of the busyness around me. Our bedroom feels like an airport, with everybody in a hurry to somewhere else. Everybody but me that is.

"Mark, do you know where my backpack is?" Elizabeth asks from the hallway, sticking her head into our bedroom.

"By the front door, near the hat stand," Mark answers, as he grabs his keys off the dresser.

"Have a good day," he says, bending down to give me a kiss and a smile good-bye. "I love you. Alyssa will be here after a while. Call if you need me."

Caroline comes in to tell me bye. At seven, she seems the same as always. Her hair half up and half down, beautifully brushed with a bow that matches her clothes. And something new. She's more and more substantial. A minute or two later, Elizabeth runs in, hollers "Bye," but then stops.

"What's the matter, Mom?" she asks.

"I don't know."

"Well, you look like Eeyore."

I laugh. "That's exactly how I feel today, like Eeyore. 'Thanks for noticing me,'" I say in Eeyore's voice. "Give me a hug and have a great day."

"I love you, Mom."

"I love you, too," I say, smelling grape jelly.

She runs out of the bedroom. Then the door slams, and the house is quiet. I slide down and try to go back to sleep. After a while, I give up. Something is bothering me. There's something I need to find. I get up and begin to open drawers, looking for whatever it is.

I hear a knock.

"Hello?" Alyssa calls out.

She's here to visit, to babysit. She comes into the bedroom.

"I'm not having a good day," I say. "I admit it."

"Has something changed?" She's learned not to ask what's wrong.

"I don't know. I need to find something, but I don't know what it is, and I have too much stuff. I need to get rid of some stuff." I sit down on the bed.

"Why don't we go out to the den? We can make a list of the things that are bothering you."

I ignore her and stand up to open another drawer. My breathing is noticeable. Bending to open a bottom drawer, I have a sharp pain in my lower abdomen. It hurts to straighten up. Then I have more trouble with my breathing. Each breath makes a horrible noise. Doubled over, I turn my head to look at Alyssa. I can't speak.

"It's okay," she says, holding onto my waist and arms. She helps me sit on the floor. "Mark told me there was some oxygen by the hospital bed. I'm going to get it. Let's don't panic. Breathe slowly."

I try to relax, but the breaths come shorter and louder. She hands me the oxygen tube, I put it in my nose, and she turns it on. After a minute or two, my breathing is easier. Alyssa brings me a pain pill, which I take. Then I lie down on the floor and close my eyes, still breathing too hard. This is so weird. Alyssa is here taking care of me because I can't take care of myself. I try to open my eyes and be a normal person, but I can't. I can't make my body do what it's supposed to.

When I wake later, Alyssa has put a blanket on my legs. She's scrunched against the wall watching me.

"Are you better?"

"Yeah." I sit up. "I can talk now."

"I checked with Meg. She said not to worry. She said when you woke up for you to sit for a while before trying to stand. Then to rest for a while before trying to move around again."

"Okay."

"And to call her if you couldn't stand."

I look at Alyssa.

"I shouldn't have told you that last part, right?"

"Right."

She looks worried now.

"I'm kidding," I say, taking a deep breath. When I take the oxygen out, I'm breathing normally. Without warning I feel as if I might start crying, and I don't want to. "It's all happening fast."

She says, "Like when I first needed reading glasses, it was only at night. And before I knew it, I needed them if there wasn't enough light. Within weeks I needed them almost all the time."

"Now I'm not feeling too good again." I look at my watch hanging on my wrist. "I can take some more medicine." I get up off the floor but sit immediately down on the bed. "Maybe you could bring it to me."

"Sure," she says, standing up slowly. "You know, it's not all that easy to get up off the floor even without cancer."

I laugh. "Thanks, I needed that."

From the hospital bed, where I'm taking a nap, I hear Caroline say, "Mom said you had a brother who died." I told her this a few days ago when she asked if Mark had any sisters.

"I did," he says. He and Caroline are reading in the rocking chairs on the front porch. The windows are open. Elizabeth is at Lily's.

"What was his name?" she asks.

"Harry."

"Who was older?"

"He was."

"So me and Harry are the oldest."

"And me and Elizabeth are the youngest," he says.

I hear the clicking of the rocking chairs against the wood floor.

"Did he die of being sick, like Mom?"

For what seems like a long time, I don't hear anything—which may only be my reaction to the question, not the reality.

Then I hear Mark. "No, he died in a car accident. Like your dad."

"I bet it was sad."

"It was very sad, and I cried for a long time."

"You did?"

"Why don't you come sit in my lap?"

A chair scrapes the floor. There are sounds of shuffling about. Then, the soothing clicking again.

"How old were you?" Caroline asks.

"Young. Well, actually not so young. I was twenty."

"Do you remember him?"

"He had red hair like me, but curlier. We loved to play in the back yard when we were little, digging up stuff. And we liked to play basketball."

"Will you teach me how to play basketball? Some of the kids at school play at recess."

This from the child I used to have to force to play soccer.

"Sure. It's easy. You'll be great."

"Do you still miss him?"

"Every day."

Lying on the couch in the den, I'm now comfortable being the still object in a room of movement. Perhaps it's just that I have less of a desire to move. My book is open to Matisse's *Still Life with a Sleeping Woman*. In the painting, the woman looks peaceful, her head resting on her arm on the table curved to fit her body, her face serene amidst the pastel colors of the sea-green plants and the soft apricot-colored oranges.

"Good night, Mom," Elizabeth says as she gets up off the floor to give me a hug and a kiss. "Are you feeling any better?"

"I am," I say, closing the book. "Thanks for asking. Have sweet dreams. I love you."

"I love you, too."

"Elizabeth, brush your teeth," Mark says. "I'll be in there in a minute to read."

"Okay, Markie."

He sits down beside me and rubs my shoulder.

I nibble on a saltine. "Where's Caroline?"

"Putting her pajamas on. I'll check on her. Do you need anything?"

I shake my head.

He looks at me. Then he kisses my forehead. He starts to leave, but instead he sits back down beside me and puts his arms around me. "I can't do this," he whispers, and I'm not sure if he's talking to me or himself. "How many more nights will I be able to fix your blanket, or bring you something, or sit beside you."

He sits up and I lift my head.

"I want you to be able to turn to me," he says. "But it's so damn hard."

"I *can* turn to you. But you're supposed to turn to me too. Remember?"

He wipes his eyes with a handkerchief—he never used to carry a handkerchief—and he leans his elbow on the top of the couch over me. Our hips are touching.

"*This* is what we have," I say. "It's not perfect, but it never would have been."

He threads the fingers of his left hand through the fingers of my right hand.

"I don't have to figure out how I'm going to be in two places at one time the next day," I say. "So when I tell the girls good night, that's all I'm doing. Usually, life goes on. With so much of it ahead, it's difficult to see the minutes and the hours, to seize the small moments, which are now the only ones I have."

"Emily—"

I reach up with my finger to touch his mouth.

"Mark, this is not just affecting me. It affects you too, and the girls. This whole family. I'm going to have bad days when I forget everything I just said. But I don't want you to censor what you're thinking and feeling." I pause. "I'll think you don't care."

"I wish—" Mark begins.

"I know. Me too." I reach up to kiss him.

Alyssa is coming today to take Caroline and Elizabeth to a Piccolo

Spoleto piano recital at Simmons Center Recital Hall. Then they plan to stroll through Wragg Square Park, looking at the exhibits. The girls have been telling me their plans all week. Another image from Piccolo Spoleto comes to mind, and I close my eyes to capture it—the year of the kites, 1987, I think. On a Saturday afternoon, hundreds of handmade kites, of all colors and shapes and tails, floating upward in the bright blue downtown sky.

I lean on Mark, trying to make it from the hospital bed to my rocking chair on the porch. It's almost dark, dusk on a Saturday late in May. These days, the girls play outside until the last minute. I hurt all over, but despite the aches, I want to be with them, and wants are coming few and far between. And still, this one overwhelming desire remains—to make it to September to see *Breakfast* again. It shocks me, and yet, it's as if it's always been there. Before Mark, before Caroline and Elizabeth. Coming up out of me, from the part that makes me, me.

On the porch, Mark scoots his rocking chair so close to mine that the chair arms knock against each other. "I remember the first time I saw you," he says. "I thought you were so cute."

I open my eyes and find Mark's.

"But you were already taken. The good ones always are."

"I remember when I first saw you," I say, breathing hard. "You were playing soccer. And I asked somebody who you were. Your hair was long and lighter than it is now. Your face was flushed."

"And I didn't even think you noticed me." He puts his hand on top of mine.

We turn to watch Elizabeth running up the steps.

"What are y'all talking about?" she asks.

"We're playing the 'Remember Game,'" Mark says.

"Can I play?"

"Sure, we're only on round one. What do you remember about the first time you saw your mother?"

"When I was a baby was the first time I saw her. I don't remember that." She laughs. "Now what?"

"Now what, what?" Caroline says, coming to join us.

"We're playing the Remember Game," Elizabeth says, sticking her feet between the posts on the banister. "You want to play?"

"Okay," she says.

"You have to say when you first saw Mom."

"I've always seen her," she says, sitting down on the steps.

My fingers clutch at Mark's. He tightens his grip on me, but he keeps his eyes on Caroline.

"She was there when I was born," she says, looking toward the street.

"Duh," Elizabeth says.

Mark has on the old dark green sweater I gave him years ago.

"Let's try another round," he says. "What's the first thing you remember about being in this house? Emily?"

"The agent showing the three of us around. We each discovered something special we liked. For me, it was the little laundry room. I knew it would be my study." My breathing is worsening. I stall for time by taking a sip of juice. "Caroline, you were four," I say, looking at her and noticing that she has on her favorite yellow dress. "You found the closet in your room and stayed there. You didn't want to leave."

I rest my head against the back of the rocking chair.

"Mom, you need some white spaces," Elizabeth says, patting my leg and then climbing into Mark's lap.

I smile at her. "Elizabeth, you were one. You had on red pants and a red shirt and a little red barrette in your hair. You loved this porch. You crawled back and forth, and back and forth, squealing and clapping your hands."

"Okay, girls," he says, "what do *you* first remember about this house?"

"Eating chocolate chip cookies under the kitchen table with Mom," Caroline says, coming to sit on the porch floor between Mark and me.

"I remember that too," I say.

"How old was I?"

"About five, I think."

"Elizabeth?" Mark says.

"I remember you pushing me on the swing," she says to Mark, "and us waving to Mom on this porch. And then we had a race to touch her, and I fell and hurt my knee, and you carried me inside and washed it and put a Band-Aid on it—and you wrote your name on the Band-Aid."

"You can't remember that," he says, giving her a kiss. "You were too little." He looks at me and brushes his hair off his forehead.

I shrug my shoulders.

"I told her about that," Caroline says. "Mark, your turn," she says, patting his foot.

And as her hand rests on his foot, I realize that this is what I would paint if I could paint, the four of us in living color. No still life. No things. Us. We're going to be okay, I think. *This family* is safe.

Mark says, "I remember your mom driving me here *after* she bought this house." He grins at me, "She had only seen it one time and hadn't even had it checked out. She showed me everything. Then she ran out to the car and brought back a picnic supper. We spread the red-and-white striped cloth on the den floor and lit candles."

"What did you have to eat?" Caroline asks.

"*That* I don't remember," he says, looking at me.

"Vichyssoise," I say. "And crabmeat salad. Bread and wine."

"Ah, now I remember."

"What is the vichy thing?" Elizabeth asks.

"Cold soup," I say.

Elizabeth makes a face at Caroline.

I look past the porch, surprised it's dark out there.

"Why don't you girls go turn on the TV and choose a movie, and your mom and I will be in in a minute?"

They scramble inside. The screen door slams. Lights go on. I look out at the stars and disappearing moon. This afternoon, Caroline made a poster about its different phases. She told me that tonight would be the last quarter moon. I wonder if she noticed.

Our rocking chairs move back and forth. I feel the moonlight coming and going. The wind blows the branches, the breezes now arriving with less calm in between. I smell rain, but it's not here yet.

After a while, Mark stands. He bends to pick me up to carry me to the hospital bed, where he hooks up the oxygen with one hand so that he can leave one hand on me. Then he covers me up and sits down on the side of the bed.

"Mark, aren't you coming?" Caroline asks, patting the sofa.

"I'll be over in a few minutes. I'm going to watch with your mom for a while." And he crawls in beside me.

How weird this is, the letting go. It comes uninvited. And my body acquiesces. It does the work so that my mind has no choice but to follow. Each of us lasts only for a time. Death is a part of life as my hospital bed is a part of the den. Nobody wants it here, but here it is. It's time to say good-bye.

Mark and I talk about the order of things. First, we'll find a time for us, a whole night, one last night where our thoughts are only for each other. We're going to give ourselves a few days in the hopes of my having a good day we can enjoy. Then it will be about the others. I'll have a special time with the girls. We'll call my parents and my brothers and sisters. I'll tell my friends good-bye.

I must reach back into my life for a memory to give me strength, to remind my body that it can push forward—all the way to Matisse. Closing my eyes, I visualize running—how I didn't think I could take another step, but I put one foot in front of the other to finish. That's what I'll do now. One step after another. I visualize Matisse— older, more relaxed, more confident, in a white short-sleeved shirt and wearing glasses, a little gray showing through the red beard. One painting after another. From now on, when I feel as if I'm starting to fade, I'll call to Henri. I'll wrap my mind around him and hold on to him in my thoughts.

Sunday morning and a good day. I know it the minute I wake up. Feeling better gives me the illusion of recovery, but I remind myself it's just the good day I was hoping for. Mark will take Caroline and Elizabeth to Martha's as soon as Meg arrives this afternoon. I hug and kiss the girls good-bye. I look deep in their eyes and tell them I love them. Then they're gone. And they were here just a minute ago.

My tears start in the bathroom after Meg washes my hair. She hands me a tissue.

"Come on now. You thought this day up. You planned for it. Mark planned for it. Here it is. A gift."

"And after this day, what?" I blow my nose.

Meg puts her left hand on my knee and bends down to put my feet in slippers. She looks up at me and says, "A good day is rough, isn't it? It makes you care again, have wishes again."

I look at her.

"Let's just enjoy the next thing," she says softly. "Focus. One thing at a time. Clean hair. Deep breath. Clean body…." Meg squeezes my knee and stands.

We both look in the mirror at the same time. She rubs my shoulders.

"Makeup?" I suggest.

Minutes later, as Meg reaches for the doorknob, I'm hit by a feeling of time going backwards instead of rushing forward. I go back all the way to high school and the anticipation of preparing for a date.

Once the door is open, I see how dark it is in the rest of the house. I hear music—James Taylor—coming from the den.

Meg helps me to the chair by the bathroom door. Then I hear her tell Mark she's leaving. A moment later he's in front of me, sweeping me out of the chair and into the den. I lean my nose into his neck, and I can smell the Ivory soap from his shower. When I look up, the first thing I see is candlelight. Mark has moved the coffee table out from the couch, covered it with candles, and spread the red-and-white striped cloth between them. He's also covered the surfaces of the two end tables in candles, creating an illuminated island for us amidst the darkness of the rest of the room. An ice bucket with a bottle of wine, a tray of bread, and what must be crabmeat salad and vichyssoise wait for us on the blanket. I look into his warm eyes. Then he steps onto the blanket, and as he sits down, he puts me in his lap with his back against the couch. He puts his hands on the sides of my face and kisses me, and then he breathes into my mouth, hugging me to him, and rubbing my arms.

"I cannot let you go," he says into my ear.

I put my arms around him and lean against his chest. I burrow into his neck, and he makes a cocoon around me.

Seconds, minutes, years later, Mark loosens his hold on me. He reaches up to the couch. Then he takes my hand and puts in it one of his carved wooden boats, one I've never seen before. It's small, maybe six inches, a rowboat with two tiny oars, and weathered white paint and ridges, as if it were made of separate planks. On one side in tiny black letters is "Emily;" on the other, in the same lettering is "Hudson." I look at him.

"I made this for you, for your journey," he says. "I hope this helps to make it safe and peaceful, and that a part of me can help carry a part of you to the other side."

I hold the tiny boat to my heart and lean my head down on his.

He rubs his hands slowly up and down my back. "Emily, I've tried to imagine walking through the front door of this house, knowing in my mind that you won't be inside. But each time I see myself open the door, I look up for you. I'll hold you in my heart forever."

Tears spill out of our eyes and down our faces as if that normally happens when people talk to each other. Mark leans his head against mine and our tears combine as he kisses me. The death ceremony. I still have my part to say.

I sit up straight and speak slowly. "Mark, when you went away, the absence of you caused me to see what had been there all along. I was finally able to *feel* you, and then to love you in a way I didn't know existed. I discovered how important it is to turn *to* each other. And I'm so proud of this life that we created together—me and you. It feels like it's full to the brim and bursting with color. Imagine that in the midst of all this. And I feel so safe. I know you'll make the girls feel safe too."

Our eyes pull in the eyes of the other. We reach and hold tight, as if it were the last time.

Later that night in our bed, my eyes open in the darkness but blink only once before they turn to the thin sliver of light coming from the window. I think back to Caroline's poster. This sliver is the waning crescent, the last phase in the moon's revolution around the earth.

The next morning, after Mark and I have breakfast in bed, he works for a while in the study.

A couple of months ago, Alyssa came over to help me clean it out. She opened the door—I was right beside her—and then she stopped. We both stood there and looked. My laptop was still set up on my desk, with the top open. I couldn't remember the last time I'd used it. There were sticky notes with reminders to do this or that, and stacks of journals and books. My to-do basket was half-full with who knows what things that were never done, and apparently it mattered not at all. But something else. Through some process I'd been unaware of, I was no longer connected to anything in this room. These things existed without me. It was as if I were already gone, and this was what was left, the remains.

She finally said, "Maybe we should just light some candles and turn it into a shrine."

And then we went to work.

We used the paper bag system, three specially marked bags— throw away, give away, relocate. We threw away stuff that only I would be interested in, like my food and exercise diaries and my "Self-improvement" file, which actually felt as if a burden had been lifted. Throwing away files and lists marked "Someday" was hard. Alyssa asked if she could have the file I kept on books. We left general files, and files on the kids, and most of the books and pictures. In one of the desk drawers, I left paperclips, sticky notes, index cards—the basics. On the desk, I left my mug of pens and pencils.

I told Mark and the girls that since he didn't have a study, we were going to share this one. Of course, if I hadn't actually been *dying*, there was not a chance I would have shared my one private spot in the house. I thought about putting one or two of my journals in each of the girl's chests, but my old fear of the written word crept up on me. So I put all my weird journals in one of those nice paper boxes with a top and left it in the corner, assuming I would eventually know what to do with it. And I did. A month ago, I started slipping a journal a day in the trash.

I spend the morning in our bed, with Mark coming to lie beside me whenever he takes a break. After lunch, he moves from the study to the kitchen to bake the chocolate chip cookies for the girls' and my "chocolate chip cookie party," and I move to the hospital bed. At four, he leaves to pick them up from day camp.

Before I know it, I hear steps on the porch. Caroline hollers, "Mom, we're home," and then the screen door slams. I open my eyes.

"Hey, girls," I say, raising the head of the bed.

"Where's the party?" Elizabeth asks, looking around.

"You're going to create it," Mark says from the kitchen. "Come take these over to your mom."

He gives Caroline a small, round tray with three cups half full of milk, and Elizabeth, the basket with the cookies and napkins.

Caroline brings the tray and puts it down on the table in front of the sofa. Elizabeth puts the basket on the bed.

"The tablecloth," Caroline and I say at the same time.

She goes to the kitchen, and Elizabeth comes over and lays her head on my arm.

"Did you have a good day?" I ask.

"Yeah, did you?"

I tell her yes as Caroline comes in with the red-and-white striped cloth, which she spreads over the end of the bed.

Mark asks, "Can I have a cookie?"

Caroline and Elizabeth look at each other.

He adds, "If I take it to the study?"

Caroline answers, "If you take it to the study."

"You girls have fun," he says, coming over and putting his hand on my head. "Are you okay?"

I nod.

"Climb up," Caroline tells Elizabeth, "and I'll pass you your milk. Mom, I'm putting yours here on the table." Elizabeth bunches up the cloth, but instead of fussing at her sister, Caroline fixes it. Then she puts the basket of cookies on the bed and asks Elizabeth to hold her milk while she climbs up. I watch my daughters move about in the world.

When we're all set, we do "cheers" with our milk glasses. "To us," I say. We talk about the gross boys at camp and the neat counselors. I let them eat as many cookies as they want, just as I usually do.

Even though I want to tell them good-bye, I don't want them to know that's what I'm doing. I'll surely be able to say that word to them later. I guess today is really for me. Some sort of ending. It's amazing how we crave, yet almost cannot bear, something more than just fading off.

"You know I love each of you to pieces. I'm so proud of the girls you turned out to be." Elizabeth is looking right at me, grinning. But Caroline looks down. Her yellow bow is all I see. She fixes her hair herself now. And I realize I didn't buy the white shirt she has on, which is trimmed in yellow, or her yellow shorts, and I don't know who did. Then I notice her hands, balled into little fists, holding tight to a napkin. I reach out and touch one. She doesn't move.

"I know you're both happy to be staying in this house with Mark. That makes me feel good. Aunt Susan will come to visit, and y'all will go visit her and Peter and Beth. You know you can talk to Mark about anything, but if you need to talk to a mom, you can always call Susan or Martha or—"

"We have so many people who love us." Elizabeth repeats what she has heard a thousand times. Even Caroline smiles at that.

"I want you to take care of each other too, okay?"

"We will," they both say, glancing quickly at each other and grinning.

"Pretty soon I'm going to feel worse. I may not be able to talk to you, but you can talk to me and touch my arm or pat my foot. I know you'll be sad when I—when I'm not here, but I want you to know that I had a really fun life. So you can feel happy too."

I start to feel desperate. I want to say, *Always wear your seatbelt. Look before you cross the street; we can buy another ball, but not another you.* I don't think I've said those things nearly enough. I want to say, *Don't talk to strangers. Don't have sex unless you want to.* I have to stop.

Elizabeth's hair is pulled back in a ponytail, but almost as much hair is out as is in the rubber band. Her small cheek has a chocolate smear across it. Her baseball t-shirt is dirty and now covered with crumbs. She takes a sip of milk then wipes her mouth with her arm. My shoulders release, as do my worries, as I realize I'm done. Their manners, and their lives, are no longer in my hands.

"Do you want to ask me anything?" I say.

Caroline shakes her head.

Elizabeth asks, "Does it hurt?"

"Not too much right now," I answer. "Come give me a great big, long hug."

Elizabeth hops down and puts the cookie basket on the table. She stretches her arms around me. I close my eyes and wrap my arms around her almost four-year-old body. She'll be fine, I say to myself. She squeezes extra tight for a second, squirms to go, and heads back to their room.

Caroline crawls over to me. I put my arms around her, and she puts her arms around me.

"I'm going to miss you, Mom."

"I'll miss you, too, Caroline," I say, fighting tears.

"I made you something. I'll be right back."

She knows what I'm doing, and I make myself breathe all the way in and all the way out.

When she comes back, she gives me a piece of paper folded like a card, standing right by me as I look at it. On the front is a picture of me holding her when she was maybe two years old. She colored a frame around it with a marker.

"I love this picture. Where did you find it?"

"In the picture box. Mark helped me."

"We have a picture box?"

Caroline nods.

I open the card and inside she wrote, "Dear Mom, you are the best Mom God ever gave me. I'm sorry you got sick. I will never forget you. I love you. Your daughter, Caroline."

I try to stop the tears. I don't want this to be sad.

"Caroline, I love this card. And I love you. And *I* will never forget *you.*" I say all this with my arms around her. I feel her crying, and I hold her. "I'm sorry I got sick too." I pat her back until she calms down. I move some stuff on the table by the bed and put her card next to my little rowboat.

"You're going to be fine," I say to her. I want her to be able to repeat this to herself when she needs it. "You're a special person."

She glances outside. "I'm going to get ready."

"Ready for what?" I ask.

"Mark said I could spend the night with Carden," she yells from the dining room.

"Tell me good-bye before you leave," I say, but I don't think she hears me.

I open my eyes and turn over. Not seeing anyone, I start to raise the bed. Then I realize it's already raised. I remember—I'm waiting for my friends. Mark is taking the girls to play at the park after camp and then to eat somewhere. Meg had to go. I glance at the time. Five o'clock. They'll be here any minute for our "happy hour."

I think I hear car doors. I do, because now I hear voices. Victoria will come in first. And she does, after a quick rap on the screen door.

"Hey, you," she says, coming to give me a hug. I wave to the others as they head in my direction.

"Are you still feeling okay?" Kari asks.

I nod.

Martha goes straight to the kitchen and then comes to speak to me. She pulls a chair up close to the bed. "I put some tapioca pudding in the fridge for later. Victoria says you're not allowed to have pudding for happy hour."

Some things never change. I relax my shoulders. I didn't even know I was tense.

Alyssa is moving stuff off the coffee table. "Do you have a cloth that will fit on this table?"

"In the kitchen. Under the candy drawer."

"Victoria picked the wine," Kari says, bringing two bowls in on a tray. "And I brought popcorn and peanuts."

Alyssa comes back in with the cloth. To Kari, she says, "Will you lift the tray two seconds?" And she swooshes the cloth out. It floats through the air to land on the table.

"Perfect," she says. "I brought sparkling water and limes and napkins."

"*Chez Alyssa?*" I ask.

She looks at me now with a grin. "*Oui.*"

"Thank you," I say, watching her arrange a bowl of cut limes, the small, green bottles, and her cream-colored napkins on the cloth.

"I'm going to get ice," she says.

"I got it," Victoria says, coming into the den with two buckets, one holding a bottle of wine. "Okay," she says, extracting the cork from the wine bottle. "What can I fix you, Emily?"

"Wine, and some peanuts."

Alyssa puts some peanuts on one of her napkins and then on my lap. Victoria passes me a glass of wine. I take a sip.

"So good," I say, resting my head back. Then I notice my hand feeling heavy. I drop the glass, and wine goes everywhere.

My face heats up and I worry, but Martha doesn't let a second go by. "At least the glass didn't break," she says as she picks it up. "I'll rinse it out and bring a dish towel back and another blanket."

"I guess I should be drinking my wine out of a sippy cup."

"I don't care if you drop the glass every time you take a sip," Victoria says. "You're not going to drink wine out of a plastic cup."

Everybody seems at ease except for me. I have moments where it feels the same, but I'm anxious.

Mostly they tell me what's going on with them, and I get to listen to their voices. Victoria and Kari talk about work. Martha talks about her daughter Charlotte, getting ready to go off to college, and her youngest, Kristin, about to start ninth grade. Alyssa talks about leaving Richard.

Then it's time for them to go, and I realize that's why I'm anxious.

Martha leaves first to pick up kids from somewhere. She gives me a hug and says, "I'll miss you, and I'll enjoy helping Mark with the girls—" She kisses my forehead and then does not look back.

After one more glass of wine, Victoria and Kari, who came together, get up to leave. I'm so happy that Alyssa is staying a little longer, that they're not all leaving at one time, that I feel shored up. I hug them good-bye without tears. They say they'll see me soon.

When they're out the door, Alyssa says, "So how are you? Do you need to rest?"

"No, I mean I'm tired, but I don't want you to leave, ever. It'll be too hard."

"But I'll be back."

"I know, but this is really good-bye. You can see as well as I can that I'm headed down fast. I mean, that's why Mark called you."

"I see you're worse, but I'll be back. You might not feel like a party tomorrow or the next day, but I'll be around. And we don't need to say any big thing to each other. We've said it all along the way."

"Yes, we have," I say.

Every time I tell someone good-bye, I feel lighter. "I think I'm ready for a sparkling water now."

She fixes it and hands it to me.

"To you, Alyssa."

"To us," she says.

Days later I wake to the smell of onions. It feels late, and I feel different, removed. I concentrate on opening my eyes. When I do, at first I'm not sure that I have, because it's dark. Then I see Mark standing over me, looking as if he's waiting for something.

"Do you want me to help you move to our bed?" he asks. Then he says quickly, "It's time for your medicine." He raises the head of the bed and pours two pills into his hands. He holds the pills out to me.

I look at the pills, but nothing happens. I look up at Mark. He sits down on the edge of the bed, squeezes my hand, and then puts one pill in my mouth. He holds a glass of water to my lips. I swallow some water and the pill. He does this again for the next one.

He bends over me—it feels as if he's inhaling me. Then he lowers the head of the bed. He sits back down and moves little pieces of hair out of my face. Then he gets up to turn out the lamp on the table. My eyes close again in the darkness. I feel him sit back down on the edge of the bed.

Mark and the girls make cupcakes. I hear squeals and smell chocolate. We watch *Mary Poppins*, and I think about jumping into the sidewalk. After pizza, we sing "Happy Birthday" twice.

I hear someone pouring cereal from a box.

Then Mark's beside me pouring water in a cup from one of the big bottles of Evian that Alyssa brought yesterday for my birthday. She said I might as well die in style. I take a sip.

"Ready for the bathroom?"

"I don't think I can," I say, shaking my head.

"That's okay."

I hear him talking, but I can't make out the words. After a while, he brings me some tea and tells me Meg is on her way.

I've made it to July, my allotted six months. Remembering Matisse's words, I know that from now on, any time I have is a gift from life itself. Another two months and "Our Favorite Paintings" opens to the public. Mark told me this morning that the paintings have begun to arrive.

In the portrait I painted of Madame Matisse, her face is gray and kindly, ageless, tilted forward, toward the viewer. And the portrait is full of blue—a blue suit against a blue background. It required over one hundred sittings. A picture is a slow elaboration.

A life, also, Emily.

I sleep most of the time. Meg put in a catheter, and the pain medication is now in a device next to the bed, some sort of pump. I remember them talking about it before.

I wake up and have no idea what time it is. Where's Mark? It's light outside.

"Hi," Meg says, coming to the side of the bed. "How about some water?"

I try to answer, but my throat hurts. I nod.

"Mark?" I ask after I sip some water.

"He said he'd be back in an hour."

"What time is it?"

"Nine forty-five. I'm going to get a warm washcloth. I'll be right back."

I hear water running. I look around. Everything seems the same. Meg hands me the warm cloth, and I put it over my face. I breathe in the warmth. I wipe off my face and then my hands.

"How about something to eat?" she asks.

"How about some ice cream?" I say.

She laughs. "I guess you're entitled to ice cream for breakfast."

After raising the head of the bed, she puts a bowl of vanilla ice cream on my lap.

"Enjoy it," she says. "There's not much left. I wrote it on the list."

Just that fast, and before I even take a bite, I know the ice cream is not going to make me feel better. "You know I should count my blessings," I say, taking my first bite of the cold. "For one thing, I'll never have to go to the grocery store again."

"True," Meg says, drawing the word out.

"I mean that is really big." I take another bite, getting used to the cold. "And I don't actually have to move to go to the bathroom. I used to waste a lot of time getting up from my desk to go to the bathroom."

Meg comes over and stands by the bed. She puts her hand on my arm. I stop eating. She looks at me. I don't want to look at her.

"Emily?"

I look past her.

"Have you talked to Mark about not being able to sleep with him anymore and about not being able to get out of bed?"

I open my mouth to put something else cold inside me, but as I raise the spoon, I meet her eyes. Gagging, I drop the spoon to the bowl and spit up the ice cream I've already eaten. I moan, and she holds me.

When I make my drawings, Emily, the path traced by my pencil on the sheet of paper is similar to the gesture of a person groping his way in the darkness. I mean, there is nothing foreseen about my path.

I hear Mark's voice. "Additional insurance, okay. Lloyd's of London. That's good."

Caroline's, "Once upon a time, there was a little girl named Emily Jane."

"By armored truck. Got it. Thanks, Sam."

Elizabeth's, "Once upon a time."

Emily, I have been no more than a medium, as it were.

I open my eyes and see light everywhere but no people. I was thinking Mark was here, or was I dreaming?

"Mark," I try to say, but it comes out all scratchy. I grope for the remote that raises the bed. Then I hear it hit the floor. My heart races. I swallow without saliva. A toilet flushes. I try to breathe normally.

"Are you awake?" Meg says, and then looking at me, she asks, "What's the matter?" She checks my pulse with her hand and then picks up the remote off the floor, raising the head of the bed. She holds the water glass to my mouth.

"I woke up. I didn't see anybody."

I glance at the note card of *Breakfast*. Mark brought it in here a few days ago. He told me he was looking at it on the table on my side of the bed, and he thought it should be in here with me. So much stuff was on this table that he took it out of the frame and taped it to the wall. Time going backwards.

I focus on the woman's face. "I *used* to be a person who liked to be alone."

"That's what you've told me," Meg says. "Do you remember I said there might come a time when you didn't want to be alone anymore? It's natural to need people."

I nod.

"You will not be dying by yourself."

I close my eyes, but I'm listening.

Emily, I continually react until my work comes into harmony with me, until the red becomes the beating heart, the life force, the jazz.

Susan opens the door before Meg gets to it. As she shuts it back, the air conditioning blares on.

"I'll see you tomorrow, Emily," Meg says.

Susan comes to the bed and squeezes my hand. "Wow, your

hand is cold," she says. "But you don't look so bad." She pulls a chair close to the bed.

"You're going to stay until Mark gets home, right?"

"Yeah, I can stay as long as you need me to."

"Thank you for—"

"Emily, you don't have to thank me."

I try to push saliva into my mouth with my tongue. "Will you do one thing for me?"

"Maybe I should find out what it is before I agree to it," she says, smiling.

"Keep up with them?"

"Emily, Lord, don't worry. I know Mark will do a great job, but I'll be here to help too, always. Even when they're fifty."

I can think of them as teenagers, like in Renoir's *Two Young Girls at the Piano*, together, leaning close to each other, Elizabeth with her long blond hair in a white dress and Caroline standing over her in bittersweet rose. The warm draperies enfolding them as I would do if I were there. But that's as far as I can go—I can't imagine them older than me.

Emily, each painting brings me closer to myself.

I fill with blue as I enter a world the color of cream. I stand in an arabesque of preparation, bending my body backwards as would an acrobat, touching the ground one last time.

Lots of voices—my mother's, my father's, others. I look around the room and see vases of flowers on every surface—purple, yellow, red, pink, and white. I close my eyes and let out a breath.

I am blue in a world of cream. I sit curved in an arabesque of acceptance with space to breathe. My left leg is bent with my knee facing the sky, and my right leg encircles my bent left leg by my ankle. My right hand reaches for my back, and my elbow forms a canopy over my left knee. My other arm hangs limp by my side.

Look toward the sky, Emily. Do you see the spire I created? Imagine a cottage with smoke coming from the chimney at the end of the day and watch the smoke that rises and rises. You get the impression that it never stops at all. That is the feeling I wanted to create with my spire.

I have less space to breathe. I sit curved in an arabesque of awareness. My right hand reaches for my face. I am more rounded, full, complete.

I try to figure out if it's night or day by the sounds. It's quiet now.

My eyes open. I can barely see the note card of my painting. I imagine seeing the real painting again. I imagine it hanging by itself in a museum. Still there long after I'm not.

Someone has moved the bed away from the wall. I have a side rail there now. I turn over, and my eyes dart around. "Mark?"

"I'm here, Emily," he says, standing.

My heart races. I hurt all over.

"The girls?" I whisper.

"Asleep."

"Their chests. Remember."

"Always."

"I love you, Mark."

"I love you, Emily."

I reach my hand through the rail, and he takes it. I close my eyes, but I hold on. When I wake, I feel his hand still holding onto mine.

The top part of my body is being forced back. My arm comes forward to my head. I am taking in more blue. As black swirls fill the world of cream and surround my body of blue, I start to separate.

My drawings and my canvases are pieces of myself, sending out beneficent radiation. I send them to my friends who are ill. Emily, I am sending this one to you.

A door slams.

"Caroline, come see the truck in the driveway!"

Running.

A pat to my foot.

Squeals. Car doors. Heavy voices on the porch. Inside.

Mark beside me. His fingers on my face. "Emily, can you open your eyes?"

"Emily," Sam says. "Look, *Breakfast* is here."

Art Referenced in *The Art of Her Life*

If you wish to see the art I describe in the novel, here's a list of links. I valued museum sites above others, and after that, I chose the site with the least commercial noise around it. This list will also be available online at Fomitepress.com so that if you leave the Fomite page open, you can click on a link as you read and go straight to the art. For the eBook version of the novel, the links will be embedded directly into the text so it will be easy to click over, view the art, then return to reading.

Breakfast by Henri Matisse
https://philamuseum.org/collection/object/63307

Interior with a Young Girl (Girl Reading) by Henri Matisse
https://www.moma.org/collection/works/78713

Interior with a Top Hat by Henri Matisse
https://www.wikiart.org/en/henri-matisse/interior-with-a-top-hat-1896

Three Bathers by Paul Cezanne
https://www.petitpalais.paris.fr/en/oeuvre/three-bathers

Gabrielle with Jean and a Little Girl by Pierre-Auguste Renoir
https://www.wikiart.org/en/pierre-auguste-renoir/gabrielle-jean-and-a-little-girl

Jazz by Henri Matisse (plate VIII)
https://www.metmuseum.org/art/collection/search/337069

Conversation by Henri Matisse
bit.ly/3IqDpI0

The Card Players by Paul Cezanne
https://www.musee-orsay.fr/en/artworks/les-joueurs-de-cartes-1312

Woman Reading in a Garden by Mary Cassatt
https://arthive.com/marycassatt/works/386023~Woman_reading_in_a_garden

Homecoming by Bo Bartlett
bit.ly/3KFK2t4

Trees in Winter by Bruno Zupan
bit.ly/3ZkV4b5

The Storm by Edvard Munch
https://www.moma.org/collection/works/80644

Nantucket by Theodore Robinson
bit.ly/3KzERL4

The Road to Lambertville by Edward Willis Redfield
bit.ly/3Y58maP

Large Gray Seascape by Henri Matisse
http://artsviewer.com/matisse-19.html

Spoleto poster by Willem De Kooning, 1974
bit.ly/3XYeeTb

Spoleto Festival dei Due Mondi poster by Joan Miro, 1981
https://spoletousa.org/wp-content/uploads/2016/04/1981_opt.jpg

Olive Trees, Collioure by Henri Matisse
https://www.metmuseum.org/art/collection/search/459161

The Yellow Curtain by Henri Matisse
https://en.wikipedia.org/wiki/Le_rideau_jaune#/media/File:Yellow_Curtain.jpg

Luxe, Calme, et Volupte by Henri Matisse
bit.ly/41qaCfw

Open Door, Brittany by Henri Matisse
https://www.wikiart.org/en/henri-matisse/not-identified-1

Still Life with Bird's Nest by George Forster (described but not titled)
bit.ly/3IWn4MY

French Window at Collioure by Henri Matisse
https://www.wikiart.org/en/henri-matisse/french-window-at-collioure

The Red Studio by Henri Matisse
https://www.moma.org/calendar/exhibitions/5344

Lorette (Laurette) in a Green Robe, Black Background by Henri Matisse
https://www.metmuseum.org/art/collection/search/489996

The Painter in His Studio by Henri Matisse
https://en.wikipedia.org/wiki/The_Painter_and_His_Model

Lorette Reclining by Henri Matisse
bit.ly/3KFKsiX

The Studio, quai Saint-Michel by Henri Matisse
https://www.phillipscollection.org/collection/studio-quai-saint-michel

Various ink drawings by Victor Hugo (described but not titled)
https://eclecticlight.co/2019/08/09/victor-hugo-the-unknown-painter/

Invalid by Henri Matisse
https://www.wikiart.org/en/henri-matisse/the-invalid-1899

Cape Cod Afternoon by Edward Hopper
bit.ly/3xUdcwN

Landscape Viewed from a Window by Henri Matisse
https://en.wikipedia.org/wiki/Window_at_Tangier

The Thousand and One Nights by Henri Matisse
https://collection.cmoa.org/objects/c5864a0a-c9e2-4e64-9751-3a275e3cbb13

The Blue Nudes by Henri Matisse
https://www.youtube.com/watch?v=_Ek9gt18X-s

Studio Under the Eaves by Henri Matisse
https://fitzmuseum.cam.ac.uk/objects-and-artworks/highlights/PD14-1964

Mademoiselle Yvonne Landsberg by Henri Matisse
https://philamuseum.org/collection/object/51047

The Creation of Adam by Michelangelo (described but not titled)
https://www.thesistinechapel.org/the-creation-of-adam

Interior at Nice (Room at the Beau Rivage) by Henri Matisse
https://philamuseum.org/collection/object/53946

The Dance by Henri Matisse (described but not titled)
https://collection.barnesfoundation.org/objects/6967/The-Dance/

The Snail by Henri Matisse
https://www.tate.org.uk/art/artworks/matisse-the-snail-t00540

Jazz by Henri Matisse (plate I)
https://www.metmuseum.org/art/collection/search/353770

The Promenade by Pierre-Auguste Renoir
bit.ly/3IWvLXu

The Laundress by Henri de Toulouse-Lautrec
https://www.christies.com/en/lot/lot-4595620

Train in the Snow by Claude Monet
https://www.dailyartmagazine.com/claude-monet-train-snow-painting-week/

Harmony in Red by Henri Matisse
https://www.dailyartmagazine.com/henri-matisse-harmony-red-painting-week/

Harmony in Yellow by Henri Matisse
https://www.wikiart.org/en/henri-matisse/harmony-in-yellow-1927

The Painting Session by Henri Matisse
https://www.nationalgalleries.org/art-and-artists/694

Composition with a Standing Nude and Black Fern by Henri Matisse (described but not titled)
bit.ly/3xSOKvA

Walking Wall by Andy Goldsworthy
https://nelson-atkins.org/exhibitions/andy-goldsworthy-walking-wall/

The Fountain of the Muses by Carl Milles
https://www.loc.gov/resource/highsm.44056/?r=-0.116,0.038,1.232,0.617,0

Ivy in Flower by Henri Matisse
https://www.wikiart.org/en/henri-matisse/ivy-in-flower-1941

Still Life with a Sleeping Woman by Henri Matisse
https://www.nga.gov/collection/art-object-page.66424.html

Portrait of Mme Matisse by Henri Matisse (described but not titled)
https://www.wikiart.org/en/henri-matisse/portrait-of-mme-matisse-1913

Two Young Girls at the Piano by Pierre-Auguste Renoir
https://www.metmuseum.org/art/collection/search/459112

Acrobats by Henri Matisse (described but not titled)
http://bit.ly/3EZsuo5

Blue Nude (II) by Henri Matisse (described but not titled)
https://www.moma.org/audio/playlist/6/316

Blue Nude (III) by Henri Matisse (described but not titled)
https://www.wikiart.org/en/henri-matisse/blue-nude-iii-1952

Blue Nude (IV) by Henri Matisse (described but not titled)
https://www.wikiart.org/en/henri-matisse/blue-nude-iv-1952

The Flowing Hair by Henri Matisse (in my imagination)
https://www.wikiart.org/en/henri-matisse/the-flowing-hair-1952

Acknowledgments

Although I didn't set out to be a writer, I'm grateful that's where I landed. Back in 1989, pregnant with child number three, something had to go. So I stopped practicing law. I've always been a reader, and during the years I focused on raising children, the worlds created by Ellen Gilchrist, Anne Tyler, Pam Houston, and so many others were a lifeline. When I looked up again, it was 1995, and my kids were two, six, eight, and fourteen. I didn't want to go back to the law; I wanted to create one of those worlds. That year, I had enough free time to write three times; in 1996, seven times. Simple paragraphs about women and the different choices they'd made, women who became part of this novel.

By the time 1999 rolled around, I was hooked and started making time for writing. I worked on *The Painting Story*, the title my mother gave to this novel, for ten years before I felt it was finished enough to start something new. Every few years after that, I would come back to it, able to make it a little better and also to update car phones to cell phones, videos to DVDs, paying the pizza guy with cash to no mention of cash.

As much as I'd hoped this book would be published years ago, I don't think I had the skill to make it all it could be until now. So I'm grateful for the years.

I'm also grateful for the people. To each person who encouraged me or loved something about this story, thank you for keeping me going and for sending this novel a little further along its way.

Thanks especially—

To Elizabeth McCracken, the first writer to read pages of this novel, and the 1999 Napa Valley Writers' Conference.

To Tony Eprile, the first writer to read the entire manuscript, and the 2001 New York State Summer Writers Institute.

To Howard Norman for clasping a copy of the novel to his chest, as if he might love it the way I loved those novels that made me want to be a writer, and for sending, in January of 2002, eight hand-written pages that would take my words closer to creating one of those worlds.

To Cal Martin and Amandah Turner who read this novel over and over again in the early years, each at least five times before 2005.

To other friends and family who read the novel—Catherine McCall, Suzanne Murphy, Evelyn Newberry, Monterey Hiett, Kim Davis, Faye Melton, Catherine Henschen, Suzanne Saunders, Cynthia Strange, Kathleen Levens, Amelia Baker, Jodi Paloni.

To Adam Braver for reading a complete draft in July of 2006 and Pam Houston for reading the next version in December, and for all their efforts to help me see the difference between the writer's work and the reader's work.

To the readers of Catching Days, created in September of 2008, for making me feel like a writer even without a published book.

To Frances Badgett and Jeff McMahon at *Contrary Magazine* for publishing, in the fall of 2009, "The Empty Armchair," a story based on this novel.

To Katie Shea Boutillier, my first agent, for loving this novel enough to sign me in 2011 and for giving it its current title.

To Karen Nelson, Cal Martin, and Lesley Dahl, my 2022 readers, for their attention to detail and good questions.

To Jack Martin for designing another cover I love.

To Marc Estrin, Donna Bister, and Fomite Press for giving this novel a place in the world.

To Cal, Kathleen, Sam L., Mack, Lily, Wynn, Bobby, Claire, Ro, Ruby, Jack, Taylor, McLin, Sam, and Katherine for everything.

About the Author

Author photo by Alyssa Pointer

Cynthia Newberry Martin's first novel, *Tidal Flats*, won the Gold Medal in Literary Fiction at the 2020 Independent Publisher Book Awards and the 14th Annual National Indie Excellence Award for Fiction. Her website features the How We Spend Our Days series, over a decade of essays by writers on their lives. She grew up in Atlanta and now lives in Columbus, Georgia, with her husband, and in Provincetown, Massachusetts, in a little house by the water. Her second novel, *Love Like This*, was published in April of 2023.

Fomite

More novels and novellas from Fomite...

Fomite

Ron Jacobs — *The Co-conspirator's Tale*
Scott Archer Jones — *And Throw Away the Skins*
Scott Archer Jones — *A Rising Tide of People Swept Away*
Julie Justicz — *Degrees of Difficulty*
Maggie Kast — *A Free Unsullied Land*
Darrell Kastin — *Shadowboxing with Bukowski*
Coleen Kearon — *#triggerwarning*
Coleen Kearon — *Feminist on Fire*
Jan English Leary — *Thicker Than Blood*
Diane Lefer — *Confessions of a Carnivore*
Diane Lefer — *Out of Place*
Rob Lenihan — *Born Speaking Lies*
Colin McGinnis — *Roadman*
Douglas W. Milliken — *Our Shadows' Voice*
Ilan Mochari — *Zinsky the Obscure*
Peter Nash — *Parsimony*
Peter Nash — *The Least of It*
Peter Nash — *The Perfection of Things*
George Ovitt — *Stillpoint*
George Ovitt — *Tribunal*
Gregory Papadoyiannis — *The Baby Jazz*
Pelham — *The Walking Poor*
Andy Potok — *My Father's Keeper*
Frederick Ramey — *Comes A Time*
Joseph Rathgeber — *Mixedbloods*
Kathryn Roberts — *Companion Plants*
Robert Rosenberg — *Isles of the Blind*
Fred Russell — *Rafi's World*
Ron Savage — *Voyeur in Tangier*
David Schein — *The Adoption*
Rana Shubair — *And No Net Ensnare Me*
Charles Simpson — *Uncertain Harvest*
Lynn Sloan — *Midstream*
Lynn Sloan — *Principles of Navigation*
L.E. Smith — *The Consequence of Gesture*
L.E. Smith — *Travers' Inferno*
L.E. Smith — *Untimely RIPped*
Robert Sommer — *A Great Fullness*
Caitlin Hamilton Summie — *Geographies of the Heart*
Tom Walker — *A Day in the Life*
Susan V. Weiss —*My God, What Have We Done?*

Fomite

Peter M. Wheelwright — *As It Is on Earth*
Peter M. Wheelwright — *The Door-Man*
Suzie Wizowaty — *The Return of Jason Green*

Writing a review on social media sites for readers will help the progress of independent publishing. To submit a review, go to the book page on any of the sites and follow the links for reviews. Books from independent presses rely on reader-to-reader communications.

For more information or to order any of our books, visit:
fomitepress.com/our-books.html

Printed in the USA
CPSIA information can be obtained
at www.ICGtesting.com
LVHW090000091123
763404LV00002B/237